Elean Thomas is a journalist, teacher and writer. She has written extensively for newspapers and magazines as well as performed her poetry in the Caribbean, Europe, Africa and North America. She has published two collections of poetry and prose with Karia Press: *Word-Rhythms from the Life of a Woman* and *Before They Can Speak of Flowers*. *The Last Room* is her first novel. After living in London for several years, Elean Thomas has returned to Jamaica where she is at work on a new novel.

Praise for *The Last Room*

'A nicely sustained mixture of shrewdness, acceptance and despair . . . Elean Thomas can write' – *Guardian*

'Caribbean contrasts of sunshine, sorrow and straight-from-the-gut wisdom colour this lilting, cautionary calypso' – *She*

'The rich musical dialect of Jamaica dances under her power – this is a confident first novel . . . a joy to read' – *Helena Kennedy*

'A first novel of great power and poignancy' – *Today*

'This novel speaks to the mind's ear with a compelling eloquence. It enthralls, mesmerises and beguiles one into the heart of Jamaican culture that is both particular and universal' – *Jan Carew*

PUTUS'S JAMAICA

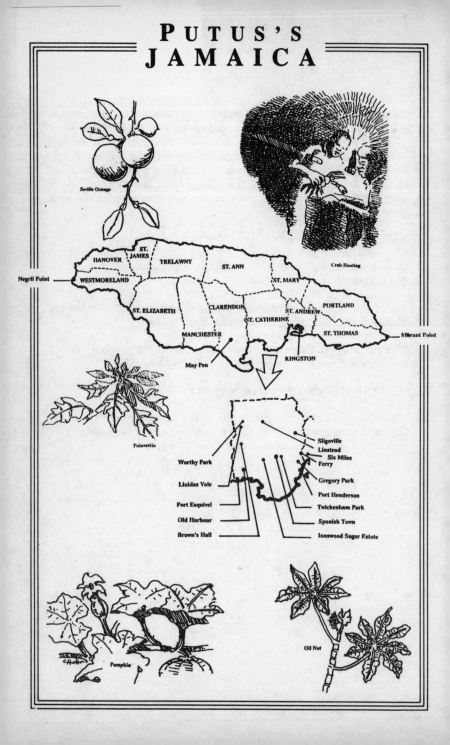

Seville Orange

Crab Hunting

Negril Point

HANOVER
ST. JAMES
TRELAWNY
ST. ANN
ST. MARY
WESTMORELAND
ST. ELIZABETH
CLARENDON
ST. CATHERINE
ST. ANDREW
PORTLAND
MANCHESTER
ST. THOMAS
Morant Point
KINGSTON
May Pen

Poinsettia

Worthy Park
Sligoville
Linstead
Six Miles
Ferry
Lluidas Vale
Gregory Park
Port Henderson
Port Esquivel
Twickenham Park
Old Harbour
Spanish Town
Brown's Hall
Innswood Sugar Estate

Pumpkin

Oil Nut

Elean Thomas
The Last Room

Published by VIRAGO PRESS Limited 1992
20–23 Mandela Street, Camden Town, London NW1 0HQ

First published in Britain by Virago Press 1991

Copyright © Elean Thomas 1991

The right of Elean Thomas to be identified as author of this work has been
asserted by her in accordance with the Copyright, Designs
and Patents Act 1988

A CIP catalogue record for this title
is available from the British Library

Printed in Great Britain by Cox & Wyman Ltd
Reading, Berkshire

FOR MAMA LOU
and
MISS BELLE

Part of whose story
This is
But not all of it.

FOR TONY

Who gave such all-round
Support
To help that story be told.

The Last Room
       Is
Not a Dead-End
Not a Finish
Not a Death

The Last Room
Is a Moment
Of Decision.
Which must be grasped
For Life
Or Death.

Elean Thomas
1990

ACKNOWLEDGEMENTS

There are many individuals, many collectives of individuals, past and present, who directly and indirectly helped me to produce this work. Some, in the example of their life experiences and their own response to those experiences, helped to strengthen and inspire me. Some helped me to survive materially and spiritually while producing this work. Some gave legal and technical advice.

Some helped me to get it together by contributing to the technical means, like word-processing, typing and photocopying.

Some made critical remarks and suggestions which improved the work.

Some helped by just being there and giving of themselves when I needed them.

There are millions of little and big moments which come together in realising any creative output. It is sometimes difficult to recognise all of them and their contributors. So, please forgive me for all those whom I may leave out. Even as I give thanks to:

Mama, Jennifer, Hortense, Bishop.

Linnette Vassel, Dickie Vassel, Elaine Molly Wallace, Sharon Henry-Stair, Easton Lee, Alafia Samuels, Daphne Kelly, Bruce Kelly, Rupert Lewis, Hopeton Dunn, Leith Dunn, Aggrey Irons, Pat Ramsey, Muta, Pam Bodden, Sister Ina, Trevor Munroe, Sharon Atkin.

Buzz Johnson of Karia Press, Cleston Taylor, Feli Taylor, Nana, Koki, Amandla Thomas-Johnson, Yvette Thomas, Wanjiru Kihoro, Sister Alice, Joan and Maurice Frankson.

Avis Hart, Dick Hart, Beverly Provost, Sola Coard, Jah T., Errol Powell, Livette Powell, Helena Kennedy, Carolyn Cooper.

Buchi Emecheta, Merle Collins, Ruth and Paul of 'Apples and Snakes', the sisters of the *Spare Rib* Collective, Clinton Hutton, Jan Carew.

Joshua Higgins and his painting, *The Orange*, Terry Shott, Anne Carrera, Michele Egan, Winston James, Michael Seifert, Nick Allen, Mervyn Morris, Melanie Silgardo.

PART ONE

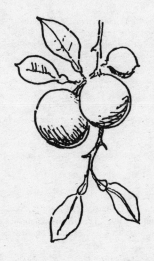

PUTUS

Jamaica is shaped like a nice, big, fat Negro yam. The type that's thick in the middle with white, floury food under the rough, dark-brown skin and has little, cute, tender-tasting toes on each side. Jamaica has two big toes and one little toe. The big toe on one side is Morant Point and the one on the other side is Negril.

With some big, fat Negro yams, the toes sometimes end up tasting watery and bitterish. Some people who live here say that this is the case with the Negril Jamaica big toe. But those are the people who feel that a certain type of tourism eats away the flesh and sweetness of a country. Be that as it may.

Go through the capital, Kingston, then bear west. Until you get to Six Miles, which really marks the border between Kingston and the next parish of St Catherine. Cross the border by going straight before your nose. It's June, which everyone knows is rainy month – the start of the hurricane season. If you make it through to the end of September and you haven't experienced a hurricane or at least a 'breeze-blow' (which is the baby hurricane) then you can count yourself lucky . . . or unlucky. Depending on from where you look at it.

Lucky if you live in one of those strong, big colonial-architecture houses on the Liguanea Plains of St Andrew and can just cuddle-up closer to your loved (or unloved) one. Snuggle-up into the intimate sounds of the rain bucketing down on leak-proof roofs and the wind lashing against impregnable walls.

Lucky if you are a visitor to the island who is staying in the grand Myrtle Bank Hotel in Kingston (no Blacks allowed, certainly no local Blacks) and can then regale the guests at your next dinner party back home with your unique experience, or even write a book about tropical hurricanes and the little 'native boy' you so courageously saved from drowning in the flooded street outside the Myrtle Bank.

Unlucky, if you are the little 'native' boy or his mother. You would have your hands full fishing yourself out of the river after your house was carried away like paper before the raging winds. Anyhow, that's just for preparation if you are a visitor. Most people who live here try their best to figure out beforehand – once they have a choice – where to be and where not to be in case they hear a hurricane warning.

However, lucky for everyone, the rain eased up last night. Now, the sun is shining warm and steamy. All the trees and bushes are washed clean. You never saw so many colours and shades of colours, have you? All touched with numberless shades of the light and shadows of gold . . . from that sun.

It is best if you come to Six Miles after dark. 'Velvet' is a hackneyed word. But there is no other word to describe the night around you. Only that the smells of the sugar-cane plants, of the woodfires off somewhere which you cannot see, of the rain-made mud, baked by the day's sun, of the saltiness carried by the warm sea-breeze, will mingle with the smell and the feel of the velvet dark caressing every part of your body (even those which you didn't even know you had while bathing). These are the days long before fluorescent electric street lights. Those little twinkling lights you have been seeing all around you are peeny-wallies or the lights could be just before your own eyes, coming out of your own head – so charged up are you on the sheer delight of this night.

Look to the left, across the swamps just after you pass Six Miles. You see some bigger lights there, don't you? Ah, those are bottle torches. You may want to stop here and go in search of the carriers of those bottle torches.

If you have a crocus bag and can get hold of a strong stick, then you may indeed be in for a unique experience and one which is pleasurable at that. You are going to catch yourself some land crabs – free of cost. If you haven't yet experienced crab catching, don't leave it too long. For in later years, especially during the big development boom of the sixties, high-flying entrepreneurs are going to mark out much of that swampland as prime for their development. They are going to blast out and dump up most of this land, killing generations of land crabs and crayfish and destroying all their holes . . . for ever.

So, hopefully, you have stopped to join the crab catchers. They have made up a bottle torch for you, wetting a bit of old rag with kerosene oil, then wadding it into the neck of a bottle (it's not a Molotov Cocktail, so don't get jumpy). See how it flares up when you light the top end of the oil-soaked rag, then burns down steady. Almost as good as a proper lamp, isn't it – except for a little black smoke and the acrid stench of the kerosene. The crab catchers have shown you how to hold your crocus bag in one hand, the bottle torch in the other, to tread softly to where the crabs are hiding in the bushes after their holes have become too waterlogged and hot for them – and to shine the bottle torch in their eyes (oops! not the crab catcher's eyes, you would be treading on very dangerous ground there).

You have to be quick and ready for when the crabs are disorientated in their fright. You have to, in one motion, shove the crocus bag under your arm (not the one holding the bottle torch), get the strong stick from under the arm where the bag now rests, into your hand where the bag was, give the crab a gentle tap with the stick in the region between its two protruding eyes and then bring the crocus bag back down into your hand, using the stick to bring inside it the stunned and blinded crab. Make sure that the mouth of the crocus bag is now tightly secured and that you don't hold the bag with the now angry, definitely protesting crab too near to any part of your body.

A bit too much for you, is it? But that's only for beginners. The seasoned crab catchers, as you will no doubt have noticed, don't need to go through all that. They only find it necessary to stun the crab when it has left its hole sometime before and is running about. Once the crab is stationary for even two seconds, the seasoned crab man pounces upon it with his bare hands (women don't go much into crab catching except in exceptional circumstances) and holds it firmly on both sides of its shell in a way which leaves the wicked claws dangling uselessly, then pops it neatly into the crocus bag. Those are the sweetest crabs to eat because the meat is unbattered.

Oh, but the crab catchers have suggested that you not try that method, have they? Quite correct. Don't mind the crab catchers' abrasive exterior and their seemingly superior manner. Jamaicans are very warm-hearted people. Would share our last dumpling with another person or even give it all to them if we felt the person needed it more (qualification – most Jamaicans). But we are not too up on the little European polite niceties and have a disturbing (to some) penchant for talking the brutal truth in an equally brutal tone of voice. So don't be vexed when the crab catchers grind out some curse at you when you try to use the seasoned method, ignoring their instructions. It is for your own good. They are even more concerned than you could be for you to continue your journey with all of your fingers intact.

Ah, the crab catching is over. Caught any? Doesn't matter, you will still get crab to eat. They have found a reasonably dry spot in the swamp. They'll get a fire, so long as they can find some reasonably dry wood. Fire starts with too much smoke. Someone blows on it. They put on the kerosene tin (in case you don't know, don't be misled, it didn't contain kerosene oil before, more likely coconut oil, it's only called that). Salt and lots of red, yellow and green peppers into the kerosene tin. Water begins to bubble. In go the crabs from the bags. Don't bother to try this one. Let the seasoned ones take over here. You would probably lose three-quarters of the crabs and end up missing pieces of your anatomy as well. They put one hand down into the crocus bag. Several crabs try to make a desperate jump for freedom. But the other hand is holding the mouth of the bag . . . tight. Just enough room for the one hand to expertly grasp the crab nearest the top of the bag . . . in its back . . . and . . . pop! . . . into the kerosene tin . . . making the supreme, involuntary sacrifice to the gastronomic desires of the crab catchers.

You wait until the crabs are boiled, telling yourself that you want to get on with your journey. But the night and the crab catchers are embracing you. This type of Jamaican is asking nothing of you or about you. They didn't want you to help them to get to America, did they? Or to get a job in Kingston? They don't want to know whether you are rich or

5

poor? Whether you have come from good family or not? To them, your only qualification for joining the crabbing community is for you to comfortable-up yourself in whatever situation you found yourself, to be one with the community and not try to be a conqueror over the community. And to have strong loins, which is their word for personal courage.

You have apparently passed the test. In humility and thankfulness, you sit on the swampy ground with the crab catchers around the crab-filled, bubbling kerosene tin. They have stuck the bottle torches into the ground, creating an oasis of fire and light in the dark swampland. As you listen to their ribald laughter, rough sex stories, their duppy stories, as you feel that night, smell the intimate stink of the swamp, hear the sounds which form the undertone of the night, you are thinking that you will move on soon, but certainly, not too soon.

You are very worried, aren't you? One side of you is saying, 'just relax and enjoy yourself'. But another side of you is feeling guilty as hell, isn't it? You oughtn't to be feeling so happy. Look how many things there are for you to do and to worry about. And you ought to be getting on with it (whatever 'it' is), oughtn't you?

You resign yourself to the moment. Whatever 'it' is, you will deal with 'it' when you leave this spot and this moment. You relax and watch the crab catchers as they take out the condensed can (got its name because it originally contained condensed milk but now made into a tin cup). They pour something into the condensed can. You sip from the condensed can as it goes around the whole group. If you are a certain type of visitor from America or Europe or some upper-class Jamaican topanaris, you have literally let down your hair (or hairpiece) by this time. You cannot be bothered if Black people and especially these rough Black people have 'foot and mouth' disease.

You sip, just like all the others. Your face becomes another shade of red in the bottle-torch firelight. You try hard not to cough as the fiery contents of the condensed can attack your throat and guts. You haven't coughed but they guess what you are going through. They pass you the butter pan (that is the one which used to contain butter from America). Yes, the contents of the butter pan do cool your burning throat, settle over your fiery guts, calm it down, send a bolt of energy through your whole system. Make you feel that you want to charge out into the swampy night and kill a lion (there are no lions there) or that you just want to snuggle down even more within the circle of the bottle torches, let your senses take you over and make this place, this time the centre of your earth . . . even your universe.

Incidentally, the condensed can contains estate rum, the first stage of processing of the rum from the sugar-cane juice – sometimes called 'Steel Bottom', sometimes called 'Jack Iron', sometimes called 'John Crow Batty' – this last from a suggestion of how strong the intestines and anus of that scavenger bird must be to process all the wastes which it takes in.

You get the picture, don't you? Maybe you didn't notice, but that was what they used to light the fire on the swamps. Yes, that which you just drank and continue to be sipping whenever the condensed can comes around.

But luckily there is the butter pan to cool you off. That is just quarts of 'wet sugar wash'. What some people call the Muscavado sugar, mixed with water and the juice of sour oranges, with a dash of molasses (good for putting lead in your pencil, too, as the crab catchers are laughingly telling you).

The crab is ready. They tell you just dip into the kerosene tin and eat. You do. You are now sated with tasty, meaty land crab. You have put your lips and the tip of your tongue into the last crab claw and sucked the roughish, tart-tasting meat into your mouth. You are being encouraged to top it off with a little more of the contents of the condensed can, just to heighten the supreme taste orgasm. Don't fall for it. Leave well enough alone. You see, since you are driving a vehicle and the others will just walk hurriedly through the bushes to wherever their women wait and on whom they will selfishly wreak the zenith of the crab-catching and crab-eating orgasm – you had better not indulge in that last course. Not really because the Law says: 'if you drink, don't drive and if you drive, don't drink' but rather because, when you get further down the road to Spanish Town, you are going to be in some real trouble if you develop four eyes (the eyes which see four roads before them).

It's coming on to daylight, and you are ready to continue your journey? Carry straight on. You are nearing Ferry police station. All the policemen there seem to have responsibility for only one area of law enforcement – to catch motorists.

Your licence may be a little or a lot out of date. Your third-party insurance may have expired. Your rear-view mirror may be hitched up with a piece of wire. Whatever – as any driver knows, there are a million and one things that can make your vehicle 'unroadworthy' to an over-conscientious traffic cop. And most of all, don't speed. It is in the days before electronic speed traps. But the human speed trap is a hundred times more efficient. You scoff? OK, try it. Go above a sedate 30 miles per hour.

As you start to feel the breeze rushing by your ears you will, first vaguely, then with dreaded certainty, discern a crisp, shiny, black, white and silver motorbike roar out seemingly from the bushes behind the big silk cotton tree. And seated loose-limbed, confident, sadistically gleeful, upon this throne, will be 'Killer Mack', the most awesome traffic police-man in all of Jamaica. If you fall foul of Killer Mack you won't be going any further . . . till next week . . . or next month . . . or next year . . . depending on when you are released from the Ferry police station . . . or how long the case takes to come up in the traffic court in Kingston or Spanish Town. Some people say that some policemen at

Ferry have been able to buy plenty property and build big houses off motorists. Be that as it may.

Hopefully, you didn't have that topper on the crab meat. Hopefully, you are one of those people who obey the law, slavishly; ignoring the nice piece of smooth road (it's a trap) and sticking to 30 miles per hour. (You wouldn't be the one who set up for Killer Mack as his bike roared out of the bushes at Ferry and ran straight through his shiny bike . . . and him, when he tried to stop you, would you?)

Go straight on. If you turn anywhere, you will get off course. You don't want to go to Port Henderson . . . or to stop at Twickenham Park . . . or go up into the hills of Sligoville . . . do you?

Come to Kingston Bridge. That's the sort of 'hog's back' bridge leading you into Spanish Town. Don't mind the shacks perched precariously on the rock-face to your left. Don't waste time to be one of those bleeding-heart European charity liberals who are always taking photographs of 'poverty-in-the-colonies'. These people will not allow you to take their photographs, anyway. Shed no tears for them before the television cameras (television hasn't reached Jamaica yet, at the time of your journey). Let others weep at the thought that, every hurricane season, the existing inhabitants of these shacks are washed down into the gorge under the Kingston Bridge. Your concern is how quaint and picturesque those shacks look, perched on the rock-face.

Pass on. To Spanish Town Hospital. Keep straight. Don't turn, unless you want to go to Bernard Lodge Sugar Factory . . . or to Gregory Park . . . or on to Port Henderson. You don't want to go right . . . to the Spanish Town Prison . . . do you? If it is a holiday, when they have the big fairs at the Prison Oval, you may want to stop. But you don't want to take the chance of coming upon some of those prisoners in their flour-bag calico short pants suit. Even worse, you don't want to see the death row block of the prison? Might you not recognise someone you know? Might it not upset your stomach more to see the gallows, with its little efficient trapdoor, which takes the body underground, whether it's fully dead or not . . . after the neck has been broken?

Pass on.

Keep left of the Munamar roundabout at Spanish Town – that's where they have the political party meetings. There won't be any crowd to block your vehicle because it's a few years before another general election time and the politicians won't have any reason to be meeting with people now.

People say that Spanish Town is a major monument to the nearly two hundred years of Spanish colonial rule in Jamaica (you know, of course, that it was their capital of the island). Well, you might be more inclined to agree with them if you had turned right at Spanish Town Hospital, gone past the Cathedral and round to the official square. But that is not your mission. You are going straight on. If you turn anywhere off that main road as you are passing through Spanish Town you are more likely to come upon filthy, narrow little streets along which the latifundistas' chariots could ride in style but which crunch against each other the people going about their day-to-day business of making a living.

Pass on. Keeping to the left. Don't bother to turn to the right on Cumberland Road, even if you want to buy something in the market – too many vehicles. That will hold up your journey too long. If you have space in your vehicle, you may want to help out some from the crowd of people who have been waiting for hours and hours to get transportation to Old Harbour and May Pen.

Keep on, pass the cemetery called 'Number 5' for some reason not too known; over the train line . . . on to Sydenham. Remember it's the days before the big highway and the housing developers' boom, so you will see mainly trees, bush and shine-Black people. In approaching Innswood Sugar Estates, if you see that Grey Donkey . . . drive straight through it. It's the duppy of one of the thousands of West Africans whose blood, sweat and tears fertilised the fat, green sugar-cane leaves. This duppy does not know yet of Abolition and he or she takes the form of a Grey Donkey and lies in wait for the slavemaster's chariot. Many before you have gone to meet their Maker, when they have tried to brake in front of the Grey Donkey. The sign of the blood on your doorpost will be if you have the clear-headedness and sheer nerve . . . to drive straight through the Grey Donkey.

You have some West African blood? Or American Indian? Or Irish? You have survived the Grey Donkey! Good. Pass on. Don't bother to stop at the goat market at McCook's Pen – you are not planning to buy any goats, are you? You don't have time for a curried goat and rice feed now. Swips past Red Ground and turn the deep corner into Old Harbour.

All of a sudden, it seems to you, there is the wooden, sand-dash Catholic church, right on the left, at the entrance of Desire Lane. Later when the politicians want to sound up to date and modern – but more to hide the unhideable fact that they haven't done anything to develop the town – they will rename Desire Lane 'Patrick Street'. But that won't make it anymore a 'street' than a lane.

As you see, Old Harbour is a one-road town. But don't make the mistake of taking Old Harbour people lightly. Some people say that the reason the local British–America Party always win elections there is because the other people up in the St Catherine Hills who own a biggish amount of land are afraid that the Garveyites in Old Harbour will win and force them to share the land with those who don't have any. Be that as it may.

You are at the post office now. You are stopping? At the market? You can't resist getting some of that bleeding fresh fish just caught three miles away at Old Harbour Bay and selling for only one shilling for a string of eight fish. OK, but don't stop too long, you may be there till the horse-racing begins at Little Ascot, just round the corner to the right and, if you are a gambling person, you may stay there for the rest of your journey. If you are going to the left, after the market, to get petrol at the one gas station, it's all right, but don't turn behind the gas station to the building with the 'Club' sign, because you did not come here off one of the ships which dock at Port Esquivel, did you? Your crab orgasm would have settled down by now. You wouldn't be so dry and thirsty for woman as at the beginning, would you?

When you get to the town clock (with the police station on the left) don't bother to go straight to get fried fish and bammie. You need to turn right, at the clock. Up into Mountain Road. Later, in the rush of their pretentiousness, the politicians are going to rename it 'Darliston Drive', maybe because the houses are bigger here. It is, however, a mountain road. You see, that name is more appropriate because it leads from the township of Old Harbour up into the villages in the hills of St Catherine; like Brown's Hall, Point Hill, Ducksies, and on to Lluidas Vale, and so on.

Before you follow Mountain Road to where it leaves Old Harbour behind, just pause a minute at the bend on your right – just after you pass the Church of England on your left. The sprawling, sand-dash wood mansion surrounded by the croton fence will immediately catch your attention. Not only because it's the largest house in that area but also because its owners somehow captured the only hillock in that section of Old Harbour, on the Mountain Road, and placed their residence there, surrounded by a fence of blazing colour, with yellow, deep red, pink and green crotons, pinky-red rice and peas bush, morning glories, sun fat, yellow sunflowers, white, pink, red hibiscus, flame-red poinsettias, white and green Aurelia bush.

If you can tear your eyes away from all that richness of colour, peep through the fence. You see an older, but strong, handsome woman on your side of the large, circular verandah surrounding the house? That's Aunt Sisi. You will know more about her soon. She is getting up from the verandah even as you are peeping.

Go up more to the side of the house, further up Mountain Road. Peep through the croton fencing again. You can see her plaited head and fattish round shoulders through the window of that outhouse (they call it a buttery). See that young girl? Oh, yes, that's Putus. You know that name? That's not the name on her birth certificate – not her 'proper' name. Putus is her 'pet name'. Everyone has a pet name. The proper name is the one given before or immediately after birth. The pet name is given in the course of the child's growing up. The pet name is usually descriptive of some perceived outstanding characteristic of the child. Or it may reflect how the child is looked upon by its family and those close friends who count as family. That girl you see there in the buttery was born sixteen years before as Valerie Barton. By the time she was one year old, she became Putus – meaning SWEET AND SPECIAL.

PUTUS

'Putus . . . ? Putus . . . ?, please come inside here a minute, Maam.'

It was Aunt Sisi's peremptory voice. Putus was standing up over the big washtub behind the buttery. She was just in the act of sucking her teeth in vexation and cussing Aunt Sisi and her three 'wrenkin, boasty pickney-them' when she heard the call from inside the house.

'Yes, Aunt Sisi, coming now Maam.'

She washed off the brown soapsuds from her hands under the back pipe and dried them on a piece of the still unwashed clothes. Aunt Sisi was not in fact her blood auntie; maybe if she was, Putus was thinking, she wouldn't treat her like maid to she and her pickney-them!

Aunt Sisi was really Mrs Bennett to most people. Her family had known Putus's family since before Putus was born. The Nicholsons (which was Aunt Sisi's family name) owned the big property right next to Putus's father's land in Brown's Hall – up into the hills from Mountain Road in the town of Old Harbour.

In those days before the birth of Putus, Mas D, Putus's father, owned a little over ten acres of land next to the back boundary of Mr Nicholson's property. The Baptist people had helped Great-Grandfather Barton to acquire it some years before Emancipation became official. And on his dying bed, Great-Grandfather Barton had made his eldest daughter, Maisie, promise him never to 'mek this ya piece a land go out – a de Barton name'. Maisie had promised. Some people say that is why she named all her children from her own family name and not that of her husband. Great-Grandfather Barton died satisfied that he had done his best to leave his family 'a legacy fe generations to come . . . so you can lef' slavery back-a-door fi-ever!'

But time had worn hard on the Barton family for the generations to come. Over the years, many of the children, grandchildren, uncles, aunts, nieces, nephews and numerous cousins came to be scattered all over the parish – indeed from east to west, north to south of the island.

The Barton land could only be properly worked with the labour of the extended family but in turn it could only provide a meagre living for a small part of that family. The inevitable feuds and quarrels arose as each member claimed direct lineage to Great-Grandfather Barton and therefore the right to sell his or her piece of the land.

In the third generation, Da Da Barton (Putus's grandfather) settled the matter. One day, it began to be whispered around the District that

Da Da had been sitting in the middle of the yam field near the back border of the land for two whole days and nights. Not eating. Not even smoking his usual tobacco hemp. Only drinking stream water now and again. And sharpening his machete. On the third day, Da Da came up out of the bushes into the yard. He declined any food, accepted only a little bush tea, 'to wash the cold offa mi stomach'. Then he took his little stool to the middle of the wide packed-earth barbecue, used for drying coffee and chocolate beans. And he sat in the boiling sun, his legs crossed at the ankles, the glistening machete in the space between his legs, its hand-carved wood handle resting loosely in his crotch. Da Da Barton was usually a man of soft voice and few words. He hadn't raised his voice then either. He called two of the small children and he told them the names of twelve members of the Barton family he wanted to come to the barbecue. The two children had run off to get them, quick, quick.

Da Da had chosen those he judged to be direct descendants of Great-Grandfather Barton. His own son, the young Mas D, was among them. They came in ones and twos to the barbecue, depending on how far away they had been when the children delivered Da Da's summons. No one who had not been summoned dared to come. But all eyes and ears were keyed into what would transpire on the barbecue under the boiling sun. By sundown, even the smallest child in the District would be able to tell the whole story, with a few big and little embellishments here and there but basically constant in all its essentials.

Da Da had waited until all twelve were gathered before him on the barbecue. There were eight men and four women. From where they stood, the blinding sun fell directly in their eyes, glazing their vision with little rivers of salty sweat. It fell on Da Da's back, scorching and tingling the muscles. And it struck fire, like little shards of lightning, from the blade of the ready machete, nestling in Da Da's crotch, between his legs.

The story goes that for the first five or so minutes of the assembly, Da Da did not even twitch an eyebrow, much less speak. The assembled heads of the branches of the family sweated. None dared to lift a hand to wipe a streaming face.

Then Da Da moved. With the thumb of his right hand he eased the machete ever so gently from his crotch. In one movement quicker than the eye could ever follow, the machete handle was firmly grasped within his fist, its blade standing heavenwards. The sun was flashing bolts of lightning from its sharpened edge. The machete had become an avenging sword. It took one minute by the clock – a seeming-century for the standing assembly – till Da Da lowered the machete and leaned it gently, on the inside of his right leg, this time.

Da Da was a man of few words. And soft manner. The story goes that the following exchange took place between Da Da and his assembled family:

Da Da: 'Tenk-ye to all you, mi blood, who leave you living tede-day fe come and change taat wif me. The good Massa teach that sober taat can stop blood from run.'

Mas D: 'Pa, is what? Is what make you so vex?'

Da Da quieted him with one little look.

Da Da continued: 'When Old Barton from inna slavery a take every penny him could a get him hand pon, fe clink pon the other, till him save up the first pisspot full a penny, then same ting, till the second pisspot full – was anybody a quarrel? Did tongue and teeth meet, even with him very wife who-fa face him blow inna a-night-time?'

Da Da paused. Total, sun-hot silence.

'When Old Barton did call all the fambily and some who wasn't even far fambily but him did take them to him heart – when him call all a-them an' say "dis lan' buy with labour and it can only keep with labour", was any quarrel an' fight? Was no so it did go, that everyone did work on the lan' and the lan' did feed them?'

Da Da paused again.

Licky-licky Tommy Barton, Da Da's younger brother, ventured nervously:

'True word, true word me Bredda. Some a-them don't know a ting bout how this lan' buy, they just come an' reap the sweet.'

Da Da ignored him. Tommy turned around as if to address the others. Da Da began to tap the point of the machete softly on the packed-hardened earth beneath his feet. Tommy's voice trailed off with: 'A true word Da Da a-talk.' He straightened up himself to face Da Da full again.

Within the space of half an hour, all had heard and accepted, without any quarrel, Da Da's suggestion.

And it was this:

Only he, Da Da, had the right, under law, to sell any of the land, as his father was the son of Maisie the issue of the direct seed of Old Barton. Point One.

No one could question that. 'That was facts', they all thought.

Old Barton set it up that the land must never pass from the Barton name. Therefore, if ever any part of it was to be sold, it would have to be to a Barton. Point Two.

Some immediately thought: 'That's logic, so far.' But especially the family by marriage grumbled tumultuously in their heads. They did not feel able to do it through their mouths.

If any Barton now living and working on the land wished to leave, then he, Da Da Barton, and after him, Mas D Barton, and after, his direct descendant – would give that person money to the value of one-twelfth of the land. Thereinafter, that person, their present family, and all descendants for ever more would have no claim to live, work, eat or otherwise benefit from any part of the land. Assembly dismissed.

Tommy Barton was the first to ask for his one-twelfth in cash. And used it to pay his boat fare to Colon, Panama, in 1926.

Mas D got married to Miss Belle Thomas whose family came from the

Districts of Ducksies and Lluidas Vale. By 1930, when Putus was born, it was mainly Da Da, Mas D and Miss Belle left to work whatever portion of the land they could manage, except for help from some far family and neighbours during planting time and crop time.

Some of the Barton women had married and gone to live with their husbands' families. Others had joined the trek of mainly the men to Kingston, overseas, or to other parts of the island – in search of work which would enable them to become independent.

And Da Da Barton passed away peacefully in his sleep one night. He got even more respect in death than in life because everyone was so impressed with how peacefully and calmly he had died. Certainly no one could say that 'Da Da Barton did dead bad' – usually seen as the ultimate negative judgement on the life one had lived. Every man, woman, child, even the numerous mongrel dogs, in the District and from far afield came to his funeral. He was buried just beyond the border of the yam field he was so fond of staying in when doing his 'thinking work'. His grave was placed beside that of Ma Tata, his wife and Mas D's mother, who had passed on while giving birth to Mas D. Da Da had never married again because as he used to say when the question was raised about the house 'needing a woman',

'Fi some man, is one woman the Great Massa mek. Tenk-ye to Him that I did find the One. The good Massa choose fi tek her before her time. That is not for me to question why? Only to praise Him for the time she spen' with me.'

After a time, people had stopped raising the question of Da Da's widowhood. But they had whispered at the Set-Up on the night following Da Da's death, and at the funeral, that Ma Tata had not been able to stand the loneliness anymore and so had just taken Da Da away in his sleep to keep her company. Be that as it may . . . The main thing, everyone agreed, is that Da Da had died good.

With Da Da's passing, Mas D became head of the Barton family. This did not bring him any great glory. Sometimes Mas D would think, and then be ashamed of it, that as long as Da Da was alive, it was he and not Mas D who had to find the money to pay to those members of the family who were claiming the value of their one-twelfth of the land. And since more of them were doing this near to the end of Da Da's life it would be he, Mas D, who would have to find the money and he didn't know where it would come from. So even as he shed genuine tears as he, along with some others of the direct descendants of Old Barton, lowered Da Da Barton into this hallowed ground, he couldn't help thinking realistically, of the burden which had now fallen on him and wondering how he was going to manage to fulfil all the obligations which fell to the head of the family and support his own wife and child.

Putus's mother, Miss Belle, used to go to Old Harbour or Spanish Town market on Fridays and Saturdays to sell whatever crop was reaped. Mas D would also add to the family's income by doing paid day's work on Mr Nicholson's property, which was planted out mainly in coffee, chocolate, coconuts and citrus fruits.

Even with the money coming in from the day's work, things were difficult. Especially since the sales in the market were very much up and down. Whenever dusk was falling in the market on a Saturday evening and Miss Belle had not yet been able to dispose of much of the provisions at the originally set price, she not only had to slash prices: sometimes she had to give the goods away almost for nothing, hoping to clear enough to pay her fare for the country truck back home and buy some corned meat and salt fish to supplement the family's dinners through the week, till next market day.

Putus's mother was not a complaining woman. But there was one thing she insisted on from Putus's birth and never wavered on: Putus Barton will never work like a slave on the land, as she had to. Putus will never sell in the market. Putus Barton will become, at the very least, a teacher or a postmistress.

PUTUS

'**P**utus, how much longer I must wait on you, Maam?' Aunt Sisi's voice, loud and harsh with vexation and impatience, dragged Putus back into the present.

'I coming right now, Aunt Sisi.'

Putus hurried into the house. Aunt Sisi was in her bedroom, so Putus was forced to stand just inside the door, looking harmless and respectful. Aunt Sisi was sitting on the big four-poster bed with the chenille bedspread. She was looking serious.

Aunt Sisi never usually called Putus into her bedroom, certainly not while she or Mr Bennett was in it. But even more worrying to Putus was the tone of voice in which Aunt Sisi had called her and the fact that she had used the term 'Maam'. It must indeed be a very serious matter that Aunt Sisi was calling her about.

Putus stands respectfully before Aunt Sisi, waiting for whatever is to come. So how did Putus get here, from the hills of Brown's Hall, to this austere bedroom of the wood mansion of Mountain Road, in Old Harbour? She would not have chosen to come to live in this house, among the Nicholson-Bennetts, for whom, at best, she felt indifference; at worst, resentment and, sometimes, even hate.

At the insistence of Miss Belle, Putus had to be taken to school as soon as she could walk and talk reasonably clearly. In vain Mas D said: 'B, she too young! I want her edicated too, but you taking this thing too far. She just pass two years old, wait till she six. Then they will take her at the Elementary School.'

Miss Belle would retort:

'That's what they tell we poor Black people. Don't bring them to school until them is six. You think the whiteman whey you see in charge of the police station dung a Old Harbour, or the manager-them at Port Esquivel, did waste whole-a six years before them start them edication?

'Think you head good, D. All of them who make something of themself and can now turn topanaris over we who work so hard, did have private teacher from them go "wa, waa" just as them come out a them mother womb. Ask them, ask them if you don' believe me.'

'But B, we cyaan afford private teacher for Putus.'

'That's not what A asking. What A saying is that we have to get her into Teacher Nicholson private school. She take them from three years old.'

'B, where we going to get the money from to pay the school fee?

Teacher Nicholson charge a whole five shillings a week. That is almost five days' work for me on her brother property.'

'Don't we did find the money fi gi you wutless cousin when him want was to go to America?'

'A had was to do that because him did own one-twelfth of the lan'. A had was to find it. Is a agreement. A cyaan bruk it!'

'Oh, but you can bruk you responsibility to you own blood, you own seed? Ah so, eh, D?'

And on and on.

Putus went to Teacher Nicholson's private school at three years old. Putus's mother now worked one day a week cleaning Mrs Nicholson's house. At this time, the main extra expense was the five shillings a week school fee, since the private school was just next door. Every time Mas D would look more and more tired and broken down, Miss Belle would smother her growing unease with the flushful pride that Putus was being educated right along with the children of the big property-owners from Brown's Hall, Point Hill, Ducksies, Lluidas Vale and even Old Harbour.

Sometimes it wrenched her heart when she could not avoid noticing that Mas D hadn't laughed in months. Hadn't playfully dragged her to the back of the yam field to have a little impromptu picnic and romping under the moonlight on a warm summer night.

Their life became one long grind of working, quick-eating, exhausted-sleep, jumping-up before daylight, quick-eating, working, slumping into exhausted-sleep – to start the round again.

When thoughts came into Miss Belle's head that 'we cyaan live so! This cyaan be life?' – she would straighten her tired back and retort to herself:

'I still fine time fe laugh and I working even harder than him. I doing everything that him doing. But who washing the clothes-them. Who washing the plate-them. Who cleaning the house. Who taking care of Putus. No me? Hey! No wonder they say woman is the stronger. I don' dwell into mi misery.'

One dusk when Mas D returned from that day's work on Mr Nicholson's property, he came and sat on Da Da's little stool right beside the fireside in the kitchen outside. This night he said to Miss Belle: 'B, A going to take me food right ya so.'

Miss Belle was horrified. At the worst of times, whenever Mas D finished work, he usually took his bath, changed his clothes and then sat down round the dining table in the front room for his dinner. Now, he sat slumped on Da Da's stool, the wool on his head caked and matted with dirt and sweat, his coppery face a multi-shade from dust, dirt and sweat, his green-khaki clothes brown-black. And he wanted to eat here, by the fireside, in this condition!

Miss Belle said in her mind: 'Lawd God almighty, give me strength to face this trial!' She swallowed two times. Then she swallowed eight times more. To calm herself.

17

'What de matter, D? You not feeling well? A think you working too hard!'

Some of the coconut oil in the Dutch iron pot bubbled over the edge and sizzled down its side into the wood fireplace. The flames reared up, with an acrid stench and black smoke.

'B, we cyaan go on like this.'

'What you mean, D?'

'A mean we cyaan live so.'

'So what we going to do?'

'A don' know full, yet. But A know we have to mek some change in wi life. Suppose you sick? Suppose Putus sick? What going to happen to we? We don' even have a penny fi rainy day. I going soon have to start borrow from people just fi live. And no Barton ever borrow money.'

'You saying all this is my fault? I there head and head with you. A not a lazy woman, sleeping in the bed while you working?'

'B, A not blaming you. A not blaming anybody. Is just so it go. All A saying is that it cyaan go on like this. We have to mek some change.'

'I know what you thinking. You want to move Putus from Teacher Nicholson. Don't think A don' have no heart. A know that you have to tek on slave work so we can pay the school fee. But think D, think! Fi we daughter is the blackest mongst them white and brown pickney. You know them keep the best for themself. And fi we own blood getting the best, right along with them white and brown people. You don' think any sacrifice wort' that? Think D, think!'

'But what going happen when she reach Elementary School? The school way dung a-yonder before you ketch a Old Harbour. She going want uniform an' book. We going have-fi get a little bicycle fi her . . . or how she going reach the school? Is going be more expense, don't it, B? don't it?'

D was right, Miss Belle thought, but they would have to manage somehow, because Putus must keep on getting the best of education available.

'We have-fe manage somehow. The good Lord will provide.'

'Him provide Mr Nicholson, B, but is me who have fe work out mi soul-case fi get the little pittance in mi han'.'

'Mrs Nicholson did want me to work full-time in the house, Monday to Friday. She say that she won' ask me fi come pon Saturday cause she know say me have-fe go to market. Maybe A should tek the full-time work over there.'

'And how you would-a fine time fi work pon fi we lan', B? How you would-a manage fi tek care a Putus?'

'You only know how fi say no, no. Don't bother to gi me no argument bout teking Putus out a school. We have fi think of some other way. Trust in the Lord.'

'Well, maybe is the Lord put this way before me. A never tell you before, but Mr Nicholson want to buy the part of the lan' that have on the stream.'

The Dutch pot boiled over again.

Mas D felt apprehension, mixed with an oncoming sense of supreme relief. There it was. Out in the open.

'That's no secret, D? Everybody in the District know say Mr Nicholson covet that lan' long time. What them don' know is that any Barton would-a even consider selling it to him and him generation-them! Remember, Old Barton say the lan' cyaan sell?'

Mas D had carried his intention heavy in his heart for many months. He had turned it around and upside down in his head for many months. At least three weeks before, he had finally come to a decision, in his head. The problem was how to communicate it to Miss Belle, first, and the scattered descendants of Old Barton second. On this second he didn't feel so bad, because between his father and himself they had sucked the family's accumulated resources dry, to pay cash to all the descendants who had wanted to leave the land.

But three things still bothered him. The first was that Great-Grandfather Barton never wanted any of the land to go out of the Barton name. For this, at least three generations had sacrificed. Starting with Maisie, his eldest daughter, who had wrecked any chance of a fulfilling relationship with her husband, because unto his dying day he could neither understand, nor accept, why his children had to be named after their mother's family. He had kept up the marriage for appearances' sake. But it had been an open secret in the District and beyond, that after he had impregnated his wife with the wash-belly child of four children he never slept with her again, but sought out and cohabited with leggo-women far and wide.

Then there were the numerous nieces, nephews and cousins who came to help from time to time but who looked on the land as their only roots – wherever they were scattered. Even those of the family who had given up all their claim by taking money still saw the land as a base.

Mas D felt that he was going to betray them, even though they had gone off and left him with all the work and the burden of maintaining the land.

The heaviest burden on Mas D's heart, however, was how he was going to tell Miss Belle. Their child, Putus, was a direct descendant of Old Barton. All of the land was her legacy. That she could 'lef' slavery back-a-door fi-ever', as Old Barton would say. Only, Mas D thought, that Old Barton could not know that land was not enough, in these times, to keep slavery back-a-door.

One had to study the slavemaster's ways, his education – or forever remain a slave.

'That is what A trying to break out of. Them is chains that even tougher than slavery chains!' Mas D had been saying over and over to himself as he lay in the coir-mattress, four-poster bed beside Miss Belle. That's part

19

of the reason he was so broken down after a gruelling day's work, he could not sleep peacefully.

On Da Da's stool, in the wattle kitchen, beside the stone fireside, surrounded by the smoke-blackened walls, he prayed that Miss Belle would understand. He didn't want to lose any more of her than he had lost already. And that is really why he had taken the decision to break Old Barton's trust. Because when all was said and done, what had kept him going was the sight, the laughter, the unquenchable light of Belle; the smell of sun and rain and wind and earth and woodsmoke and sweat of her body that he lay next to every night – even when often he couldn't find the energy to take this body into his own, suck up its juices, and eat it up.

And little Putus was such a joy! At first, just after the birth of the child, he was irritated and jealous that B paid so much attention to it. But then, as she grew and became almost a replica of B, with her shine-Black skin and Black-white knowing eyes, her little tendernesses, like climbing upon him in his work khakis and putting her little face right between the top of his chest and the bottom of his chin – and just laying her face there – he began to feel that this child was his blood and he would kill for it.

He had taken the decision to sell a portion of the land to Mr Nicholson when he knew that the land was not worth his life.

Miss Belle wanted passionately for Putus to have all of Old Barton's land as her legacy. But she wanted with equal passion for Putus to be equipped with the slavemaster's education. What to do? D was right. They couldn't go on living like this. But to sell the land? To take it out of the Barton name? 'Jesus Christ,' her mind screamed, 'how much more?'

'So, D, you mek-up you mind. A know you sufficient to know that you mek-up you mind.'

'Yes B, A mek-up mi mind.'

'Well, there is nothing more to be said.'

This was the response that usually brought most tremors to his heart. It meant that B would do whatever was necessary, but he would never know what she really thought, as this part of B would be closed to everyone, including himself. He bled in his heart. But knew it did not make any sense to pursue the matter further.

'Come D, A set up a nice tub of sun-water for you bath. Bathe an' change you clothes. By the time you finish, the food wi on the table.'

Mas D hesitated a moment. Then went to the zinc-enclosed bathroom in the yard, where the tub was resting on the stone-packed floor.

By the time Putus was of an age to go to the Elementary School, Mr Nicholson was the proud owner of about 8 acres of the Barton land. He got the part with most of the stream, but since a part of the stream ran near to Da Da's and Ma Tata's graves, he couldn't get the whole stream, not to mention the whole 10 acres, which was what he really wanted.

After the sale, Mas D did not feel the happiness he thought would have followed. But the land sale did allow the family to put away something for a rainy day, as well as meet the expenses for suiting out Putus to the Elementary School.

Putus did well. All her teachers said she was very bright. The head-master suggested to Miss Belle that Putus take the First Jamaica Local Examinations when she was thirteen. He said he knew she could get through, especially if she was able to have extra lessons.

She passed with flying colours. Mas D was still bowed down but ever so proud of his daughter. And as for Miss Belle, the people at the shop on the main road began to call her 'edicated Mama', behind her back, because she boasted so much about Putus.

Putus was then going on in her studies for the Second Year (Jamaica Local) exams. The road seemed clear. Everyone felt that she would pass and then go on to Third Year. After that, she couldn't be stopped again. Because with the Third Year certificate, she could become a pupil teacher, a postmistress, or begin training as a nurse. All that was necessary was for her to concentrate her mind, behave herself and study her book.

Just one month before Putus was to sit the Second Jamaica Local Exam, one event changed their lives, for ever.

That morning, Miss Belle thought, Mas D had looked even more burdened down than usual, as he put on his work khakis. She was worried that he was sick with something.

'D, when last you take a wash-out?'

'A don' need no purgative, B. A feeling arright.'

'But you don' look arright. Come Sunday morning-ya, A going dose you with a little senna and salts – just fi clean out you system. You wi feel much better after that. Don' mek up yu face so – is not even castor oil A suggesting that you take – just a little senna and salts.'

'A don' need no wash-out B. But arright, A wi drink a little senna and salts Sunday morning.'

Mas D then did something he didn't often do. He went to the door of the bathroom, where Putus was taking her bath before going to school, and told her:

'Hurry up, Putus, A want to see you before you go to school.'

Then he told Miss Belle to come out of the kitchen and asked for her and Putus to accompany him to the little opening in the side fence leading from the Barton land to the Nicholson property. At the fence, just before he left to go into the property next door, he hugged his wife and his daughter and said to them:

'A try mi best. A try mi best to mek you happy. Sometime tings don' work out arright, but A try mi best.'

Both Miss Belle and Putus wondered what this was all about. But both of them loved him so much, in their different ways, that even if he had

21

chosen to strip himself naked and do a rain dance, they would just have taken it in their stride.

Mas D went through the opening in the fence, and just at the point beyond which he would have disappeared from their sight, he turned around. His almost copper skin (from a long-ago Portuguese woman whose blood got mixed up with his Ghanaian ancestors) was bouncing reflections of light in the tender early morning sun. His khaki was stiff, with the starching and ironing B had given it. But it was his eyes. They were a cross between hazel and brown, normally. Now, they seemed to have gotten the blue-black depths of the sink-hole just off the fishing beach at Old Harbour Bay. Mas D's eyes seemed to be saying something. In some language that the two women could not understand.

He looked at them for such a seeming-long time, that Miss Belle had to say:

'D, D, yu going late. Sun come up arready an' you don' reach full pon the property, yet.'

Afterwards, Miss Belle wished she hadn't said that. She wished she had run through the opening in the fence and squeezed him one more time. Buried her nose in his sweat-sweet armpits, one more time. Smelt all his little dark corners, one more time. Tasted the salt and the sun of him, one more time.

PUTUS

'Mrs Barton, Mrs Barton!' The call was coming from the front gate of the yard. Miss Belle was in the kitchen. Putus had not yet returned from school.

It sounded like the big man himself, Mr Nicholson. But Miss Belle wondered why was he coming to their house? And at this time of day too?

'Miss B, Miss B, we have something to tell you.'

That was his eldest daughter, Sisi's voice. She was not a bad woman. Even used to be kind to Putus when she was at her aunt's private school. But she had never deigned to come to this house before. Even though Miss Belle had once extended an invitation to her, her husband, her mother and father, in whose house she sometimes worked, to pass by on a holiday-day when family and friends were gathered at Mas D's and Miss Belle's house. They had always given her some excuse. Mr Nicholson hadn't even come to their house when he and Mas D were negotiating the land sale, Mas D had to meet him in the lawyer office in Spanish Town. So it was a marvel to Miss Belle to consider what could have brought Sisi and her exalted father to her gate?

Miss Belle's heart became heavy and her head swell-up big, big, like when duppy visit the yard. And all of a sudden, she knew. Or at least she knew that it could not be anything good they had come to deliver.

'Greetings to you, Mr Nicholson. Miss Sisi, hope you hawty. Your mother in the best of ealth? Come in, come in.'

The pair hesitated. It appeared they wanted to deliver any message they had brought from outside the gate. Of course, there was no way Miss Belle was going to allow this. It would have compounded too much, their higher status and her lower status. They came through the gate and allowed her to seat them properly in the front room. Only after she had served them with some sour orange lemonade, cooled with ice, did she seem ready for whatever they had come to say.

'So, whats-it, Mr Nicholson? Whats-it, Miss Sisi?'

Mr Nicholson paused a minute. He didn't know how to begin. When the silence had gotten embarrassingly long, Sisi prodded him.

'Pa, jus' tell her. It happen already.'

'What happen, Mr Nicholson? What happen, Miss Sisi? Whats-it?'

'Well, Mrs B, you husband had a little accident.'

'What kine a accident, Mr Nicholson?'

Mr Nicholson paused again.

'Miss B, he fall off the coconut tree. Pa don' know how to tell you it.'

'Fall off coconut tree, Miss Sisi? But what him doing on coconut tree? A thought mi husband was doing day's work supervising the field. Him not boy to climb coconut tree. What him was doing on coconut tree?'

Miss Belle turned her black eyes full on the father and daughter. Mr Nicholson cleared his throat.

'I had a little problem getting coconuts picked in time for the contract at the soap factory, so Mas D said he would help me out.'

'And you send him pon the coconut tree. What happen to him? What condition him in now? Where him is? Eh, Mr Nicholson, eh, Miss Sisi?'

The question now raging in both their minds was, who would answer. Sisi continued to be the bolder one.

'He dead, Miss B. Him neck broke when he fall down off the coconut tree.'

'Dead. Dead. Ah, A see. Dead. You sure him dead?'

They nodded.

'Well, there is nothing more to be said. Tenk-ye for coming to tell me.'

All she wanted now was for these people to go. She knew she had to find out more of the details, like where the body was now. But she wouldn't be able to gather the strength to hear anything more or attend to anything else, until she got these people out of the house and could vent her feelings in private.

'Miss B, we will help in whatever way we can.'

Mr Nicholson found his tongue.

'We will pay for the funeral . . . '

'Pay for the funeral? Pay for the funeral? That can bring him back?'

'Mrs Barton, Mrs Barton, pull yourself together. I know that you are upset but these things happen, you know.'

'Happen, Mr Nicholson? Happen to who? A never have a husband before who drop offa coconut tree and bruk him neck? It never happen to me before?'

'Miss B, don't take it so hard. Is nobody fault.' That was Sisi.

'Yes, you right, mi dear, is nobody fault. Arright, tenk-you.'

Miss Belle rose to take them to the gate. They were not satisfied, so they lingered. The father clearing his throat, the daughter rubbing her hands together and looking everywhere except into Miss Belle's face.

'Miss B, we know it going to be hard for you and Putus now, with Mas D gone. Mama say that you can come and work full-time in the house. You won't have so much work as before because me and Mr Bennett and the children moving to wi new house down Old Harbour next month. If you want anything, I willing to help.'

'Tenk-ye, Miss Sisi. God bless you. But A don' need nothing. A will manage. Tenk-ye for coming Mr Nicholson, Miss Sisi. Let me take you pass that old cross dog.'

By this time, Miss Belle had succeeded in guiding them to the gate.

PUTUS

'Mama, God have to forgive me for saying so but is so I feel. I hate them. I hate them. I hate them.'

'Shush yu mout girl! Is not everyting good fi eat, good fi talk. Have respeck for yu dead father. Him body don't even cold yet.'

'They did have any respect for him, eh, Mama? They did respect him when they send him like a little leggo-boy to climb coconut tree? Don't Mr Nicholson could find idle boys and pay them something to climb the coconut tree?'

'Mi child, we all suffering. But is not for us to question God's will. Thy Will Be Done, the Good Book tell we . . . '

Putus interrupted sharply, 'Thy Will? Thy Will? – is only Mr Nicholson and him family Will! They take away wi land, then they take away mi father. Then they bright enough to come up in the funeral an' preach sermon over mi father who they kill . . . '

Miss Belle's face became purple-black. Only by the redness of her eyes and a slight puffiness under them could anyone guess that she had wept continually, in private, every night since Mas D's death. And only once, at the funeral, just before they lowered the cedarwood coffin into the grave beside Da Da and Ma Tata, did she lose her composure, for a minute or so. She had grasped on to the coffin and let out three wails – wooy . . . wooy . . . wooy! The sound had fled to the surrounding hills and bounced back into the funeral gathering. Had condemned and confounded all the guilty among the mourners.

Then in a rough, hoarse voice, coming from the bottom of her belly, she had raised her own adaptation of the popular funeral hymn:

'Farewell my love
Mek sweet angels speed your rest
We love you
But Massa Jesus love you best
Farewell my love
Sweet angels speed your rest
Farewell, farewell, farewell.'

Then she had whispered, as if only to herself, or to Mas D, 'Nothing, nothing more to be said.'

'Ashes to ashes, dust to dust,' Parson intoned importantly, as the coffin hit its final resting place and close family threw handfuls of earth on it, before the men would begin shovelling to fill the grave.

But Putus had been a problem. For her, there was much more to be said. Luckily, Miss Belle thought, she had so far not said these things in public. And although she fully understood Putus's feelings, yea, even shared them, she felt that Putus had to learn from now to suppress her true feelings. Or else she would have an even harder time in the world. Miss Belle responded angrily to Putus's outburst.

'Wait girl, yu forgetting yu manners! Yu sudden-sudden turn big woman? Mine A don' have to soil yu father memory by boxing yu teeth down yu throat, even before him body full cold.'

Putus started to roll herself on the floor of the main bedroom – the one her mother and father slept . . . used to sleep . . . in. She now slept there with her mother. Putus began a deep, low groaning but it wasn't of helpless mourning, it was more a growl of aggression. Miss Belle continued to speak, more calmly, slowly and deliberately this time.

'Putus, Putus, listen to me. Yu have to understand yuself good, or world will mash yu. Yu have to consider yu head and understand good, before yu open yu mout, no matter how much yu vex. An' mos time, wat yu understand, yu have to keep it to yuself. "Let not yu lef' han' know wat yu right han' knoweth." Yu listenin' to me, girl?'

'Yes, Mama' – between the aggressive groans.

'Mr Nicholson an' him fambily didn' tek yu father lan', is him who sell it to dem an' dem pay money for it. Is dat money dat help send yu to school an' pay for yu private lesson-them. They didn' kill yu father wilfully. They sen' him pon the coconut tree but him didn' have to go. The good Lord give every man a free choice, no matter how poor dem be . . . '

'Free choice? Free choice? How you can say that, Mama? What choice mi father did have not to sell the land? What choice him did have not to obey Mr Nicholson order, to pick coconut? You call the choice for we-all to starve, choice?'

'Girl, don' interrup me. A talking. Have manners. Sometime A wonder if dat white man edication not bad fi yu. It mek yu feel dat yu can pass yu place with yu elders and betters. Even with yu own mudder.'

'Beg pardon, Mama, A listening.'

Putus backed down. From experience, she knew better than to get Miss Belle too riled up. And, after all, she thought, I don't have to tell even her what A really thinking.

'Now Putus, A want yu to tek-in good, good, wat A saying to you. A not goin' to repeat it again. Is for you to put it in yu head an' mek it teach yu how to ack when the right time come.'

'What it, Mama? What you talking bout?'

'Tings goin' change-up. Some-a de change-dem, we wi mek wiself, some wi jus come down pon wi. A cyaan tell yu now, wat all de change-dem will be. The good Lord will reveal all in His own good time. A don'

26

wan' fi yu to frighten an' lose yu head like bruk-neck fowl when de change-dem come, Putus.'

Putus stopped her rolling and growling. She wanted to listen to this good-good. She knew her mother enough to know that she would have to listen both to what was said and as well to what wasn't said, to be able to read the meaning within the meaning of her mother's words.

'Yu father did leave back a little something from the sale a de lan'. We can always fall-back pon dat if tings get too tough. But, as yu know, if yu tekking-out everyday an' not putting anyting back in – what was in, mus run out one day.

'A mek-up mi mind – A not goin' turn Mrs Nicholson full-time maid. But A goin' to do some more days' work over there, to help we out. A wi work more pon what lef of yu father lan'. Is now your legacy. A don' want it fall into cassia macka an' weed. So A have fi cultivate it as good as A can manage. A don' know how A goin' do it by miself, but the good Lord wi help those who help themself.'

Two or three times, Putus had made to interrupt. But the intensity and seriousness with which her mother was telling her all this held her tongue.

'Putus, A don' wan' you to help me on the lan'. A don' want you fi do even one minute work over Mrs Nicholson house. A wan' you to go on studying yu book. Putus, hear me, when all things change, dats one ting dats not goin' change. You mus concentrate on yu book an' on nutting else. You mus pass yu exam-them. You wi be de Barton who true lef' slavery back-a-door. You wi be a teacher, or a postmistress, or dress-up in yu stiff white uniform – mi little nursie.'

Here Miss Belle went into one of her very rare demonstrations of tender feelings. She picked Putus up from the floor, like she was a baby. Sat on the bed with her on her lap and in her arms and began to stroke and cuddle her all over. Putus began to weep.

'Don' cry, mi baby. Don' cry. Jus promise yu Mama. Promise yu Mama dat yu not goin' lose yu way. Promise yu Mama day you wi be the one who bruk dem slavery chain fi-ever. Promise yu Mama. Ol Barton wi laugh an' yu father wi res in peace.'

Putus got out, behind her tears and grief, 'A promise you, Mama.'

'Come, mi chile, eat something. Drink little a the soup. You don' eat nothing much since yu father dead.'

This whole episode helped Putus to face life without her father. She did become more withdrawn. She did perhaps spend a little too much time, even by Miss Belle's standards, studying her book. She passed Second Jamaica Local, at the top of her class – at fifteen years old. It was now the last stretch of this particular stage of the race to which generations of her family had committed her. She settled down into her studies for the Third Year exams.

Nothing much, as far as she could see, had changed. Except that her mother worked even harder than before and she missed her father badly.

And only that the Nicholsons were more mixed up into their lives than when her father was alive. Mrs Nicholson was now giving her mother little things, like clothes that she didn't wear anymore, like clothes that her children and grandchildren had grown out of. Even when Miss Belle pointed out that some of them were almost new, Putus absolutely refused to wear them.

'I prefer dead first, than wear Nicholson "what-lef".' But she did accept the new school clothes and books which Sisi bought in Old Harbour and brought to her in Brown's Hall on one of her weekend visits to her parents.

Now, different ones of the Nicholson family called at Miss Belle's house fairly often, whether to bring messages or 'just to see how you getting on, Mrs B'. Mr Nicholson himself had even come over to put it to Miss Belle one evening that he thought herself and Putus would get on better if she sold him the rest of the land, just keeping the house-spot which they lived on. Miss Belle had responded demurely, her head respectfully bowed:

'Tenk-ye Mr Nick fah tinking so much bout me an' Putus. You right, yu know. Maybe it would be de bes ting for wi to sell de lan' but the fambily-dem wouldn' agree. A don' wan' no trouble wit dem, Mr Nick.'

Miss Belle had boiled inside to think that Mr Nicholson would dig out the Barton very graves. But she kept her face looking concerned and respectful. At the same time, turning her smoke-thunderous eyes towards the keyhole of the door leading into the main bedroom, where she knew Putus was peeping and listening. She would not put it past Putus to shout out their true feelings about Mr Nicholson's 'suggestion'.

As for Putus, she was vexed enough that Mr Nicholson had become 'Mr Nick' to her mother and Sisi had become 'Aunt Sisi' even though she was younger than Miss Belle. But by the time Sisi brought the new clothes and books to the house and her mother had called her into the front room to receive them, she was able to say meekly: 'Thank you very much, Aunt Sisi' – without choking.

PUTUS

If Putus had thought that she had by then seen all the changes her mother had warned her were to come, she had much to learn.

She began this phase of her real-life education one Sunday about a year after her father's death. A cousin of theirs had come by on the Saturday evening and killed one of the young fowls in the yard. Normally only on special occasions was a fowl, and especially a young one, killed. They were needed to lay eggs to be sold in the market to provide part of the money to buy the salt meat and saltfish. Miss Belle had picked and cleaned the fowl and then seasoned it up, from Saturday night.

Putus wondered what they were celebrating. But she didn't dare ask her mother. Miss Belle was silent, like a brick wall. Putus decided that she would wait and see, even as her mouth watered at the thought of how sweet the fowl meat was going to be when it was cooked the next day.

As the Sunday wore on, Putus wondered more and more. It wasn't only that her mother told her from early in the morning that she didn't have to go to Sunday School that evening, it was more that her mother, although silent most of the time, could not hide the excitement in her heart. Normally, Sunday was a day of rest, apart from going to church. This Sunday morning, her mother told her to give the yard a 'little sweep'. And it was as if Miss Belle wanted every leaf in place in the yard. She shouted at Putus when she left a little mound of dirt under the mango tree, as usual, telling her to spread it out and damp it down with water. And as to the house! When a little piece of thread found its way on to the centre table, her mother got into a rage and accused her of not being able to tidy a house properly.

By 2 o'clock, the dinner was ready. Brown-stew fowl with Irish potatoes cooked-down in the gravy; rice and peas with coconut milk; salad tomatoes sliced and sprinkled with salt and black pepper; carrot-and-beetroot juice for drink, soft-top sweet potato pudding for dessert.

'Putus, look in the Atoman. Tek some tings from dere to set the table wit.'

Eh, Putus thought, Is what this?

The only time in her life that she had seen her mother take any of the house things from the Atoman at the foot of the four-poster bed was when she was keeping up dead house, at the time of her father's death.

By the time she finished setting the table, her mother was decked out in one of her church dresses, Putus's favourite – the black one with the big red and orange flowers.

'Putus, go change yu clothes. Put on yu little bird-eye frock that yu did wear to the harvest at church,' Miss Belle commanded. 'An' put on yu good shoes and socks. We having visitor.'

Putus felt that much she had guessed. But who could this visitor be, that was so important? She thought the question, she was not going to ask it. She obeyed Miss Belle's instructions.

She bathed quickly and dressed herself. The dinner was being kept warm. The house was spotless. The yard was all packed-earth orderliness. Putus and Miss Belle were immaculately dressed. Putus hoped that the expected high and mighty visitor would come on time. Because although Miss Belle did not say so outright, it was crystal clear that no eating was going to take place until this visitor – whoever he or she might be – came.

Right on the dot of 3 o'clock, there was a knocking at the gate. Mamby, their dog, set up a loud barking. Putus jumped. Miss Belle sprang up from her seat in the sitting-room.

'Don' worry yuself, Putus. A tink is wi visitor. A wi let him in.'

Her mother literally ran from the front room but closed the door behind her as she went to the gate. Putus peeped through the window.

At the gate stood a Brown man. Putus couldn't see his whole figure. But she could see his face and his curly hair. She decided she didn't like the Brown man.

'Putus, this is Mr Boysie McKenzie from Linstead. His family keep business in Linstead. Him come to break bread wid we.'

Silence. The Brown man stood uncertainly just inside the front-room door.

'Putus, say How-di to Mr Boysie!'

'How-di, Mr Boysie. Hope you well. All you family well?'

He smiled. Or rather stretched his pink lips.

'Glad to meet you, Putus. Yu mother tell me a lot about yu.'

Putus looked surprised. Not pleasantly surprised but vexed-surprised. She didn't say a word.

'Thank-you for asking bout the family. Yes, them all well.'

'Come, come Boysie. Sit down. We going to dish up the dinner.'

Her mother rescued the moment. Putus didn't like the Brown man. She didn't know him. But she thought that he had puss eyes. And he grinned too much. She didn't trust anyone who grinned too much. She prayed that he wouldn't try to become too friendly with her. She hoped that he would be one of those red-niggers who didn't know how to conduct themselves. Then her mother would surely throw him out of the house.

He wasn't. He was the soul of manners and decorum. Seating himself quietly at the table, complimenting the food but not hogging it. Using the knife and fork well (normally they ate with spoons). Not talking loud. Not laughing loud.

Putus still didn't like him.

'Is who him, Mama?'

They were in the four-poster bed, after the visitor had gone and they had cleaned up everything, putting the special things back into the Atoman.

'Him fambily come from Linstead. Them keep shop and furniture business there. Them is Brown people who did have a whole heap a lan' but dem had was to sell some to the Clarke-dem.'

'So how you know him, Mama? You don't go to Linstead. So how you did meet him?'

'Him is a furniture-maker. An' sometime him mek furniture for de Nicholson-dem. Is him mek all the furniture for Aunt Sisi an' Mr Bennett house in Ol' Harbour.'

'So you meet him over by Mr Nicholson?'

'Yes, Putus.'

'So why him come here and eat with we? What him looking?'

'Putus, him not looking nuttin'. Is I who invite him fi break bread wid we.'

'He not coming back, Mama? He not coming back?'

Miss Belle turned over . . . and, ostensibly, went to sleep.

He did come back. He began to be a regular visitor after his work on the Nicholson property. One night, Putus had to go to bed while he was still in the front room talking to her mother. When she came to say goodnight to Miss Belle, her mother told her:

'Putus, go to yu old room. You is a big girl. You suppose to can sleep by youself.'

Putus went to her old room. But she couldn't sleep. When they blew out the lamp in the front room and left to go into the main bedroom, she crept into the front room and clapped her eye through the keyhole to the bedroom. There was no light in there but she could still discern shadows in it. The main one being the Brown man . . . grunting and groaning . . . on top of her mother. Putus went back to her single bed in her own room. She couldn't sleep the whole night. In the early morning, long before the sun came up, she crept out of her room and went into the outdoor kitchen. She placed a note she had written in the night, right on the stone fireplace. The note said:

'I saw what you made that Brown man do to you. I hate you. You have betrayed my father. May God burn you up in hell.'

She went back to lie on her single bed. She didn't want to live in this type of change.

PUTUS

B oysie and Miss Belle's wedding took place one week after Putus's sixteenth birthday. Many of the Barton family didn't attend. Quite understandably, Putus thought, 'since she married so quick after Papa died'. A lot of Miss Belle's family came from Ducksies, Point Hill and Lluidas Vale. The biggest family group at the wedding were the McKenzies, who had travelled over from Linstead.

Putus had played with the idea of boycotting the wedding. She had made up her mind that even if she couldn't stop the relationship between her mother and this Brown man, at least she was not going to do anything to encourage it. On a Friday evening in May her mother had called her into the main bedroom while she was getting ready to go to the market in Spanish Town. Boysie was there but out in the field, behaving like 'man-a-yard' (or so Putus thought). Miss Belle had said to Putus, 'A ave someting to say to yu, Putus.'

Miss Belle sat on the bed. She wasn't finished putting on her clothes. She was in her full slip.

'Come up here pon de bed, Putus. A want we fi look into wi one another face when we talking.'

Putus climbed up on the bed but she kept her face averted from her mother's.

'Putus, A did see the letter you lef pon de fireside.'

Putus's body stiffened defiantly.

'Don' worry yuself, A not going beat you, though is a true wrenkin' letter. Me is a big woman an' Boysie is a big man. You is a child. You not suppose to tek such tings an' put pon yu head. You losin' yu mannas. Howsomever, A understan' how yu mus feel, an' dats why A not going beat yu, A going talk to yu. The fus ting is dat A don' want you fi go practise wat yu tink yu see me an' Boysie doing through the keyhole . . .'

'Then how you doing it?'

'Shet yu mout girl! Befo A ha fi shut it fi you. We is big people, you is a schoolgirl. We going married, you jus start yu studies; you wi ave plenty time fi dat when yu grow big an' ave yu big profession. A don' wan' no man spoil yu prospec, so A begging yu, keep yuself circumspec.'

'Mama, I not coming to the wedding.'

'Wat yu say, girl?'

'I say, A not coming to the wedding.'

'Look like yu drink mad-puss milk? Look like yu lose yu head?'

Putus raised up her head and stared straight into her mother's face, for the first time since she sat on the bed. Miss Belle knew that stubborn look. It was, after all, the same like hers. It meant that no force or threat of force could budge Putus.

'Putus? Putus, mi love? A know how much you miss yu father. A know seh dat you don' like Boysie. But tink again, Putus, tink again. Don' you see Boysie work hard? Don' tings better since him is here? Look how de lan' plant-up nice? An' don' him treat you arright? Him ever even raise him voice to you, much less fi lick you?'

'But he couldn't mad fi go lick me, Mama?'

'No, Putus, A wouldn' llow him fi do dat. But him is yu stepfather an' him ave a right fi discipline you if you don' behave yuself.'

This, even more than anything else, sent rivers of alarm through Putus's bloodstream. She felt that she would kill Boysie if he ever raised a finger to touch her. He wouldn't dare! That wasn't the problem. What shook her up was that her mother could sit there and tell her that he had 'a right' to do it.

At last, she began to understand what her mother had been trying to tell her those months ago about the type of change that just came down upon a person.

'Arright Mama, since is him you love and cyaan do without, I will have to manage the best way A can.'

'Putus, why yu looking on tings dat way? A love Boysie but dat don' prevent me from love yu same way like before. It don' prevent me from love yu father. But Mas D was in the pas', so A can only love him memry an' him spirit.'

'You going to give away Papa labour to Boysie. You going to make him and him family take over the rest of the land. You going to spend out the little savings that Papa leave, cooking big-food for Boysie.'

Miss Belle had pledged to herself that she wouldn't get vexed. But these last accusations of Putus brought her perilously near to the edge.

'Is who putting them things in you head, tell me, is who? You couldn't think up them lie all by yourself. Is who you bin talking to when A think you gone to school?'

'Mama, A not been talking to nobody. Is what I notice me ownself.'

'What you notice, what you notice? That sometime A cook beef an' kill a fowl some a the Sunday-them? Putus, Boysie bringing-in more money than you father. Him get more pay fi the furniture-them that him make. Him have more time fi work pon we lan' an' him bring man from him furniture business and fren an' fambily fi help out. Putus, me cyaan work the land by meself? You cyaan see that?'

Putus did see all that. But although she had highlighted those things, they were not the root of what was really worrying her. What was really worrying her was the change in her mother. She had never peeped through the keyhole at her mother and father in their bed. She had never even thought of whether they did anything there but sleep. She had never felt threatened when her father hugged-up her mother. She hadn't seen

33

anything strange when her father playfully patted her mother on the bottom. But when Boysie did any of these things with her mother it seemed, somehow, dirty. And the worst part of it was not only that her mother did not protest when Boysie was always touching her, touching her-up, all over the house and the yard, but she also would respond like a little 'leggo-girl' (or so Putus thought), laughing and grinning-up whenever Boysie touched her. Running to get into bed as early as possible whenever Boysie slept there. Having eyes for no one else but Boysie, when he was around. It was as if, it seemed to Putus, her mother was in a dream. She had the feeling that anything Boysie wanted, Boysie would get. This was confirmed by her mother's position on Boysie's 'right' to beat her.

And what further worried her was the attitude of the Nicholsons to this relationship between her mother and Boysie. Putus started her analysis from the base that the Nicholsons could not wish their family any good. After all, had they not stolen their land? Had they not killed her father? Yet Aunt Sisi had the nerve, on one of her visits to the house, to proclaim:

'Oh my, I never see Miss B so happy for a long time. Is you responsible for that, Mr McKenzie?'

Putus had thought that she would vomit when Boysie looked so pleased, with his Brown face lighting up and his puss eyes dancing. It was one of the Sundays when they had both brown-stew beef and fricassed yard-fowl for dinner. The Nicholsons – father, old wife, daughter and her husband – had, at last, come to dinner.

They had all been paying homage to Boysie and the McKenzie family, asking about their business in Linstead; discussing the war which had just finished in Europe, talking about the man called Hitler, the British, the Americans, the Russians and a whole heap of other things which Putus could not work up an interest in, although some Bartons, like Tommy's son, had died in the war overseas. She was concentrating on the main thing that was clear to her – that the Nicholsons did not mean her family any good; therefore the Nicholsons were not her friends. They liked Boysie, therefore she must be right, that whatever the appearances, Boysie could not be a good man. Her mother was simpering and glowing through all this talk and general fraternity. Therefore her mother must be in the total control of these people. She could not depend on her mother anymore to be sensible and to know the right thing to do and the right way to act. What Boysie wanted, Boysie would get . . . and the Nicholsons would support.

She was clearly the one on the outside. She decided that she might as well go to the wedding. She would have to now begin to practise much more one of the things her mother had always said to her: 'let not yu left hand know what yu right hand knoweth.'

She wasn't surprised when shortly after the wedding Boysie moved in his 'bastard' son with a woman in Linstead, to live with them. Mannie was fifteen and Putus's mother said that it was not right for Putus and himself to sleep in the same room. Mannie slept, for the time being, on a cot in the front room.

By Christmas-time in December, her mother was looking fat around the waist. And Boysie was saying: 'Belle, as soon as the holiday done, A going have to build on a little room pon the house. It getting crowded.'

Putus wasn't surprised when her mother said to her during the Christmas holidays: 'Putus, A think it bes' for you studies if you stay down a Old Harbour with Aunt Sisi, till you tek you Third Year Exam. It nearer to the school an' since you only going in the evening now, you could learn dressmaking with Aunt Sisi, help her out in the house and study you lesson, same time.'

Putus was silent.

'A not sending you to turn dressmaker. But is a good thing for you to know to mek you own clothes, when you turn teacher or postmistress.'

Putus was still silent . . .

'Putus, Putus, mi love. A not sending you way? You can come up weekend. This will always be you home. An' as soon as you finish you exam you can come up an' stay here. Is just that you wi able fi concentrate more pon you studies if you stay there, an' you wi have the chance fi learn how fe run business from Aunt Sisi an' Mr Bennett. All A asking you is fi behave youself and have manners to them. Is only few months till you take the exam an' once you pass it, you can start out a the school as pupil teacher, an' later on, we try fi get you inna the Teachers' College. Boysie ask Mr Nicholson arready fi help we with that.'

'Oh?', Putus said, and then used one of her mother's favourite sayings: 'Then there is nothing more to be said.'

35

PUTUS

At the time when Aunt Sisi called Putus so imperiously into her bedroom, Putus had been living there for four months. She worked in Aunt Sisi's dressmaking shop and she worked in the house. Mr Bennett owned a big citrus farm near to Bodles on the way to May Pen. He exported fruits overseas. Putus had only been to the farm twice, when Aunt Sisi had sent her with something for Mr Bennett.

Aunt Sisi let go the washerwoman at the house, one week after Putus came to live there, and Putus had to take on the washing for the whole family. Some days there was so much to do that she couldn't go to school. And she was there for a whole month before she had been able to spend one weekend at Brown's Hall. Her room was now Mannie's and she slept on the cot in the front room. Her mother was fatter than ever and seemed preoccupied. Even as she asked Putus how things were going at Aunt Sisi's, she seemed not to be really listening. The only thing of all that Putus was trying to tell her that seemed to penetrate was that Putus was managing to keep up with her lessons.

When Putus left on the Sunday evening after dinner for Old Harbour, she pledged that she would not go back any more weekends.

Putus was managing to keep up with her lessons, mainly with the help of two people. One was a pupil teacher at the Old Harbour Elementary School – Miss Haughton, a big woman in her forties who had never advanced beyond pupil teacher because she had not been able, for twenty years, to get admitted into Teachers' College. This made Putus feel that it might not be as easy to get into Teachers' College as her mother thought – even with the help of the Nicholsons. And why should they help her? Did they not have their own children and grandchildren to help? Whenever Putus missed school, she would steal away when all the Bennett family were gone to the Church of England on a Sunday morning and go around to Miss Haughton's house. The woman was a God-bless soul, although not a regular church-goer, and she would take the time to help Putus with her lessons.

The other person who helped Putus was the man who had the little tailor shop next door to Aunt Sisi's dressmaking establishment on Old Harbour Bay Road. He had passed Third Jamaica Local, long ago, but did not want to be a pupil teacher, he told Putus. He wanted to be a parson but he would have to go to America to study for that. And in any event, they wouldn't allow him to head any established church, since the parsons for those came from England or America.

In the meantime he was content to be a master tailor, like his father before him, during the week. On Sundays, he was the most powerful preacher in the Pentecostal tent, further down Old Harbour Bay Road. Putus had to pass his shop every time she went to the dressmaking establishment. One day he had called out to her and asked her if she was family to the Bennetts. Putus was afraid to stop in his shop to talk to him. Somehow she felt Aunt Sisi wouldn't like it. Although he was old enough to be her father, she felt he was the only one who paid her any particular attention, since he began to look out for her every time she passed the shop and would always call out to her:

'God-child, how the lessons going?'

One Saturday, they met outside the market and she found herself telling him about herself and the problems she was having with her studies. He couldn't help her often, like Miss Haughton, he said, but he was going to give her some advice on the way to study. She would practise that way and tell him, whenever she saw him again, whether she got on better using that way:

'God-child, don' try to learn everything by heart. Fine some time to sit down and read the book. Don' think of nothing else while you reading it. When you understand full what it saying, write down what you understand. Then read over the book again. If you understand anything more, write it down in you notebook. If it better for you, draw a picture of what you understand. Then write out the picture in words.'

She had tried Mas Rupert's method, after that day, outside the market. And it was hard, at first, but after a week of trying it she did find that she remembered the lessons more. She began to use that method consistently.

Many people came to the Bennett house. Mr Bennett was a high official in the Jamaica Agricultural Society (St Catherine Branch) and sometimes the Executive meetings took place at the house. The Bennetts' three children – Marvin, who was in his father's business with him; Althea, who was at a girls' boarding school in Malvern, St Elizabeth, and would graduate at eighteen, next year; and Donette, who was eight years old, but still going to private school – stayed in the drawing-room whenever the Bennetts' friends came to dinner. Putus stayed in the kitchen with the domestic help and the other girls brought from Aunt Sisi's dressmaking establishment to help out whenever the Bennetts entertained.

The wood mansion had ten rooms. There was a big drawing-room at the front, right off the large, circular verandah, which ran all around the house, from front to back. Then to the side of the drawing-room, but going into the middle of the house, was an almost-just-as-big dining-room. There was a smaller room just off the dining-room to bring the food into, from the outside kitchen, after it was cooked. And in which the crockery and utensils were stocked. Then there was a big room with books and easy chairs, into which Mr Bennett and his friends would go after they had eaten, to smoke and to talk. There was a smaller room in which Aunt Sisi had a foot-pedal sewing machine and some easy chairs. She would take her friends into that room, when the men were in the room with the books. That room in which Putus went to answer Aunt Sisi's call was the master bedroom. Master Marvin had his own bedroom, Miss Althea had her own bedroom and so did Miss Donette. The last, little room at the back was for the live-in domestic help. Putus slept in a cot in this room with Miss Mabel, the live-in cook. The kitchen, bathroom and shower, as well as the toilet, were in the back of the yard. Each was joined by a covered pathway to the main house. An outhouse, called the buttery, was set further back in the yard. It was a general utility and storage room.

After Putus had served the guests, saying nothing, doing whatever was asked or expected of her, she would retire to the last room in the ten-room mansion.

PUTUS

Putus stands respectfully before Aunt Sisi just inside the door of the master bedroom. She keeps her face bland. Bland and innocent. But anxious in case she has inadvertently done anything to offend Aunt Sisi or her family. Adoring of the Bennett family and what good people they are. And most of all, adoring of Aunt Sisi's red skin, her Brown-womanness. Her plenty, long, thick, curly hair, falling to her shoulders as she sits in bed. Normally, it is plaited in two thick plaits and wound around Aunt Sisi's head, just like she had seen in a book about French women. But today it is falling all around her face and on to her shoulders, reaching almost to her waist.

In all of this, Putus wishes that her own kinky, woolly hair fell to her waist. Even keeping her shine-Black skin, she would be able to feel more equal to Aunt Sisi if her hair also fell, even to her neck.

'You did call me, Aunt Sisi? You want to talk to me, Maam?'

'Yes, A want to talk to you, Putus.'

(This woman can't even speak proper English. Yet she has to bow and scrape to her. It isn't as if she is even white. She is a 'red-nigga'. She is a red-nigga!), Putus is thinking.

'Putus, A don' see you washing any small clothes this month?'

(Lawd God Almighty, what this mean?)

'A see you small clothes on the back line las' month, but A don' see any this month?, eh Putus?'

(How did this woman know whether she washed small clothes or not? None of them noticed her enough to know when she washed small clothes or did not? What was it all about anyway? What did it matter to them? What did it mean, not to wash small clothes?)

'Putus, you see any blood, this month?'

(Oh! that is what it's about.)

'No, Aunt Sisi. But sometime it don't come when it suppose to. It hurt mi belly so much when it come, that I glad it don't come. It will come soon.'

'Putus, A don' know what you mother tell you bout when you blood don' come. But is not a good thing when it don' come.'

'Aunt Sisi, Mama tell me the same thing. But is plenty time it don't come when it suppose to. So A don't worry bout it. A just glad. Because when it come, it hurt me so much, A cyaan lay down, A cyaan stand up, A cyaan walk, A cyaan do nothing.'

'Putus, you make any man trouble you?'

39

'What you mean, Aunt Sisi? What you mean by "trouble"?'

'You make any man trouble you little vagi?'

Putus's face became purple-black. How dare Miss Sisi go so far into her business as to mention her private parts?

'I don't know what you talking about, Aunt Sisi.'

'If the end of the month come and you don' see blood, I going to have to send for you mother. I hope is just cold you have, why you blood don' come. If you blood don' come by nex' week, A going to send for you mother. She make me promise to take good care of you. She make me promise to see that you pass you Third Year Exam. You only have few month before you finish the exam. A don' know what A would tell her if anything happen to you.'

'Me arright, Aunt Sisi. I doing mi lesson good. I going pass the exam. You don' need to worry about anything.'

'A hope so, Putus, A hope so. Anyway, if you don' bleed by nex' week, le' me know. Don' hide it from me, if you blood don' come by nex' week, you mus' tell me.'

Putus went back to the last room in the ten-room wood mansion. The interview being over. As far as she was concerned, the 'blood' could stay away for ever. It was just an extra burden on her. She couldn't understand what Aunt Sisi was so heat-up about. If she didn't have the blood, she would be able to concentrate more on her lessons. There was no one she could tell how much she hated the coming of this 'blood'. It gave her so much pain that she couldn't even study when it came. And all those bloody napkins to soak and wash, she could do without them. It was just like the Nicholsons to be liking something she hated. She had the feeling that her mother would take their side. That her mother would get upset because she hadn't seen the 'dyam blood'. She didn't care what they thought. She was glad the blood hadn't come. She would prepare her mind. Just as she had done when she had to deal with the fact that Boysie was there to stay. She would keep herself to herself. She wouldn't let any of them know what she was thinking. But she would be the happiest human being, if the blood stayed away. And that happiness, none of them could take away.

PUTUS

Next week, Putus fell asleep under Aunt Sisi and Mr Bennett's four-poster bed in the master bedroom while she was cleaning it.

Next week, Putus discovered that chocolate tea, with all the oil on top, which she used to love so much, made her stomach sick.

Next week, Putus couldn't stand to look at the blood-raw goat and wild pig meat brought into the house. Her stomach turned over at the smell and she vowed that she should rather die than touch the meat, to prepare it; much less to eat it.

Putus vomited outside, at the back of the yard, behind the buttery, most mornings.

Putus's mother arrived from out of the hills of Brown's Hall District, on urgent summons from Aunt Sisi.

It was a day in March between the cool weather of Christmas and New Year and before the Caribbean sun would have started to gather up its fury to climax in the burning months of July and August. So that Putus's mother was cool, coal Black. Her face ebony-purple with disappointment, pain, the murder of her dreams. Her belly hanging heavy with Boysie's child.

After the customary preliminaries of greetings –

'My respects to you Aunt Sisi. Hoping everything arright with you, Mr Bennett and the children-them. Boysie sen' respect to you and all the family. Everybody in the District hawty and sen' them greetings to you and the family. We pray for you everynight that you and all the family will keep hawty and go from strength to strength. That no evil walk near you house and that God will always bless you and yours for all the kindness of you and you family to we-all . . . '

And so on and so forth.

Aunt Sisi, Mr Bennett, Putus and the mother went through all the motions. Because even if the sky was falling down and the earth was being consumed in fire, the proper greetings and thanks would have to be said before discussing the real business of the visit. That was just manners and only those poor lost ones, the ones who – poor souls – forget their manners and culture, would even think of behaving in any other way.

But after the customary preliminaries of greetings, there was this combrucktion to be faced. It was not going to go away. Because there was Putus before them all – in her little bird's-eye church dress, now too tight around the waist and too short-up under her high bottom – a little child, just past sixteen years old but beginning to show signs, in her eyes and the thickening of her skin, that she was soon to say goodbye to childhood, for ever.

'Putus, talk to me. Tell me everything. Don' fraid. A not going to beat you. You always know that A never tek mi hand to you, when A vex, cause A might kill you when A never did mean to. So don' fraid, just tell you mammy everything. Who is the man?'

Miss Belle was by now seated, her legs drawn up under her, her arms cradling her pregnant belly, her shoulders and back bent forward, her head up, looking into Putus's eyes. Her whole body rocking like some small canoe cast eternally adrift. Putus just stood there in the big drawing-room. Her whole body was hot and cold. It seemed as if she had two hearts. One was like a hard rockstone in a hole in her chest and it was spinning around and knocking and bumping up and down all around in her chest. It, itself, the rockstone, that is, was like the biggest heartburn she had ever had or anyone could ever have. In a moment, she felt, it was going to explode and shatter her whole body into fragments, some of which would be flown up Mountain Road on to the hills of Brown's Hall, others of which would fly past the Bodles Agricultural Station to May Pen, then some would pass Red Ground, and go on to Kingston. The rocking, spinning, jumping heartburn of all heartburns would clamp its skin on the Old Harbour clock in the centre of the town and the remaining fragments of her body would float towards Old Harbour Bay . . . and the sea . . . the sea . . . and be washed clean . . . and start again? . . . oh, and start again? In that very salt and warm sea . . . to start again?

But the other heart was staying put. It was beating lower down in her belly somewhere. It didn't want to move . . . or explode. It clung to her lower belly. It eschewed the violence of the first heart. But it was no less violent. Its violence consisted in its determination to cling on where it was . . . and not be moved. And it beat warm . . . then icy cold. It was this heart, she knew, though nobody told her, which began to force urine down her legs. And as she looked with consternation at the urine filling up her crepe-sole shoes and beginning to creep out on to Aunt Sisi's immaculate floor, this heart established its rule over the other heart, hardened her pain . . . and shame. This heart forced her short coarse-black plaited-hair-head up, straightened her back. With ramrod body, Putus stood there.

'You see how you stiffening up you neck like Miss Matty old bull? You going to tell me who the man is today. Go clean up youself, change you clothes and come back here, mek we get to the bottom of this thing.'

'Yes, Mama', Putus whispered past the nauseous water that had filled up her mouth. She grasped the chance to leave the scene, if only for a few minutes.

Mr Bennett spoke for the first time: 'You know, people always say, before you spend money on girl-pickney, it better you throw it down sink-hole. All girl-pickney good for, is to start breed baby as soon as them start ripe-up.'

Putus's mother snapped:

'Is the low-down, crowbait man-them. Them only go round loking pon the young girl pickney-them and as soon as them little bubby begin to sprout-up pon them chest, there comes a Mr Man fe jump pon them and spoil them prospec'. Girl-pickney want advance themself like anybody else, but the man-them just won't leave them alone fe prosper.'

'But, Mrs B, is Putus you have to blame. Is she know how much you sacrifice to make her get an education. She should-a keep herself more circumspect.'

Silence fell. A silence made even more charged up by the fact that Putus's mother had stopped rocking her body and cast that awful blackness of her suppressed-tears-red eyeballs across at Aunt Sisi and Mr Bennett, with a glare that seemed to freeze them to the spot.

But her voice was ever so quiet and gentle, when she said:

'A put Putus here, that she could be safe and carry on her studies in peace. A put her here, so that she could be safe . . . from Boysie . . . when she would start to ripe-up . . . from him constant botheration for me to take her out of school. I put Putus in a Christian, decent, respectable home. If she couldn't safe here, where she was going to safe?, eh, Aunt Sisi?, eh, Mr Bennett?'

And the 'canoe' started again its eternal rocking. Now accompanied by low moans of despair coming from deep, deep in the belly-bottom.

'Woooy . . . woooy . . . wooo . . . huuummmm. Woooy . . . woooy . . . hummmm . . . woooy . . . What else A could-A do? woooy . . . A is just a poor woman trying to do the best A can. Wha else A could do? Somebody, tell me? Massa Jesus know that A try me best? When man on earth have done their best, angels in heaven cyaan do more – so the Good Book say – don' it? Aunt Sisi? Don' it? Mr Bennett . . . ?'

Without moving, the Bennetts seemed to move closer together. Seemed to lock ranks against the suffering, despairing woman, in her polka-dot maternity shift barely able to cover her protruding belly.

This woman was nothing. Had been nothing . . . would forever be nothing. That's what they got from trying to help these people. She should be kissing their feet, showering them with praises for taking in her no-good daughter. How dare this woman seem to be suggesting that they were somehow at fault because her daughter had just done what all of these types of people did best? Did she really think that that daughter of hers was going to be different? The uppityness of this woman. They had been too kind. These people needed to be put in their place, whenever they forgot.

'Come now, Miss B. What you saying? That we should turn policeman on Putus and be watchdog? You have to understand that we have our own children to take care of . . . don't be unreasonable . . . ?'

43

'Woooy . . . woooy . . . hummmmmm . . . A not asking anybody to be policeman fo' mi daughter. All A saying is that if she living in the District and a man smelling round her, A would ha' fi know who him is. If him didn' come to the house, A would go seek him out and fin' out what him up to, what is him intention. All A asking you, Mr Bennett, all A asking you, Aunt Sisi, you never see no man smelling round Putus? She never bring no man to you house? How come you don' have no idea who get her in the family way? eh? eh?'

That awful black glare begged them to say something that showed they had cared enough to know.

'Look, Miss B, is a decent, respectable Christian house here. We try to do good to our fellow men but we can't take responsibility for bad-breed pickney . . . '

'Aunt Sisi, you never tell me that Putus was bad-breed when you agree to take her to live in you house? All the time she live here, don't you tell me that she work hard and she obedient and she doing her studies good, good? You never tell me that she interested in man? You never tell me that she was behaving like leggo-beast an' staying out to catch man? A wrong or A right?'

A direct question had been put. The Bennetts couldn't shift around anymore.

'Miss B, A don' know if she meet any boy at her school. But the only man-them who come here is Parson, Mr Bennett friend-them from the Agricultural Society and sometimes Mas Rupert, the tailor from the Pentecostal Church. It must be some leggo-boy she meet on the street when she going to school . . . or one of them boys who in the school with her . . . Miss B, I try to fin' it out . . . but nobody don' see her with any man . . . and Putus won' talk to me bout it. What A could do Miss B? What A could do? I try mi best?'

'Aunt Sisi, God know, A not trying to blame anybody. A just want to get to the bottom of this thing. Don' you have somebody who is gardener in you house? You have any man work in the dressmaking shop? You see, Putus is mi own pickney. She not bad-breed. A don' think she would just pick up any and any man from the street. It have to be somebody who she see often. So A don't want to get anybody vex, but it have to be somebody who befriend her in this house or at you dressmaking shop . . . '

'What you saying woman? None of our friends would do that. They are all men with their wives and children, upstanding people in the Church . . . '

'Mr Bennett, don' one and one always make two? It ha' fi be one of you upstanding friends-them unless . . . ? A don't mean it the way it may soun' . . . but one and one always make two . . . so if it not some man in the dressmaking shop . . . and if is not the gardener . . . then it have to be one of you upstanding friends-them or else . . . God forbid . . . God forbid me to say who it would have fi be then . . . '

44

'You ungrateful Black bitch. Is mi husband you talking bout? You think mi husband would stoop to you little nasty daughter? See here, woman, don't make I have to sin meself here today . . . '

'Is not Mr Bennett, Mama.'

They had been so immersed in their accusations and denials that none of them had seen Putus re-enter the front room.

There was a moment when there was no sound audible to the normal ear. But there was a sound that everyone felt. It was as in the sound of a pipe letting forth pent-up steam, relaxing all muscles, easing the acrimony. Yet freezing all as in a black-and-white photograph.

Putus's mother was the first to come out of the frame.

'Putus, you wase enough time. If wi don' min' sharp, you going to cause bad feeling between we and this good family who take such good care a you. Mek we put a stop to all the specilation. No woman can get her own self into the family way by herself. Tell us who the man is and done the argument.'

'Mama, is not a leggo-boy. Him is a good man. Him is like a father to me and him never mean to make this happen . . . '

'Lawd Jesus Christ, help me! Putus, you mean to tell me that is married man get yu in the fambily way? Woooooooy . . . wooooy . . . wooooy!'

'No, Mama, him don't married.'

'So why him don' present himself to the fambily? Why him hiding out like bruk-kitchen? If him don' have anything fi hide, why him not here with you?'

'Him fraid for you, Mama. And him fraid that them will read him out of the Church because them will say that him commit fornication.'

'So him not man enough to stan-up to him action? Him more fraid of what the Church wi say than what God must tell him conscience is the right thing fi do? But God is the head of all Church, don't it, Putus? Don't it . . . ?'

'Mama, him want to get married before the stomach start to show but I not sure I want to married, Mama. I want to become something in the world. Just trust me, Mama. A fall into this problem but A don't want it to make me stop here. A want to go through the mansions of the whole world and A want to go into the last room of the last mansion of the world . . . '

'What kind-a nonsense yu talking, Putus? You now in the las' room. Everything A work for . . . Everything A sacrifice for . . . woooooy . . . woooooy . . .

'And to think yu end up breeding, like all them leggo-gal. Is the end of yu life. You still don' tell me the name of the man. Putus, tell me who him is. Yu don' understand? A must know who the man is.'

Putus stood with ramrod body. Her mouth clamped tight. Both to prevent her from throwing out the nauseous water on to Aunt Sisi's floor, as well as to keep in information she had no intention of giving out. She swallowed the water.

'Mama, don't make me tell you. I don't want to bring him full into my life. And if you don't know who him is, then A can cross this bridge and carry on with mi life.'

'But girl, whey yu ever hear sey woman in the fambily way an' won' call the name a the man? Is whey you get them type a thinking from? The man, whomsoever him be, have to stan-up to him responsibility. If him don' come to me, A have fi go to him, so that him can face-up to this thing, like a man . . . '

'Him want to come to you, Mama. But I don't want to tie-up meself. Mama, I promise you, after I have the baby, I going to take-up back with mi studies again. Please, Mama, don't make me have to married.'

PUTUS

In this moment, Miss Belle hated her daughter. The hate rumbled in her stomach, making her belly-bottom weak. Then it began to crawl its way up into her throat. It would have spewed bitter water out of her lips, did she not have the presence of mind to quickly bend her head as far over her pregnant belly as it would go, with the aim of trying to get her head between her legs.

'Lawd Alvin, A wonder if she going to get a heart failure in we house?' Aunt Sisi hissed a whisper to Mr Bennett.

'Alvin, do something, nuh. We can't let her dead into we house.'

Mr Bennett remembered that he was late for a meeting with the manager of his farm and he quickly shuffled sideways until he was out of the room. Aunt Sisi stood up and went towards Miss Belle. She didn't touch her. Instead she turned to Putus and said:

'See what crosses you bring into we house. I should-a listen to Mr Bennett when he did tell me not to bring you here. Now you going to make you mother dead into mi house. You is a wutless slut.'

Putus had been standing there. Looking only at her mother. Hoping that her mother could read and understand all the things she hadn't said and wasn't saying. For quite a while she had been talking only to her mother, blocking out of her mind the presence of the Bennetts. When her mother put her head between her legs, she didn't think that her mother was going to die. She knew that when she had lived with her mother, whenever she ate too much and got colic or when she had a bad stomach, her mother had always told her to put her head between her legs and that way she wouldn't vomit or faint. She couldn't understand why her mother wanted to faint now but she could understand why her mother wanted to vomit. Because she knew that her mother's stomach must be empty, since she would have had to leave from Brown's Hall before-day-morning to get a taxi to Old Harbour. Aunt Sisi had not offered her mother any of the hot chocolate or coffee-tea, the steamed callaloo and boiled green bananas, the boiled eggs she put with Mr Bennett's breakfast. When her mother arrived, Aunt Sisi had only offered Miss Belle a little of the stone-cold oats porridge left over from the breakfast that Putus herself had eaten and which was only one course of the family breakfast. At least, they had eaten it when it was hot. Aunt Sisi did not warm it up and no one else could warm it up unless Aunt Sisi asked for it to be done. She was her mother's daughter and she lived in this house. She had even helped to prepare the breakfast with the cook. But not even she could give her mother a proper breakfast because it would have been bad manners – it was after all Aunt Sisi's house and only Aunt Sisi could say what should or should not be given to a guest.

She knew her mother must be hungry but she couldn't feed her with the food she had helped to cook.

When she saw that Aunt Sisi was not going to offer her mother a proper hot breakfast, she had swallowed her pride and tried to be well-mannered. Even though she knew that Aunt Sisi must know that Miss Belle got sick whenever she ate cold food?

But, Putus thought, that was then, before they all spoke. Now, Aunt Sisi, far from admitting that she was to blame for Miss Belle's condition, seemed to be saying that it was Putus who was causing her own mother's bad stomach.

As if that was not enough, this woman then went on to call her a slut. It was more than she could bear. Putus decided to throw good manners out of the window.

'You red-nigger bitch! What you mean by calling me slut? Is you an' you husband an' you family who killing mi mother! Just like how you kill mi father.'

Aunt Sisi sat down plop in the middle of the floor. Her face turned more yellow, then red, then blue, then purple. Then she held her chest and then she began to gasp through her mouth like one of them big fish that the fishermen sometimes catch in the sea at Old Harbour Bay.

Putus sprung her whole body towards Aunt Sisi. She wanted to choke some sense into this woman.

'Valrie, leave Aunt Sisi alone.'

Putus stopped with her hand inches away from Aunt Sisi's throat. Miss Belle's head was no longer over her pregnant belly between her legs. It was raised high and looking into Putus's eyes.

Miss Belle got up from her chair. Putting her hands under Aunt Sisi's arms, she said:

'Come, Mrs Bennett. Sit down in yu chair. A not going have heart failure. Yu don' 'ave to fraid dat A going to dead in yu an' Mr Bennett house. Calm yuself. Everything going to be arright.'

VALERIE

Aunt Sisi was now settled in her queenly chair. She was over these people again. She ignored Putus and settled her queenly stare on Miss Belle. She knew that normally, Miss Belle would have sprung on her (as her daughter had) for calling her daughter a 'slut'. But she was not going to take any of these people's feistiness. She was now on top again. The daughter had failed this woman who wanted to behave like a topanaris, as if she was equal to her and her family. She had her now. She would have to go down on her knees and beg her to keep this sluttish daughter of hers. And still she wouldn't.

Miss Belle returned to her own little chair. She began again her motion of canoe-rocking in stormy waves. But she was not moaning anymore. Putus stood like a black-stone statue.

Aunt Sisi leaned towards Miss Belle:

'Well, Mrs B, I suppose you will all have to work it out 'mongst youself. But as you would expect, I can't keep Putus here any longer, I have me own children to consider . . . you know.'

Miss Belle was rocking her pregnant body. If Aunt Sisi could have read her mind, she would have read the following:

'You own pickney-dem to consider! A trus' you as another woman to help me guard me own pickney but fe mi own pickney mus' be destroy, so fi you pickney-dem can live an' prosper. Is jus' now A understan' what mi husban' Mas D used-to sey to me. Is jus' now A understan' why him come home so silent from you father property every evening. Is jus' now A understan'.'

But Miss Belle didn't say any of these things out loud in this grand wood mansion. She didn't tear her tight maternity shift from her body. She didn't bawl and roll herself on the floor at the smashing of all her work and dreams. Among her own people, Black people who saw Jamaica as 'Little Africa', this would be what was expected. But those tainted with the European blood, the blood of the white slavemaster, the Brown ones, whom her daughter had called 'red-nigger', they would never understand.

They, the white and Brown ones, like Aunt Sisi and Mr Bennett, would think that she was less of a human being if she let go and showed how she really felt. They would look down their noses at her in a way which shouted that they really thought how uncivilised and savage her people were.

If she did what was normal for her people before such as Aunt Sisi, she would be baring herself and her people naked before them. And that she could never do. So she said:

'Of course, Aunt Sisi. A quite understan'. A know that yu cyaan keep Putus in yu house anymore. I taking her away today. Yu don' ave to worry. By eveling we will be gone from yu house.'

Aunt Sisi was comforted. No one was blaming her for what had happened. If Mrs B understood, then everybody would understand. Aunt Sisi's conscience was clear. She could now, like her husband, leave the room and these people to sort out their problems by themselves.

Miss Belle was still rocking as Aunt Sisi got up to leave and without ceasing her rocking-canoe-motion, she said:

'Valrie, pack up yu things. Hurry up an' come. A waiting for you.'

Putus hurried out of the room behind Aunt Sisi.

Miss Belle got up and walked slowly to the back of the yard to sit on the little bench under the breadfruit tree.

She is surprised that the sun is still shining. It is brushing the slimber, pointed leaves of the coconut trees with yellow gold. All the other leaves of the other trees are either kissing-up with the sun or flirtatiously or coquettishly playing hide-and-seek with it.

Miss Belle wishes the sky would get dark and send thunderous rain on to the land, washing away all these crosses. And most of all, washing out from her soul the hate she was now feeling for her daughter.

She thinks that the sun must be mocking her. What great sin had she committed to deserve this unbearable trial that was now her lot? For the first time in her life, she can't pray. Not even for forgiveness. She had always thought that those who hated, even for a good reason, should continually pray to keep their minds and bodies free of the poison of hate.

She wants to help Putus pack up her things but she doesn't want to go into the last room of Aunt Sisi's mansion. She feels that if she doesn't see the room that Aunt Sisi had put her daughter into, then she wouldn't have to believe it. So she waits outside for Putus, under the breadfruit tree.

She hears a sound and raises her hanging head. Putus is approaching her. In the little bird's-eye dress of innocence. But even so soon, too tight around the waist.

'Take off that dress.'

'But is me dressing frock, Mama.'

'Is you church frock, an' it not 'propriate for today. Furda-more is the same one that you just done vomit pon. Go take it off an' put on something else.'

'But Mama, I wash it out and dry it with the self-heater iron, look . . . '

'A say to tek it off!'

Putus opens her mouth to say something more. Takes another look at Miss Belle and thinks better of it. She turns around and goes back the way to the little room at the back of the house, carrying the little suitcase with her.

She is so long in the room that Miss Belle has to come to get her.

'Lawd Jesus, what I going to do, Mama? What going to happen to me?'

'You should-a think of that before you make man trouble you. An' since you won' even tell me the name a the man, an' you don' want to married to him, look like you going to have to bear yu burden alone.'

'Mama, du, help me. Don't leave me alone.'

'Come, hurry up, we have to get on wi way. We should-a leave the Bennett-them house long time. If we hurry, we can still catch a taxi to take we to Brown's Hall before the rush come down.'

Putus wants to talk more. She feels a great need to have a really private-time with her mother before they would have to face Boysie and the rest of the world. She needs to hug-up her mother. She needs her mother to hug her up.

Miss Belle says:

'Valrie, if you don' hurry-up an' come now, A will turn mi back an' lef you right here an' mek Aunt Sisi and Mr Bennett throw you out on the street.'

Amidst the shock of everything, including her mother calling her 'Valrie', Putus hurriedly changes her dress, folding the little bird's-eye dress neatly and putting it in the little cardboard suitcase.

VALERIE

Boysie's puss eyes are very knowledgeable. He is a big man in the District now. He can't help knowing that the men don't particularly like him or trust him. It is enough for him that they respect him.

After all, had he not succeeded where many of them had failed? He had gained control of the rest of the Barton land through the door of the bed of Mas D's widow.

He had gained control of Mas D's widow herself – the beautiful and hoity-toity Belle – by his brown skin and his 'sweet stick'.

He had somehow been able to get the 'edicated Mama' to get her edicated daughter out of the house. He had brought in his own son. The two of them had added on to the house, planted-up more trees and flowers in the yard.

On a holiday-time, there was always a goat bubbling in the kerosene tin and plenty of white rum to spare for anyone who wanted to stop by for a little refreshment. Then, many of the men would laugh loudly, slap him on the back and call him 'Big-man'.

It was mainly the women he couldn't win over. They were polite enough, 'how-de-do Mr Boysie' and so on when they came into contact with him, but nothing further.

Boysie did not let the attitude of the women worry him. They must be just jealous, he told himself. Especially since he did not play with any of them. He had long decided that whenever he wanted to whet his appetite with a 'little something' outside the house, he would look for it in another district. Caused a man too much trouble to graze too near to home.

So not even the old toothless grannies who were always mixing-up into other people's business could find a good enough reason to be against the partnership. Belle had a man who was from a Brown family, worked hard, did not have other women in the District with her and did not beat her.

Only Miss Mack, the shopkeeper at the little grocery shop at the corner where the road turned to come into the District, had dared to voice openly a criticism that many of the women no doubt had. And she had not done so before his face. She had said in the hearing of Mannie, his son:

'Shouldn-a listen to that man an' sen' Putus to Old Harbour though.'

Boysie had thrown back his head and laughed when Mannie reported this to him.

'If they don't like it, bite it,' was all he had said.

Everyone knew that Putus had returned from week-before-the-last. Some also knew why. Not because anyone had told them and not because the stomach was showing all that much – in any case, Miss Belle had made Putus band it down with a stiff piece of cloth. But the women, especially, could guess. And some of the more thoughtful men shook their heads in sorrow and clamped their jaws shut, to think that Mas D's daughter had gone the age-old way of girl-children whom poor parents sacrificed for. The mothers and grannies cursed the multitudes of men who were always waiting to spoil the prospects of their girl-children.

There were many discussions in the shop but Miss Mack would not allow them to get out of hand. Her own daughter had to be stopped from school last year and she knew what Miss Belle must be going through.

But not even Miss Mack could resist elaborate and concerned enquiries from Miss Belle whenever she came to the shop about how Putus was coming on with her 'sickness'.

When Miss Belle had returned from Old Harbour with Putus, she had let it be known from the next morning that Putus had caught some strange fever down in Old Harbour and she had had to go for her and take her home so that she could recover in the bosom of her family.

Boysie had been away at the big-man Clarke's house over near Worthy Park at the other side of the parish when Miss Belle and Putus came back from Old Harbour. The son, Mannie, was still at school.

Miss Belle and Putus had not spoken a word in the taxi from Old Harbour to Brown's Hall. Even if either of them had a mind to, they couldn't anyway, not with eight people packed into the little old car, some kotching on another's lap.

Miss Belle had moved Mannie's things into the new room that Boysie had added on to the house and put Putus into her old room. She knew that Boysie would not like it.

He hadn't.

His puss eyes had glinted ice-blue when he came home and heard that Putus was back. The following conversation had taken place between them.

'But Belle, you should-a let Aunt Sisi keep her in Old Harbour. It easier to get doctor for her there an' she would be nearer the school where she going to do her exam.'

'You don' understan', Boysie? She sick. The best place for her is here, with her fambily.'

'Then you should-a did put her into the new room for the time being, since she not staying long. You know how Mannie like the room that him into.'

'Yes, Boysie, I know how Mannie like that room. I like it meself. It get all the cool breeze-them blowing over the yam field. But is Putus' old room an' she will get better quicker if she in the room that she used to.'

She had confined Putus to the room. Not even the biggish Mannie would dare to go into the room for fear of Putus's contagious fever.

Enter the room he didn't, but he couldn't catch the fever by peeping through the blinds of the little jalousie window to see what Putus with a fever looked like.

Earlier this evening, he had whispered to his father, 'Papa, Putus don' look sick, you know.'

Shortly after Boysie had taken Mannie away from his mother in Linstead and brought him to Brown's Hall and the Barton house, he had come to rely on Mannie as his chief and most reliable 'news-carrier'.

'What you mean, Mannie? You don' hear her mother say that she catch one of them bad fever down a Old Harbour? I hope you not been going into the room. Take care you don' catch it too. I going to have to jeyes-out the room when she get better an' leave.'

'Papa, A see her through the window yesterday. She don' look sick at all. Fac' is, she look very hawty an' she fat so till!'

'Fat? What you mean by fat? Which part of her?'

'Particular her belly, Papa. An' her little tittie-them get bigger.'

'You sure you talking the truth Mannie?'

Mannie wet his forefinger on his tongue and lifted it over his head, in the accepted sign inviting God's wrath and retribution upon himself and his family should he be lying.

'Arright, arright, you don't hear A tell you not to take oath. Don't say nothing to nobody bout this.'

'What you going to do, Papa?'

'Go inside an' go do you homework. Is not only Putus one who can pass exam. You better see to it that you pass you exam-them too.'

Boysie waits until after they have all eaten their dinner. It is coming on to 8 o'clock. They will soon go to bed because tomorrow is another early work-day. But this is the hour or two, after the evening meal, when they sit up to digest their food.

Belle is embroidering a baby chemise. It is the last of the baby clothes she has to get ready before the new little one comes. Delicate pink (for girl), blue (for boy) and yellow (for either) chemises are neatly folded in the baby's bathpan, awaiting its arrival.

Boysie has been going in and out of the sitting-room, since he ate his dinner. He tells Belle that he cannot find one of the goats. Then when he has found the straying goat, he has to fill up the water drum because enough rain has not been falling recently to keep it full. He is now back in the sitting-room and has come to stand over Belle. There is a smirk on his yellow face and his puss eyes are knowledgeable.

VALERIE

Putus comes down off the single bed near to the window and goes across the room to the keyhole in the middle door between her room and the sitting-room. She cannot see much of what is going on in the sitting-room but she can certainly hear better than when she is on the bed. She clamps her ear to the keyhole.

'Belle, what the doctor say bout when Putus can go back to school?'

'Him say must carry her back to him nex' week an' him will sound her an' tell me if she getting better.

'Whats-it Boysie? Sit down, man. Why yu standing-up like dat an' keep looking down pon me so for?'

'What kind a fever him say that Putus sick with?'

'Me no 'member the name whey him call it – you know how them doctor business full-a pure big word – but is a bad fever.'

'Hmmmnn. Maybe you should-a make me take a look pon her. Me see some bad fever inna Colon an' it have bush that can get it better . . . '

Putus hears Boysie's footsteps coming towards her room. Then before she can scamper away from the keyhole, as she means to, she hears her mother moving towards the door of her room. She feels a heavy vibration on the door. She hears a sharp intake of breath and a grunt. She hears a 'woom'!, which she thinks must be her mother's back on the door.

She feels the stiffness of the door which she thinks can only be coming from her mother pressing her back on to it. She decides not to scamper away from the door because she wants to be there, in case Boysie goes past the mountain of her mother's pregnant belly and tries to break down the door.

Footsteps, grunts and puffs now give way to Boysie's voice, raised, angry:

'Belle, move out-a de way. If yu don' move out-a de way, A going have to move yu. Yu an' yu daughter take me for idiot. Yu take me for coonu-moonu! Move out-a mi way!'

Then she hears her mother's voice. Quiet-quiet.

'What you want to go into Putus' room for, Boysie? You is doctor?'

'Belle, A say move out-a mi way. If you an' Putus don't have anything to hide, why you don't want me to go into the room?'

'Why you want to go into Putus' room? What business you have in there?'

'What business A have in there? How you can ask me that, Belle? Is my labour an' money sen' her go to school, suit her out to go to Old

Harbour. is because a me, because me is them friend, why the Bennett-them take her in, an' you asking me what business A have in there? Move out-a mi way!'

'What yu say, Boysie? Fi-yu labour? Fi-yu money? So what happen to fi-mi labour? Is yu one work? What me doin' don' count?'

Silence. Then her mother's voice again.

'When me here from morning till night weeding an' planting an' cleaning-up, that not labour too? When mi have-fi sleep inna de market a Spanish Town pon Friday night fi sell di provision-dem, that no labour?

'When mi buy fish an' salt-meat out-a what mi sell, an' lif'up di load, an' ride inna the back-a de country truck an' bring home de meat-kine for wi dinner fi de week, dat labour don' count?

'When A keep de house clean an' tek care of yu bastard son, is not labour dat too? When A cook de curry-goat an' rice an' de soup, dat yu frien-them can come here holiday-time an' 'ave a nice time, yu don' call dat labour?

'Is what yu saying to me, Boysie? Yu drink mad-puss milk or wat?'

'Belle, A don't want to hear none a yu feistiness. A put up with this thing too long, so you an' yu wrenkin' daughter think you can tek step wit me. Tell you what, make we done the argument. Whatever . . . fever (eh, eh!) Putus have, it have to get better somewhere else. She can't stay under mi roof an eat offa mi labour no longer.'

A cool night-breeze is blowing off the hills, finding its way into the sitting-room through the backdoor and the windows. It's coming first into Putus's room through the half-open jalousie blinds. But Putus is covered in cold sweat. She can smell the sweat from her armpits. There is a stirring at the bottom of her belly. All of a sudden, she knows that there is something alive there. At the same time, she hears another 'wump!', but the pressure on the bottom of the door does not ease. There is a moment of dead silence in the sitting-room.

Then the silence is broken. Her mother's voice is hoarse and breathless. But still very quiet, when she says,

'Don' force the issue, Boysie. We can talk bout what happen to Putus but you cyaan tell her not to live here. This is her father dead-lef' lan', an' his father before him. Great-Grandfather Barton buy dis lan' from inna slavery. Fi mek all him generation-dem free. Fi mek him generation-dem lef' slavery back-a-door fi-ever. Putus is direct descendant from Ole Barton. Putus is Barton blood. The name on her birth cerfiticate is Valrie Barton. No one can tek her off-a dis lan'. Dis is Barton lan'.'

Smash! Woom!

The sound vibrates the door to Putus's room. The sound shakes the foundation of the entire house.

'Murder, murder! Him killing mi mother, him killing mi mother.'

Her cry reverberates around the entire Brown's Hall District.

VALERIE

She had never known Mama Belle to stay in bed late on a morning before. It was now after 10 o'clock and Mama Belle was still in bed.

After Boysie had hit her last night, it was Miss Belle herself who quieted Putus's cries. Putus had wanted to open the door, run out of the room and claw Boysie to death for hitting her mother. Miss Belle had blocked the doorway. And before Putus could decide what to do – step over her to where Boysie was standing or hold up her mother – Miss Belle had said:

'Tan-tuddy, Putus! Shet yu mout! Yu want to bring down more disgrace pon wi house?'

She hadn't been able to understand her mother's reasoning. Was she to keep quiet and allow Boysie to kill her mother? Mannie's room did not open out into the sitting-room but he must have heard what was going on? Yet he was quiet as a mouse. Still, she had obeyed Miss Belle when she commanded:

'Go back into yu room, Putus.'

She hadn't been able to sleep the whole night. She had heard Miss Belle leave the sitting-room and go to her and Boysie's room. Then the rest of the night had been dead silence. At the breaking of dawn, long before sun-up, she had heard Boysie go into the outside kitchen. She had heard him calling Mannie to wake up to go to school. After a while, she had heard Mamby, their dog, barking and she knew that Boysie had opened the gate to leave. Then she had heard Mannie singing out, 'Gone, Aunt Belle', meaning that he was saying goodbye before going to school. She hadn't heard her mother stir.

At the time when the sun was just about to begin to flex its muscles Putus crept out into the kitchen, rekindled the dead fire and made some mint tea. She sweetened it with more than usual dark sugar, cut off two thick slices from the hard dough bread, covered them with salted butter, put two mugs with the tea and a plate with the bread and butter on a waiter and went to call at her mother's door. Her mother had said, 'Cum Putus.'

Miss Belle was lying in the bed with her face turned to the wall. She must have been to bed in her clothes because she was dressed as she was the night before. Only that she had tied her coarse black hair tightly in a red tie-head.

Putus drank her mint tea and ate her bread and butter. Miss Belle only drank the mint tea, keeping her head turned away from Putus to the wall.

'Mama, you not going to leave him? I did know him was no good from the first time when I see him at wi gate. I did tell you too, but you wouldn't listen.'

For the first time since Putus came into the room, Miss Belle looked full at her.

'Leave him? Where A going leave Boysie an' go? You father lef' me pon dis lan'. No more lan' no lef' with fi-mi side a fambily. At fe mi age, me cyaan go turn trouble to mi fambily. We would-a be two more mouth to feed an' dem can barely feed who is there now.'

'But Mama, Cousin Henry and Grannie Lou have land up by them. We couldn't live with them?'

'Putus, A don' know how yu goin' to manage into the worl'. A always tell yu that yu take tings too simple. Is pure rockstone grow pon dat lan'. Hengry try him best with it but him will soon have fi sell it an' go a-foreign go look work. Him is a young man an' him soon wan' get on in life. Mama Lou old arready, so she can stay pon de lan' till she dead. What them get from the lan' not even enough fe themself.'

'Then if the land so worthless, where Cousin Henry going to find somebody to buy it?'

'Maybe one-a them big man or a foreigner might want it fe them own use. Them no need have fe depend pon it fe feed them an them fambily.'

'Then why you don't tell Boysie and Mannie to leave, then? Don't is my father house this?'

'No because yu turn big woman an' mek man get yu in the fambily way, dat you tink yu can tell yu elders an' betters how fe run dem life. If yu did behave yuself an' study yu book like A tell yu, all this wouldn' happen. Is because yu is me own pickney an' out-a respec' for yu father memry, why I don' box you down an' kill yu, like how Boysie box me down. You cyaan expec' him fe tek what happen to yu like how I tek it. I goin' to have to bear mi burden like Job an' hope dat one day de good Lord will deliver me. But if a ketch dat man who tek advantage a yu, may God forgive me fe what A would-a do to the bruk-kitchen wretch.'

'But Mama, what we going to do? Boysie say I can't stay here and he mean it. Him is going to make our life a misery if I stay.'

Her mother didn't answer. Instead she told Putus to get a piece of ice out of the ice-box behind the kitchen, wrap it in a piece of clean cloth and bring to her to put on her swollen, purple and blue face.

VALERIE

Putus was beginning to realise that even in moments of time when everything one knew is tumbling down, life goes on. And life had gone on since that night when Boysie hit her mother and that morning when she begged her mother to leave Boysie.

By the evening, Miss Belle had gotten up out of the bed. She had prepared Boysie's dinner. Mannie had come from school. He had watered the plants in the yard, just as he did every day. Boysie had come from Linstead, had his bath in the outside bathroom, sat at the dining table in a corner of the sitting-room, had his dinner and licked his lips. Putus had taken to her room, especially when Boysie and Mannie were at home.

There was a day when she had an overwhelming feeling that things had gotten to a bump, when she knew that something big was about to happen. If only because things could not go on as usual. The night of that day, Miss Belle came and got her out of her room.

'Putus, A cyaan come on this journey wit yu. You goin' to have to travel dis road alone.'

'Yes Mama.'

'God know A try mi bes fi yu get a good edication. God know A try mi bes to prepare yu to hold up yu head in the world, an' when man on earth have done their best, angels in heaven cyaan do more.'

'Yes Mama, you tried your best for me.'

'Putus, A don' want to cry over milk that throw away arready but how yu could-a kick over yu bucket a milk so? Look how much A work? Look how much A sacrifice? An' fah everyting to turn to ashes?'

Miss Belle started to moan. Putus couldn't stand it. Her body kept switching from burning hot to ice cold, out there on that barbecue to the back and at the side of the yard where Da Da Barton had, generations before, held his land council. She felt very fragile and alone.

When she had realised that her not seeing the monthly blood meant that she was going to have a baby, somehow she had not seen it as a great tragedy, even after all the fuss with Aunt Sisi, Mr Bennett and her mother. She didn't like to be sick each morning and her clothes were getting so tight, very soon she would have nothing to wear. But she had seen this baby-business as something she could easily get through, take back up her studies and in time, become a teacher or a nurse, just like her mother had planned.

It was only on the morning after Boysie had taken his hand to her mother that she began to suspect that nothing would ever be the same again. It was worse than when her mother had married Boysie. Then her mother was still queen of the Barton land, if only because it was Boysie who had come to live on their land and he could do nothing with it unless her mother agreed.

It was worse than when her mother had sent her to Old Harbour to live in Aunt Sisi's backroom. Then she knew it would only be until she had passed her exams and that she could re-establish herself in the house and on her family's land, when she began working.

That Boysie could lift his hand and strike a Barton woman down. And get away with it! That Da Da Barton, Ma Tata Barton or especially Mas D Barton, from their graves, had not called down lightning and thunder to consume him in smoke and fire. That he could calmly leave to make furniture in Linstead the following morning. That he could have calmly returned in the evening and licked his lips with the delicious dinner prepared for him by the hands of the very Barton woman who still wore the black and blue scars of his beating – all this brought to Putus a fear she had never known, never even knew existed.

She didn't only then stay in her room as before. She cowered in it. She didn't come out to eat. She didn't come out to bathe in the outside bathroom but cleaned herself either in the pail or face basin inside her room.

During this time, her mother had called through the locked door. Knocked and called through the little jalousie window. Broken out two of the blinds and pushed through Putus's daily meals. Putus had answered not a word.

But on this night, there had been a different quality in Miss Belle's voice when she called at the window:

'Putus, A mus talk wit yu. Is either yu come out or A goin' to have to bruk down the door an' talk to yu in dere.'

It was the week after the beating. She had raised herself up off the single bed and gone over to the little window facing Da Da's yam field. She had moved the curtain and looked through the space left by the two broken-out blinds.

There is a greenish-gold light which comes from the moon at a certain time of night. That time when all plants and lower animals are at rest. When even crickets are quiet. When all self-satisfied human beings are at rest and one with nature. When only the dissatisfied and restless dead and living refuse to lock the door on the terror and sweat of their daily existence.

Boysie and Mannie are asleep. The yam field is asleep. Miss Belle is standing before the jalousie window.

Putus looks upon her. She is covered in green and black and gold. The flowers on her housecoat appear like dark sleeping leaves. Her belly is like a mountain. The moon's light is cruel. Because as black as her face is, it shows blacker still the bruise marks.

To Putus's eyes, the form of Miss Belle keeps constantly changing. One moment she is the tall shape of a Negro-yam hill, the next she is melted down and dissolved into the fat vines and broad leaves of a giant pumpkin plant on the ground under the window. The next, she is a Scotch Bonnet pepper tree, the leaves turned all gold, like the peppers. But in whatever form, her face does not change. Always Black and grieving. Now a roundish Negro yam, next a big dark-green pumpkin, and then a bright-yellow vast Scotch Bonnet pepper.

Putus leaves the window, goes to the door, opens it, comes into the sitting-room, opens the front door and goes outside, into the yard. Miss Belle turns from the window and goes towards the barbecue. Putus follows. The moon has made the barbecue its playground.

Miss Belle sits on a part of its ledge, Putus sits on its recently laid concrete floor.

Miss Belle sharply tells her to sit on the ledge, that she might catch a cold from the concrete floor. Putus obeys. Neither of them speaks for some time. Then Miss Belle begins to speak.

'Putus, Putus, always remember A luv-yu. A did luv yu fada when him was alive. A luv me own madda. But A neva luv anybody de way me luv yu who come from mi own womb. A want yu to understan', A still luv yu, even though yu let me down bad, bad. But A cyaan come pon dis journey wit yu. Dis journey is fe yu alone.'

Putus is listening quietly, her eyes big with apprehension.

'A don' expec yu fe understan' everyting dat A sayin', but one day, one day, yu wi' understan'. A don' expec yu fe understan' why A cyaan leave Boysie, although him beat me. Yu see, Putus, worl' tough fe woman an' yu goin' to learn dat. A try mi bes' no to mek yu have-fi learn dat but is you dat put yuself in de way. So yu goin' to have-fi learn dat by yuself. After yu learn dat, an' if yu survive, den yu will understan' why yu have-fi travel dis journey alone. Yu no longer Putus, yu is Valrie now, an' yu 'ave to tek yu medicine as Valrie. Walk Good, Valrie.'

Putus got down on her knees in the middle of the concrete floor of Da Da's barbecue. Her father and her mother had taught her to pray to a God whom she could not even picture in her mind. Da Da and Mas D were more real to her. The moon with its greenish-gold light was more real to her. She prayed to them.

She prayed to them to take this fear away from her. She prayed to them to protect her mother from Boysie. She prayed to them not to make her die. She begged them to go with her on this journey, whatever it was and wherever it might lead.

GRANNIE LOU

Study the donkey. Can anyone imagine what marvellous tales would be heard if the donkey was able to talk? In the time of cars and trucks and buses and airplanes, not many people notice the donkey. But not many people on the globe that is earth eat the donkey, though all peoples eat things which to other people may seem strange.

For many people, to eat the donkey would be like eating themselves. For the donkey is the burden-bearer of all animals, just like some people are the burden-bearers of all people.

Even the donkey is not sure-footed. It heaves its way with its two laden hampers up the hill but every now and again its hooves slip on the many loose stones on top and beneath the surface of the red, clayey soil.

That is why Henry has his toes dug in behind the donkey and his hands on the donkey's haunches, giving it a little help up the hill, whenever it needs it.

Putus holds in her right hand the rope from the bit in the donkey's mouth. She is bent forward, leading it on up the hill. Henry had said that she should steer the donkey. It is Henry's donkey. And it will only respond to her steering it if Henry instructs it.

She had begun her journey the morning after her talk on Da Da's barbecue with Miss Belle. Before the sun was up, Henry was calling-out at the gate: 'Boysie, oh Aunt B, hold dog! Is me, Hengry.' Boysie had gone to let him in. Boysie wasn't too happy that Belle's nephew had turned up but manners required that he welcome Henry as his dear 'in-law', even though he didn't know why Henry had come. He suspected that B must have sent for him. He hoped that B had not told her family that he had beaten her. Even if this was so, Boysie thought, since he and Henry were 'man-to-man' they could understand each other.

'Morning, Cousin Henry, morning. Come in man, come in. What bring yu here so early? Everybody wit yu, hawty?'

'Morning, Boysie. Aunt B de dere?'

Boysie hadn't liked this greeting, it was too bare. It said that Henry was responding the minimum acceptable for those with good manners, but that he was not going beyond. He had made it clear that he had not come to see or talk with Boysie but with Miss Belle, his blood aunt.

Boysie felt he could rest assured that Henry wouldn't beat him up, as he had beat-up Miss Belle. Henry was a small Black man, not given to violence. But if Henry came to hate him, he couldn't tell what Henry would do.

Before Boysie could answer Henry's first question, he went on to another:

'Putus arright?'

Henry hadn't moved from the gate. Mamby was keeping up his barking all this time because the gate was open. Henry ignored Mamby, although he full well knew that Mamby would stop barking as soon as he shut the gate.

Henry stood at the half-open gate and looked into Boysie's yellow eyes as if he wouldn't move until he got an answer satisfactory to him, to his two questions.

'Come in, come in, Cousin Henry. Everything arright.'

Henry had not moved from the gate.

Belle had heard Henry's coming. Putus had heard Henry's coming. Putus had remained inside her room. Belle had gone to the door of the sitting-room. She had stepped to the gate and said:

'Everything arright, Hengry.'

Only then did Henry enter. He had come into the sitting-room. Boysie had not known what to do with himself. Henry had said:

'A come for Putus. A come fah mi likkle cousin Putus.'

Then he had turned to Belle and asked:

'She ready?'

Miss Belle had answered:

'Yes Hengry, she ready. A jus have to get her from her room. Jus gi' me two minute an' den she will ready to go wit yu.'

Belle had gone into Putus's room to help her to get ready. She had taken in a draw-string bag with her and said to Putus, 'Put dis bag wit the rest a yu tings-dem. Don't open it till yu reach where yu going.'

When Belle and Putus came out into the sitting-room Boysie and Henry were there, both standing and both quiet. Henry had looked at Belle, with his eyes on Putus, when he said:

'Come, A wi' help yu carry yu load to Miss Mack shop at de corner. A have mi donkey dere. Come.'

They had travelled all day, Putus walking sometimes, at other times riding on the donkey when Henry judged that she was too tired to continue on foot. Henry had walked all the way. They had stopped in Ducksies, Henry's birth-village, for the night. She was so exhausted, she slept in her clothes. Before sun-up the next morning, they started out again.

Neither of them had spoken about the events at the house in Brown's Hall since leaving Boysie and Miss Belle. On Henry's side, he had not spoken because there are some things that cut so deeply in the heart that it is better not to speak about them. On Putus's side, she just wanted to go wherever this road with Henry and his donkey led. She had decided, from that night with her mother on the barbecue, to put herself and her life in the hands of Da Da, Mas D, the leaves and the trees as her God and she had to depend on them and Henry, to protect her and lead her where they would.

She knew by now that where they were bound for was up further into the hills from Ducksies. Way past Ducksies. No one could ever find it on a map, it was so far up into the hills. Some people from Brown's Hall didn't even know that anyone lived beyond the outer reaches of Ducksies. The five or so people who lived in this place that would never appear on any map were thought, by many outside Ducksies, to be from Ducksies.

Grannie Lou, Miss Belle's grandmother and Putus's great-grand-mother, was one of the five people who lived up there. Grannie Lou and her husband, Kayam, had originally met in one of Grandy Nanny's 'free villages' in Portland. Everyone knew that Grandy Nanny, or 'Nana Yah', as she was called in Ghana, was an Ashanti princess who was captured and sold into European slavery as the reprisal of the enemies in one of the Ashanti wars. Equally, everyone who knows anything knows that it is not possible to enslave an Ashanti 'commoner', much less an Ashanti princess. Grandy Nanny had refused to go on the auction block, after coming through the Middle Passage into the slave market into which Jamaica had been transformed. She had resolutely declared, 'I will not be a slave' and had gone on to found and lead the Maroon nation, made up of Africans from all the different nations who had been captured and sold into European slavery and who refused to be slaves.

Grannie Lou's and Kayam's forebears had fought side by side with Grandy Nanny. One had come from the Fanti peoples of the great Ghana kingdom and the other from the Ashantis. Having defeated the colonial British armies, they had been left to set up the first 'free villages', under the British–Maroon Treaty. Most people had celebrated wildly at this victory against the British. But Grandy Nanny had died of a broken heart because her brother Kojo had given in and agreed with the white men to include a clause in the Treaty which said that the Maroon nation, in exchange for being given their 'freedom' under British law, was to turn over to the slavemasters any other African who tried to run away from the slave plantations and join the free villages. It was never written in the history books but it was passed from generation to generation by word of mouth, in songs, in dances, that Grandy Nanny cursed this clause of the Treaty and told her Maroon nation only to turn over the bad ones, layabouts and informers, to the British.

Grandy Nanny's generation had passed down to their ensuing gener-ations the charge: 'never be a slave'. They also passed down to their children the idea that the possession of land was everything, yet land could neither be bought nor sold. It could only be held by those who worked it.

This was also the idea of Great-Grandfather Barton, although under the European regimen he had to buy the land.

Not so Grannie Lou and Kayam. They had seen that the free villages were getting overcrowded. So that they had begun to prepare to move before the great migrations to other parts of the island, which took place during the early years of the century.

They had moved out from Portland and struck a path over to St Catherine, where they had some relations already settled. As far as they were concerned, all the land belonged to the Arawak Indians, who were the original Jamaicans, and since they had been killed off by the Spanish and, later, the British, Grannie Lou and Kayam felt that they were the proper inheritors of the Arawaks' land. They knew that most of the land was then controlled either by the plantation owners or the Church of England, and that any land that was left over was designated 'Crown Lands'. But Grannie Lou and Kayam did not care what this meant.

They followed their African tradition which said that land could neither be bought nor sold but belonged to those who worked it. After travelling for many days, they came upon this land on a hill above the settled villages of St Catherine. They immediately staked it out and they began to live there and to work this land. The 'Crown' didn't bother them, maybe because not even the 'Crown' and its officials knew about this land, since it didn't appear on any map.

When Kayam had died at the age of ninety-four and Grannie Lou was only seventy-one years old, all the family on Miss Belle's side had tried to put pressure on Grannie Lou to leave the hill, to come down into Ducksies and even, better still, go to live with her daughter, Miss Belle's mother, in Lluidas Vale, in the same parish of St Catherine. After Miss Belle's marriage to Mas D, they begged her to live with Miss Belle in Brown's Hall on the Barton land.

Grannie Lou did not move. People further down the hill and on the lowlands, even as far as Old Harbour, talked about her behind her back. They said that she wanted to stay up on that hill to work obeah with wild animals, birds, her Ashanti and Fanti ancestors. Whenever any of the white Creole slavemasters' descendants took sick or died, some of them said that it was Grannie Lou who had worked her obeah. Grannie Lou paid them not a mind. She just stayed up on her hill.

The donkey, with Henry spurring it on from behind and Putus leading it in front, is going up on to Grannie Lou's hill. Putus can't think anymore. She has come from Henry's home in Ducksies and is climbing the hill. All she can see and remember are the oil nut trees. Among all the other trees that she sees on this journey to her Grannie Lou, the oil nut trees, with their tough, spiked, green leaves, give her the most comfort.

Even as she pulls the donkey forward, she knows it is dead tired. Just at the point when she thinks it is going to collapse, they see Grannie Lou at the top of her hill, before the wattle-and-daub hut that she built with Kayam.

What with worrying about whether the donkey will collapse before it reaches to the top of Grannie Lou's hill. What with worrying about what her life is going to be after this trial. What with worrying . . . she can only see the form of an ancient Black woman standing before a hut. She cannot see the face of Grannie Lou.

Henry brings the donkey to rest before Grannie Lou's hut. He just stands there, silent. Putus is too tired to say anything, anyway. It is Grannie Lou who speaks:

'Come, mi granny, come inside.'

Putus does not realise that she is speaking to her, until Grannie Lou takes her hand and pulls her inside the one-room hut. Then she goes back outside, where Henry is still standing by the donkey. She takes the rope which Putus has been holding.

'Come, yu tired. Come fah water an' food.'

She is talking to the donkey. The donkey follows her to the back of the yard, she ties the rope on to the big cotton tree. She puts a pan with water for the donkey to drink. She comes back to the door of the hut where Henry is still standing.

'Come Hengry, come inside.'

They are all inside now.

'Hengry, yu have fi stay tinight. Dat donkey cyaan mek de trip back down de hill. Come, Miss Val, pack-out yu tings-dem. Get yuself in awda to wait fah de likkle one.'

GRANNIE LOU

I t wasn't easy. Up there on Grannie Lou's hill. Before Putus came there, she had tried to save up every penny she could lay her hands on from she had gone to live at Aunt Sisi's house in Old Harbour.

As well, that morning when Henry had come for her, Miss Belle had accompanied them to the shop where the donkey was tied and she had pressed something into her hand, just before she said goodbye.

Putus had put the hard, little parcel into her brassière without knowing what it was. When she took off her clothes to go to bed on that first night at Grannie Lou's, she had opened the parcel. It was two 10 pound notes. She had added it up with what she had been able to save and had counted a little over 30 pounds. A vast sum of money, especially since she wouldn't have to buy any baby things. When she had opened the calico draw-string bag which her mother had given her just before she left the house, she discovered that it contained everything from baby nappies and chemises to baby powder and gripe water.

But on Grannie Lou's hill, she came to learn that it didn't matter how much money you had. Grannie Lou did not charge rent. Grannie Lou did not use money because there was nothing on the hill to buy and the last time she had been to Brown's Hall or Old Harbour was about fifteen years before. Grannie Lou had kerosene lamps but if no one brought the kerosene and the lamps became dry, she would build a fire in the yard, to keep off mosquitoes and flies, as much as to give light. In any event, when there was a moon, Grannie Lou would just open up the hut and allow the full light of the moon to come in.

When Putus had been there for two weeks, she had asked Grannie Lou if she would like her to go down the hill and see if Henry could help her to buy some things in Old Harbour. Grannie Lou had been sitting under the hairy-mango tree, marking lines in the dirt with a stick.

Grannie Lou put the stick down and looked up at Putus:

'What tings yu want to buy, mi dawta?'

Putus felt the answer must be clear. They were always short of provisions. There were enough yams and pumpkins, bananas, callaloo, coconuts, oranges, sugar-cane, guavas and jackfruit. They even had some dry gungo peas which Grannie Lou had stored up. But no meat, no fresh fish, no salted fish, no cooking oil, no butter, no flour, no rice. None of many of the things she had become used to eating. She had stammered her answer to Grannie Lou:

'Maybe some fish an' a piece of mutton an' . . . '

67

Putus stopped because Grannie Lou was looking at her in a piercing way. At last, she had said:

'Don' bodder yuself bout what dey-a Ole Harbour. Yu might harm the likkle one yu carryin', if yu try to go down de hill now. Yu should-a ongly tek dat risk if is fah someting yu cyaan do widout. An' mi chile, yu wi' learn dat is ongly one ting dat yu cyaan do widout. Dats life itself.'

Putus turned away from Grannie Lou. How could she explain to this old woman her craving for a piece of goat mutton stewed down in curry with fluffy white rice? How could she explain her longing for stewed red peas with pickled pig's tail and salt beef?

It wasn't like when she was at Aunt Sisi's house and her stomach turned at the goat meat and wild hog. Now she craved for fresh meat as if the little one needed meat to grow in her belly. The wanting of brown-stewed yard-fowl and rice-an'-peas was a physical hunger tearing her guts out some nights and keeping her awake.

And it wasn't only meat of animal or fowl that she craved for. She dreamed of fresh fish. Fish that was just caught from the sea, scaled, cleaned, marinated with lime and put into the pot to steam with fresh seasoning and a little butter. Her mouth filled-up with juices of anticipation when she remembered mackerel and banana rundown. The truth was that Putus missed her favourite foods more than she missed her mother.

But as well, she always felt hungry. She wondered what Grannie Lou would say, if she told her that she now felt like she had to feed two people and the food she ate was never even enough for one. She prayed that Henry, or someone, would come to visit them on the hill soon. Once anyone came, they would bring provisions because it was not the way of their culture to come empty-handed.

Then the rainy season started. From the end of May and all into June, then to September, the rains came on and off. A hurricane could come any time and sweep them off the hill, Putus thought. The rain came down in swords directed at the little hut. On a night in July the wind came, first with a whisper, then a moan, building-up to screams.

The more the rain thundered, the more the wind screamed, the quieter the child became within Putus's womb. By this time, her only company were whatever it was in her womb and Grannie Lou. At the most unusual times, like when she was sitting quietly or talking to Grannie Lou, the something would start up a racket. Kicking and dancing and prancing within her womb. If she was standing, she then had to sit down for fear that the child would knock her off her feet. But when nature took charge and the wind and the rain threatened to smash the little hut to bits, then the child did not move. Then it was as if there was no child there.

Fear and panic washed her. She thought that the child had died. She had felt that if this was so – and she had no way of knowing – she would also kill herself and join the child. For in the bleakness of Grannie Lou's hill, she had come to look forward to the child's movements. They had become her main evidence that she herself was alive.

Then another fear overtook her. That the wattle-and-daub hut would not stand up before the onslaught and she would be hurled down the hill to be smashed-up on the rocks.

But, morning had come. And with it, a lull. So glad she was to be alive, that she was able to laugh as she confided her fears of the night before to Grannie Lou.

'Don' fret, mi likkle dawta. Mi likkle abode witstan' many rainy season. An' it shall witstan' many more to come.'

The casualties of the night's storm were one mango tree, one guava tree. All the slimber sugar-cane plants were intact. And so was the hut, except for a few leaks in the joining under the roof.

But Putus still carried the nagging fear of the baby's death.

'Grannie Lou, A tink de baby dead!'

'How yu know?'

'It not moving.'

'If it don' move by eveling, tell me.'

She started to help Grannie Lou clear up the yard. She bent down to take up a mound of rubbish when the baby started-up a turning and a kicking inside her womb, so violent that she dropped the rubbish and sat down on the ground.

Grannie Lou smiled. 'Res' a likkle, Miss Val, den come help me tek up de branch-dem dat de storm blow off.'

They had managed to live. Upon that bleak hill. It was Grannie Lou who helped Putus to manage. Got her to stop longing for things she didn't have and couldn't get and to, at least temporarily, glory in the things she did have.

Grannie Lou had three dresses. Two were those she called her 'yard frocks' and one, Putus had never seen her put on. The two 'yard frocks' were of calico and the other was a floral cotton, which, Grannie Lou said, she would wear on any 'special occasion' if she had to go down the hill and if not, she would like the family to see that she was buried in it.

Grannie Lou had two pairs of shoes. If the sun was shining, as most times it was, she would go barefoot – 'good fah de foot-dem', she would say. If it had been or was raining and the ground was all soft and squelchy, she would put on her laced-up boots which came a little above her ankle. The other was a pair of black patent leather pumps, in which she said she had been married. This was to go with the floral cotton to dress her in at her burial.

Every morning early, Grannie Lou would go outside the hut, open-out her big, black nosehole and draw-up the chilly morning air into her lungs. And then she would open her toothless mouth wide and belch-in air. Then she would walk around the yard and she would touch the Injun-kale by the water drum, she would pat the callaloo plants, she would check the pumpkins and sweet potatoes. Then she would gather little pieces of wood and sticks and make up the fire for their bush tea. Breakfast was bush tea, a piece of roasted yam or some callaloo. Unless someone had brought some saltfish; then a piece of that would be roasted too.

There were two she-goats and a rammie, which Grannie Lou kept inside the hut whenever it rained hard. Putus could not hope for any curried goat from these goats. The she-goats were for milk and the ramgoat to keep the she-goats company, Grannie Lou said. Sometimes she would pat the goats on the head and talk to them, just like she did to the plants. Putus had asked her one day why she did that, was it some sort of obeah?

'Obeah, mi pickney? If is obeah, is the obeah of life. A do it to mix-up mi spirit wit all dat is roun' me, after a night in de small death which they call sleep. It is fe show respec fe de fac dat life start all over again every morning. An' while dere is life, dere is 'ope.'

Somehow, after that, Putus found that she came less and less to view this hill as a lonely prison to which she had been abandoned. She began to take a more active interest in getting up at the same time as Grannie Lou and taking care of the plants in the yard with her. She still hungered after the provisions they didn't have and she swore that she would never eat jackfruit again after she left this hill. But she was now able to control her hunger.

It had still been so lonely. Except as the child grew in her womb. Except as her breasts became bigger and bigger and strained to let out the milk they had been producing and storing-up, she came to feel more and more that she had company in the life she was carrying.

Her fear now was that she would get ill in the night, or something would happen to the child in her womb and she only had Grannie Lou's bush baths and herb tea to depend on.

But she didn't get ill. Up until the evening she felt the pains knifing across her stomach. She had kept quiet at first. Then one of them got so bad, she screamed out. Grannie Lou held her under her armpits, began to guide her towards the hut, while saying:

'Cum Miss Val. Cum likkle modder. Yu time come.'

ICYLANE

She named the child Icylane.

It was a full ten days after her birth that she was officially registered as having joined the human race.

Somebody had to go to the post office in Old Harbour and fill out some form, which would then be sent to the Island Records Office in Spanish Town. Grannie Lou couldn't do it, she didn't leave her hill. Putus couldn't do it. She was taken up with forgetting the pain, which she could never even have imagined, of bringing a child into the world; getting used to this little thing always sucking, sucking and drawing on her painful breasts and above all, getting used to the wonder of this 'something' that had been in her body being out and needing to be kept alive by her alone.

This 'something' had increasingly become a 'somebody' in the ten days. At first, she had been afraid to hold it, thinking that it might break. Grannie Lou had laughed and told her that she would soon get used to it.

Then she would stare at it in wonder for hours, marvelling that it had everything that she had, in miniature. And it was black, black, black, all over. She had been disappointed that it didn't look like anyone she knew. She hadn't wanted it to look like its father – she had put him out of her mind from the moment she told Miss Belle that she hadn't wanted to marry him. She hoped that it would look like her own father, Mas D.

Grannie Lou had told her: 'never pattern de look of a newborn off anybody else, the baby look like it own self.'

The baby had a long and very slim body. Its neck was particularly long. It had this head on top of the long neck that would be normal for some bodies, except for two things. One was that the top of the head was covered in coarse black hair – who ever heard of a young baby being born with so much hair, one could almost begin to plait it right away? The other was the eyes. They were black and brown pupils on a white eyeball but it was as if they came in a big person – they were so deep and serious. The child would lie wrapped up on the makeshift cot after its feeding and it would just lie there looking steadfastly up into the roof of the hut, not making a sound. When it was feeding, it would clamp its little mouth on its mother's breast and all the time be looking up into its mother's face with a set stare.

'I naming her Icylane,' Putus told Grannie Lou.

'I naming her Icylane because is a icy lane I travel through to bring her into this world.'

She waited for Henry or somebody else to come from down the hill. She would ask them to go to the post office in Old Harbour and register the child. Putus felt that they must have been tracking the months and knew that this was the ninth month. So somebody would come soon.

When Henry came on his little donkey on the eighth day after the birth, Putus had a paper ready for him on which she had written the baby's name and date of birth. Because the child was born out of wedlock, it wasn't necessary to put the father's name. Putus was glad. Henry said to her, 'that's not good, cousin Putus, every pickney have father, pickney cyaan come without father.' But Putus retorted, 'what father have to do with me and Icylane? Is my child.' Henry kept quiet.

When Henry got down to Ducksies, he called all his neighbours into his house for a drink to celebrate the birth of little Icylane. He had already sent a message to Miss Belle in Brown's Hall. But he knew that she would not be able to go up the hill, since she was then only three months into suckling her own little one – a boy. Moriah, who lived on the land next door to him, said he was going down to Old Harbour the following morning. So Henry gave him the paper to register Putus's baby at the post office.

It nearly made Putus get vexed with Henry. Because when Henry gave her the register-paper that Moriah had brought back from Old Harbour, the name recorded on it was 'Icilyn Belle Barton'. Belle was all right. Putus had given her daughter the name of her mother for a middle name, although she was not too pleased with her mother now. Barton was right, she wanted her child to have her own family name. But she got into a rage at the spelling of the first name.

Henry explained that when Moriah had presented the paper on which Putus had written, Mrs Williamson, the postmistress at the Old Harbour post office, had said there must be a mistake. She said she had never heard of any name called 'Icylane' and that it must be a bad spelling. In vain did Moriah try to point out that the mother of the baby was a graduate of First and Second Jamaica Local Examination and thus was an educated person who could no doubt spell the name she wanted for her child correctly.

Whatever Moriah said, Mrs Williamson knew better. She knew that most of these people from the hills were a little 'dark'; even when they were insisting that they had gone to school and passed exams, most times they couldn't even remember what day it was, much less to spell words properly. She had to fill up the forms for them, as she thought best. 'Icylane' indeed!

Putus wanted to go down to the post office herself to have the register-paper corrected.

'I name her Icylane. And Icylane she shall be. She is not Icilyn. That's a different baby. My baby is Icylane, you don't see how she get Icy when

72

she studying anything? I going down to tell off that woman at the post office!'

Henry stood by looking very sheepish. Grannie Lou told her that she wasn't strong enough to go down the hill yet and in any event, the 'woman at the post office' would probably tell her that the paper was gone to Spanish Town already and could not be changed.

The young Icylane was to live through her life with a confusion on her 'proper name'. There was no confusion with the shortened name. Because before she was one month old, her mother, Grannie Lou and Henry called her Icy. Her pet name came to be Icy, to one and all.

PART TWO

THE SEVILLE
ORANGE

The Seville orange is an interesting fruit, though some people just take it for granted. It is usually seen as the 'ugly duckling', 'poor cousin', of sweet oranges.

Those who don't know it probably just say when they see its tree, 'Ah, another orange tree'. And pass on. For the Seville orange tree looks like most other orange trees, only that it is taller, its bark is tougher and its dark-green leaves are thicker. Some say that's why it can withstand breeze-blows and even hurricanes.

As for its fruits, they usually come larger than the common sweet oranges. But that is not the main thing that distinguishes Seville oranges. Because the ugli-fruit is also large, very large, yet it is not a Seville orange.

The skin of the Seville orange is thick, rough and puckered. In that roughness of the skin are many submerged colours. At a glance, it appears to be deep browny-green. But if you look deeper, you will see that, as well, it has purple, black, dark and light shades of green and touches of yellow.

Some people say that the Spaniards brought it to Jamaica with them when they took the island away from the Arawak Indians and that is why it is called Seville orange. These people say that the way these conquistadores kept themselves alive on those long sea voyages was to suck the juice of the Seville orange. Its sourness would 'cut their nature' and calm their raging desire for women.

Others disagree. These say that its real name is 'Sobil' (for sour) orange and that it migrated from Africa with the forced emigration of the slaves. Still others say that it was always on the island and that the original inhabitants worshipped it as a special god.

Be that as it may, however it found itself to Jamaica, it stands there as a sacred tree.

No one eats the Seville orange. Its pulp is bitter and its juice excessively sour.

Should you be one of those know-it-all foreigners who ignore the wisdom of the local people and try to eat a Seville orange, you will very quickly feel its bitterness and sourness scorching your throat, withering your lips. As well, its tree is thorny and if you are not careful you could get your fingers all bloody-torn if you try to pluck the fruit, instead of picking it, when it's good and ready to be picked.

The Seville orange does not bear a sweetened fruit. Compared to it, sweet oranges turn out to be hypocrites because the fruit of a sweet orange tree can be sweet or sour and the eater has no way of knowing this until she or he has actually tasted the particular fruit. With the Seville orange, you know that it's going to be sour, from the beginning until the end.

Yet no one destroys it. In some societies, the people would have thrown it out, chopped down and rooted out its trees, burnt and destroyed any of its seedlings which dared to survive the onslaught. But Jamaicans have not destroyed the Seville orange.

You wonder why?

Well, the older people say that there are several reasons for this. If you asked Grannie Lou, for example, she would have summarised the reasons like this: 'in every bad there is good and in every good there is bad, what not dead, don't throw it 'way, find some use for it.'

And when you think of this sour fruit in this way, you will first of all see it as a tree. The older people say that a tree is a tree and to be loved for itself, whatever it bears. Don't know if you would agree. You wouldn't be one of those people who cut down trees and cover over the grass with concrete, to make buildings, would you?

Think, if you had been on the sugar-cane plantations, day after day, seeing endless miles of sugar-cane plants, would you not welcome and nurture the Seville orange tree which you found growing wild by your barracks?

Another thing. That long sour drink you have had so many times. That 'lemonade', which cools your guts and quenches your thirst, comes from the juice of the Seville orange! It is so good, some people cannot drink it in cups, or glasses or even mugs. They have to drink it by the butter pan-full.

Yes, that same harsh, sour juice, which would make of your mouth, throat and stomach one big sore if you tried to drink it, becomes a soothing, healing drink when mixed with sugar and water. Of course you have to know the exact quantities in which to mix the ingredients. Any Jamaican knows the recipe, just by instinct and experience.

They don't know or they don't care about patents and copyright. So it doesn't matter to them if when the visitor from Europe or North America goes back home, he sticks a nice label and a new name on it and announces to the world that he has discovered it. (Women don't go much into stealing patents, except in exceptional circumstances.)

If you ever get down to Birmingham-way, in England, you could have the opportunity to study the Seville orange when it has been removed for a long time from its home ground.

You see, when Valerie 'Putus' Barton-Mason was leaving Jamaica for England she carefully wrapped, among some of her most private garments, two young Seville oranges, picked directly from the tree. Wonderfully, the Customs officer at Heathrow missed them when he searched her luggage. She kept them with her. She carried them wrapped up in her clothes to whichever house she moved. Even when she threw out other things, she took them in her trunk from London to Birmingham.

They shrivelled up, lost their juice, became crisp, dry and hard.

MRS MASON

So help me God if it's not the same voice. Appear before my very eyes. Standing right in front of me.

It's so hot inside. But chilly . . . chilly . . . outside. Hot . . . and . . . chilly . . . cold, cold . . . all at the same time. Could be it's the heat from the Eckna . . . singeing the oilskin tablecloth once again. Yes, I can smell the burn-smell . . . creeping . . . creeping up and up . . . into my nosehole. It's going to reach into my head soon. Maybe there, it will find its last resting-place. With the Voices. Eh, eh, hope they get on together. Perhaps quarrel start already. Maybe that's why this one run out of my head.

And standing right in front of me. Before my very eyes.

'Mrs Mason, Mrs Mason . . . you up there?

Mrs Mason . . . Yoo . . . hoo . . . Mrs Mason

Somebody coming to you

Yoo . . . hoo Mrs Mason

Why you don't answer me?'

I not answering a Raas!

('Val, I don't tell you, you must stop cursing badwords. You never used to do that . . . decent woman like you.')

You, shut your Raas too! It's a pity the heat didn't drive you out of my head, just like the other Voice.

It's that woman from downstairs. Call herself *Mistress* Dixon. Like anybody would have ever choose She, to married to. She and her whole heap of Black bastards pickney . . . Eh' eh' eh. I am not answering her. 'Let her stew' . . . as the English would say. I don't know what she is bothering me for. Staying at the bottom of the stairs and shouting her Yoo . . . hoo up to me . . . just like they . . . her combolos . . . do it, from their mountain-top down to lowland and up again in their hog-holes in the West Indies. 'You can take the hog out of the wallow but you can't take the wallow out of the hog.' And always calling me '*Mistress Maay-sin*'. Decent, educated people – the ones I like to mix with – call me *Missis May-son*. Eh! These idle lower-class people just give all Black people here a bad name. With their bad talking. They don't even take the time to learn the people's language properly . . . eating up their words and breaking up the English language. Then shaking up themselves and grinning all the time . . . like they so happy . . . they happy more than anybody else? How that could be? They only trying to give an impression. Like that *Mistress* Dixon downstairs . . . she have to hide from the Social Security and clean office at night to support her five children. From early morning you hear them making noise in the building. From early morning till evening, she cleaning and she washing and she cooking and she puffing up and down and she sweating. In the night she cleaning white people office . . . cleaning them high-class shitty toilet, till late. Yet she have the nerve to come up here, from her flat downstairs . . . up here . . . to the last room at the top of the building . . . to ask me if I arright . . . how come I not been going to work . . . if I need help. Eh! What kind of help She can give me? She need help Herself. Those people, like Her, too busybody. Always poking their noses into other people's business.

Then the Black boy on the second floor. Call himself Rasta. With him stinking, dirty, knotty hair. Pushing-up himself on me too. Not that he ever touch me. I don' think he is really a criminal. But he went past his place that time when I forgot my dignity and shout down to them from the top of the stairs and told them to turn down that ungodly sound system. Morning, noon and night, 'boom, boom, boom, clacka, clacka, clacka'; blaring out from Rasta flat. Nobody else in the building seem to mind it. But I do.

You see, I am not the same as the others. They and I are not combolos. They are used to their low-down living-style. I am not. I am used to better than this building. I am just stopping here till I find my feet. They call that savage, dreadful noise 'music'. Want to put it beside the English people's lovely, nice chamber music. What cheek! Only them and those uncivilised Africans could like that noise. Jumping up and gyrating their bodies and grinning their teeth . . . they don't even have food in their pots. Cursing the English people behind their backs . . . saying they have no soul . . . they are machines . . . that they don't have any rhythm in their bodies. Eh, more fool them. Rhythm can put food in the pot? Rhythm can put money in their pocket? Rhythm can make a person dignify and prevent anyone from taking step with you?

That's why I was so vex with the boy Rasta, when he passed his place that time I shouted down for them to stop the noise. He came up here . . . stop in the middle of the top stairs . . . shake his dirty, knotty head . . . look up into my face and said:

'*Mother Mase, sorry if we disturb you, but a little music keep the soul alive. Remind we that Jah live. Mother Mase, Jah live! No matter how bad things get. Jah is in you, and you can rise above them. Mek the enemy stumble and fall trample him under you feet. No shut out the music, Mother Mase . . .*'

I was blue with vex. If I had the will of him, I would have pushed him down the stairs . . . down . . . down . . . down . . . to the last step . . . into the little dark hall . . . and I would shovel-up his lifeless body and put it outside for the garbage-man to take away.

Then the boom, boom, clacka, clacka, would stop. Inside my head. The Voices would be quiet. Would stop tormenting me. I would be at peace . . . at last. But here is the chief Voice. Standing right in front of me. No matter how much I shake my head . . . to get rid of the confusion . . . coming from the sound system downstairs . . . blow my nose . . . to push out the burn-smell from the Eckna . . . stop-up my ears . . . so I won't hear *Mistress* Dixon calling up to me . . . shut my eyes tight, tight . . . not to see the slim woman shivering at the top of the last stair . . .

She will not go away. Just keep looking at me . . . into me . . .

She doesn't say anything. Just keep looking into me.

'Dead before me, rotten before me.' We used to say this three times when I was a child in Jamaica and ghost come to the yard. 'Dead before me, rotten before me. Dead before me, rotten before me . . .'

She still there.

You see mi dying trial now? How I going to explain it to Henry and Miss Jo when they come here? According to them, they always come to see if I'm arright. But I know better. They just coming to see if I'm dead . . . or mad . . . so that they can get lawyer to give them the piece of land that mi generation-them left to me in Jamaica. It's a clear case of grudgeful and bad mind.

I knew that for sure after the first time that I told them about the Voices.

Four years after I come to Britain, the Voices were just like when echo from the mountain-top come into your ears. I wasn't even sure that the Voices were there. But the first time that I leave Fitzie and go to the Trinidad Carnival with mi friend . . . I knew the Voices were following me. Because I saw them in Trinidad. In bodily form. Like this one standing before me right now. There were thousands of them. Laughing and grinning and jumping-up and talking so loud!

They weren't satisfied to stay just in my head. They were all around me . . . and pulling me . . . to come dance and grin . . . and sex with them.

I didn't. I don't mix with such people in Britain and I was not going to mix with them in Trinidad. But when I come back to Britain – eh! it's that time the Voices get bold!

They started to talk loud . . . in my head . . . sometimes talking to one another . . . in my head. But most of the times, talking to me . . . from out of my head. They just settled themselves right in the middle of the space above my nose-bridge, at the start of my forehead . . . running up . . . and over . . . into my head . . . and down, into my neckbone.

When I moved back in with Fitzie in Brixton, they set up such a racket in my head, I had was to run from him and go rent a room all by myself in a house in Ladbroke Grove. But it was even worse there. The Voices went into my shoulders and down into my arms. They didn't stop there. They went into my chest. They clamped themselves on my heart, choking it up. Pounding their fists to the same beat as my heart. Took over that rhythm . . . then speed up the beating of their fists . . . dragging my heart along with their rhythm.

I remember one time when one of the old women I was looking after at the hospital start to tell me her feistiness again . . . calling me dirty black monkey . . . just as I bathe her off and put her in her bed . . . I remember that time, all the Voices start shouting in my head at the same time and they grip my whole body so tight, I couldn't even blow through my nose. I had was to kneel down right on the floor . . . next to the old patient on the bed. I couldn't even hear her cursing me anymore. All I could hear was the Voices and all I could see was the filth on her that I just finish washing off her.

The Hospital Administrator and the Nursing Sister were standing up whispering just inside the door to the ward . . . always whisper, whisper through their teeth (you know how they speak without hardly moving their lips). They run come down to the bedside where I was kneeling down and ask me, with their plastic concern: 'Missis May-son, are you all right? Are you all right? Do you need a doctor? You're sure you're OK?'

I just keep quiet then, only groaning softly now and again. Seemed to me that it is a foolish question they asking me. Because if I wasn't all right, I couldn't answer them anyway. In any event, what was I going to tell them? That the Voices take over my whole body? And watch them arrange their marble-white faces politely, push-up their corn-hair eyebrows, turn-on their hospital whisper and say: 'it's OK Missis May-son dear, we'll take care of everything.' I can't stand when they call me 'dear' or 'love' in their funeral voice. And when they tell me they'll 'take care of everything', I shake like leaf inside. Because of one thing I am sure, that 'care' won't do me any good.

The other day after they told that old Irish woman that they would take care of everything when she began to bawl on the top of her voice and wouldn't go into the bed; I didn't see her the next night when I come on duty. I think that she must be bawl herself to death and they move her body to the dead house. But I hear round the ward that they send her to a madhouse. I know that will be the last room for her, especially if they put her on the senile dementia ward.

Who? Me? They must be think that I am an idiot. Me? Tell them about the Voices? Not me.

But I did think that it would be different with Henry and Miss Jo. They should understand about the Voices. They must have the Voices in them too. Maybe not the same Voices as my own but some like mine, cousin to them. I think it must be so, since Henry and Miss Jo and me come from the same place. Poor fool me. I will never forget the first time that I told them about the Voices.

MRS MASON

Miss Jo came to Birmingham, like usual when it was the Convention-time for the Church of God. Miss Jo is head-cook-and-bottle-washer in that church. They give her the title 'Mother'. When the Church hold Convention in Birmingham, Miss Jo stay with Henry and that wife of his. One year, I go round to Henry's house to see her and I start to tell them about the Voices.

In the middle of my talking, Henry wife covered her mouth and began to laugh so much behind her hand that it put Henry and Miss Jo in one embarrassment! They had was to ask her to leave the room and go and see what the children were doing. I don't take any notice of Henry's wife. She is a stupid, lower-class woman, only fit for breeding more and more hungry-belly pickney. In Jamaica she would never get a sensible, strong, nice man like Henry. But in England, where he was away from all the family and where the only other Black people are them uncivilised Africans, and the small islanders, he would have to choose somebody like her or marry a white woman. And he couldn't bring a white woman back to Jamaica as his wife, except he did want everybody in the District to look on him as a coonu-moonu who get catch by white trash or look on him with pity when she leave him and go live with one of the Brown men who have whole heap of land and money and want a woman to lighten the colour of their family. So I didn't pay no mind to Henry's wife, because she could only get him in England.

But it was Miss Jo and Henry who surprised me.

We were sitting in the little lounge of Henry's council house. Not a bad house. One reasonable bedroom with two little squingy ones. A little long lounge and bathroom and kitchen. Would be quite all right for three or four people. It's not the council who tell Henry to have eight children? So he can't blame the government if people crawling over one another in the house and some of the children have to sleep in the little lounge, where is the same place that the family eat. So Henry got up and close the door to the lounge after he send out his wife. Then he went back to sit down, all this time not saying anything to me. I began to wonder what they thinking about. Then Miss Jo got up and come up to me and laid her hands on my head. She started out with a soft, soft voice, then before I know what was really happening, she start to raise-up her voice and speak out in unknown tongues. Although I don't go to Miss Jo Church – I am a Baptist – I know that how she was acting mean that some bad spirit take over my body – or so she think. She carried on like that till I

84

get so embarrassed, I had was to wrench myself from under her hand and fling myself over to the other side of the little room.

By this time, Henry stand up again and came up to me and try to hug me up. But I was struggling hard, hard. I couldn't understand why they were carrying on like that and the other thing was that I didn't want Henry's old miserable wife to come back into the room and catch Henry hugging me up. She would jealous of his very mother who birthed him, if she was alive and Henry pay any attention to her, not to mention if he seem too friendly with me, his own cousin.

But Henry never paid no mind to me struggling. He just keep holding me tight, tight, and then said: 'Putus, Putus' (Henry never call me that since I was a little girl in Jamaica, before he come to England), 'you have to take you mind off Fitzie. You mustn't consider so hard on him. What is to be, must be. What is fe you, can't be un-fe-you.'

I never understand what Henry was saying that for. It didn't seem to me that the Voices had anything to do with Fitzie and me. That is dead and done. So I was quite vex at Henry for bringing up Fitzie name that time. But another part of me was wondering how Henry know that one of the Voices sometimes sound like Fitzie and sometimes like Canute?

I don't quite remember but I must have told Henry and Miss Jo that of the two Voices which came most times, one was a man and the other was a woman.

The woman one has taken on a bodily form and is standing right in front of me, in flesh and blood.

MRS MASON

From last week I been having this heavy feeling on my mind that something strange was going to happen. I remember the night when I had just finished eating the little late supper that I prepared for myself – nothing much, just a little milk pudding and bread and butter (I didn't feel for any heavy food). I washed out the plate at the little sink, put some water in the kettle and was going to make myself a cup of tea, when I heard somebody coming up the stairs. I had was to pause a while and listen, because only two times in the last year that anybody ever come up to this room. Because it is the last room at the top, nobody don't pass by it to go anywhere.

The first time was in the middle of me groaning (which must have been loud) because the West Indian woman, Mistress Dixon from downstairs, was puffing and blowing and almost running up the stairs, calling out at the top of her voice: 'Mistress May-Sin, Mistress May-Sin, what happen to you?' She did keep knocking on the door and calling out to me. I didn't let her in (even if I did want to, I didn't have the strength to get up off the bed) but I was able to call out to her: 'It's OK, thank you. I'm all right, just having a bad dream.' She went back down the stairs, much slower than she came up.

The other time was when the Black boy Rasta come to pass his place with me.

But last week one night, I heard two pairs of heavy boots coming up the stairs. I wondered, is which officials coming to me in the night. I broke out in cold sweat. I wondered if that Mistress Dixon or Rasta make out a complaint against me. I wondered if They come to take me where They took that Irish woman. I make up my mind that I am not going. They will have to kill me first.

'*Missis May-son, Missis May-son, open the door, this is the police, Missis May-son . . .* '

Lord Jesus Christ! My heart did jump out of my chest. This is even worse! I remembered when They did come for Canute in Jamaica. It was before-day morning. Just when we had started to get a little sleep after he come off the midnight shift at the sugar factory. It's the same thing They said when They came to knock down the door. I did tell Canute at the time, let we pretend that we sleeping sound, sound and don't hear them! but Canute did say – 'it don't make no sense, Val. If we don't answer, they will break down the door. Don't worry yourself, it going be arright.'

Ever since, I hate that word all right. I never saw Canute again till six months later when They told me I was allowed to visit him down at the 'first offenders' prison miles away. But still, I know after that, Canute was right. It don't make no sense not to open the door when They knock. He told me afterward that the main reason why They never break him up and that They let him out after three years, was because he didn't give them no problems. He obey everything They tell him to do. Afterward, he recover himself and now he is better off than before.

So I did open the door.

'Yes, I am Missis May-Son.' I said to myself – 'what is to be, must be.' I committed my soul to the Great Father in Heaven. I faced my destiny and whispered to myself, 'If it is Thy Will, then let it be done.'

'*Missis May-son, Missis Valerie May-son?*'

'Yes, Sir, that is my name.'

'*We had a telephone call from Jamaica about you.*'

'Saying what, Sir? I am a decent law-abiding woman.'

'*Do you live here alone, Missis May-son? Where is your husband?*'

(What Fitzie have to do with this?)

'Yes, Sir, I live here alone. I don't know anything about my husband. I left him in London. Is he in trouble, Sir? I don't know anything about him . . .'

'*Missis May-son, we got a telephone call from Jamaica that you were ill . . .*'

'Me, Sir? Ill? As you can see, I am quite all right. Never been feeling better. Who you talk to on the phone, Sir?'

'*The call was taken by our station-sergeant. We don't know whom he spoke to but the person asked us to check up on you. Your family back there are worried about you and somebody wants to come to see how you are . . .*'

'I am perfectly all right, Sir. No need for any worry.'

'*Are you happy in England, Missis May-son?*'

'Of course, Sir, don't I look happy? Couldn't be happier. I think somebody make a mistake. Don't pay it any mind, Sir. Everything is all right. Would you like to come in for a cup of tea? Chilly night out there, isn't it? Come in and have a nice cup of tea, won't you?'

(Jesus, I certainly hoped they didn't.)

It seemed that the one in the front believed me. He got relaxed. The one behind him, who only been looking on and studying everything, don't look like he want to leave. Like he want to investigate further. I grin my teeth. I look happy. I hoped that I looked presentable in the old housecoat. I wished I had changed my clothes before opening the door. Put on my nice, curled wig. Too late now. Have to hope for the best.

'*All right, Missis May-son, the person will ring us up again from Jamaica tomorrow. We will tell them that you are very well . . .*'

'Yes, yes, no problem, Sir. Everything is fine. Never felt better in my life. Such good, kind people here. They take care of everything. Whoever ring you from Jamaica must be mistaken, Sir. Don't know where they get their ideas from. I always write them and tell them how good everything is here. Don't pay any mind to those people from Jamaica, Sir.'

'*We will be going now, Missis May-son. If you have any problems just come and see us. We will take care of everything.*'

(Eh, they must think I am an idiot.)

'Yes, Sir. Thank you kindly, Sir. No problem at all. I will come to you as soon as I have any.'

The second one didn't want to leave. He suspected something. I kept the grin on my face. I hope my heart don't jump out of my chest and roll on the piece of chaka-chaka carpet. I kept the grin on my face. The first one smiled at me and turned to go back down the stairs. The second one hesitated. He didn't want to leave. I kept the grin on my face. And looked happy. Their official, heavy boots went down the stairs. I was weak. Just as they leave, the two main Voices started to quarrel inside my head.

The man-one was laughing. The man-one was saying that I should have gone with the police. The woman-one is telling him to shut up. The woman-one was saying, 'You brought her to this. The least you can do is not to gloat over it.' I went back inside the room. Shut the door tight. Lay down on the bed.

I didn't know if I was sleeping, dreaming or waking-up. I heard puffing and blowing coming up the stairs. It must be that Mistress Dixon.

'*Miss Val, Miss Val, you arright? What the policeman did want with you?*'

None of you business, you nosey bitch.

'*Mistress May-sin, is what happen?*'

I will die first before I answer the lower-class Black bitch.

'*Mistress May-sin, A want you to know that is not anybody in the building who ring them to come and bother you. You arright?*'

Go and sex your man and get another bastard pickney, woman. Don't bother me. (They should-a lock you up. Till you learn to behave yourself. Insulting good people with you nasty word-them.)

That was the man-Voice again. The woman-Voice leap at him . . . in my head. I am tired of them. Tired of Mistress Dixon and her poking her nose into my business. Tired of everything. Tired.

MRS MASON

So when I heard the footsteps tonight, I had was to listen careful. I wondered if it was the Bobbies (no, it could only be one of them – from the sound) coming back again. There was the sound of one pair of feet but there was also the sound of a lot of things. A heavy load that whoever it was, was dragging up the stairs. Then the footsteps stopped at the landing just outside the door. There was a knock. Not like the official knock. This one was like the person was not too sure that they had come to the right place. Like the person was a little shy. I didn't pay no mind to the first knock. Then two more knocks came. I went to the door, but I kept it shut. I called out: 'Who is it?'

The person, a woman's voice, said:

'Open the door and see.'

I said, in my mind, eh, but what a bold one that is, whoever is out there. I didn't work out in my mind why, I just knew that I must open the door. I cracked the door. I saw the form of a woman there. I didn't know how I knew. But I knew from that time that it was the Voice. I wanted to go back fully inside the room and slam the door shut again. I wanted to look more at the Voice, examine its bodily form and get to know it. I wanted to get a hose and wash it away. I wanted to throw the Eckna at it. To burn it up to ashes so that it would disappear from outside my door. I wanted to touch it. I wanted to kill it. I wanted to kick it down the stairs and know that it was lying lifeless at the bottom and could not come up again.

But I just stood looking at it . . . at her.

She looked weary . . . if a Voice can be weary. She looked confused . . . if a Voice can be confused. It was her eyes that I can't take. They are deep and black – like all of her . . . except her dress, which is floral. (I know she is not from England, English people wear civilised colours – black, greys, browns, beige – never these bright-coloured clothes.)

Her eyes are looking all over me and into me. I am giddy. Perhaps it's the stench of the Eckna singeing the oilskin on the table. Perhaps it's that terrible noise of the black sound system downstairs. Perhaps the other Voice wants to take over my head now. Perhaps it's the effect of seeing this Voice in its bodily form.

She, the Voice, stands there, with her . . . its . . . black eyes boring into me. Then two tears, hardened like glass, appear on her jaws. She is lifting-up her arms. If I am not careful she is going to hug me up. I step back and put up my hands, like a shield or like a weapon. My whole body is saying, 'if you come any nearer, I will kill you . . . '

The black eyes let out a spurt of weeping. The tears are melting. They are flowing on to her uncivilised dress. She steps back, further away from the door and among the load I had heard her dragging up the stairs. She must be an immigrant. Only they bring so much things with them when they are travelling. She hasn't moved her body all this time. But her black eyes are moving all about. She drops her hands but her eyes are doing what her hands tried to do before . . . hugging me up.

I don't know how I know it but I know she . . . it . . . is going to speak. It's pure madness going on here. How can a Voice speak out of a bodily form? I am thinking that if it does not speak out of this form, then it will go away. If it speaks, it will be really here with me. I don't want it to be really here with me. I want to put the hard wood door between it and myself. I cannot move.

It speaks:

'*Mama, oh Mama, you are alive!*'

If this goes on, it's going to soak the dirty chaka-chaka carpet on the landing because it's now washing it with its tears. Its hands are at its side but it is like if one of them has thumped me in the chest so hard, it has made a hole, plunged through it, collared on to my heart, is squeezing all life out of my heart. I have to open my mouth wide to catch breath. It doesn't know it's killing me.

So it goes on: '*Mama, Mama, I'm so glad I found you alive. The policemen told me on the telephone to Jamaica that they came to your house and they saw you. They told me you seemed all right but I couldn't rest, till I saw you myself.*'

I am still in wonderland. I am still trying not to die. I still want to kill this Voice in bodily form. I don't want to talk with it. It is coming nearer to me again. It speaks again:

'*Mama, don't you know me? I am little Icy. I am your daughter.*'

I can't allow this to continue. This is madness.

'Take yourself off, young lady. Go and play your tricks somewhere else. I have no daughter. I am alone in the world.'

90

PART THREE

ICY

Icy Barton always wondered why it was called Red Hills Road. Since for more than two miles along it, there are no hills. Only dusty flatland, intersected by a ghettoised road on the sides of which board and zinc shacks and poky little shops smelling of salted dried fish, corned meat and kerosene oil tumbled and rubbed shoulders with each other.

Now and again a bright new self-service supermarket or mini shopping plaza would assert itself on the drabness of the road as if to affirm that this was in fact a middle-class area.

Blakey's 'Turntable Night Club' in the mini-plaza half-way up the road marked the beginning of its 'night-club stretch'. After Blakey's club there were two more supermarkets, the big bakery which made the wholewheat bread and the pharmacy. But in between all those were the clubs. Dickie Wung's 'Tit-for-Tat', where a closely knit community of music-lovers would gather every Wednesday, Friday and Saturday night to revel in the ecstasy of the sounds of up-and-coming Jamaican jazz, blues and reggae musicians whom the rest of Jamaica and the world were later to 'discover'.

Then there were the two other clubs. Icy had visited each about two times, under the guise that she was doing research for a university paper on Jamaican music. Two of her friends from her workplace, one a woman, the other a man, 'humoured' her in her 'research', fully well knowing that she just wanted to go to these clubs to see what was going on there, to see and get to know what the people were like who frequented such places. They didn't bother to tell her that as 'Kingston People' they had been going to 'such places' – and others which she would probably blanch at – since their eyes were at their knees.

Icy had been to the 'Tit-for-Tat' several times. It was one of those few clubs (Blakey's, which had come later on, was another) where a woman could just go to, have a little drink, sit down and listen to the music, dance, if you feel like, or not even talk to anybody, if you don't feel like. Leave when you were ready to leave – without anybody, especially any Man, feeling and acting that since you are there by yourself, you must be just waiting to be molested by Him or any of his brothers . . . or uncles, or fathers, or . . . 'good buddies'.

In the other clubs where Icy went with her friends from work there were a few drunken men, usually of the type who couldn't get a woman to say hello to him unless he had just won the Irish Sweepstake. And even then . . . some women still wouldn't even spit on such types. But, she felt, those types were a few. Most of those she met, briefly or over a long period, came with no wicked intention . . . but only to try in that atmosphere to obliterate, for even three or four hours, the uncertainties, the boredom – and, above all, the fears – of their daily existence. To blot out these fears, in sound and feel and unnecessity of thought.

For in 'such places', Icy learned, everything is loud. All sounds and feel and taste and smells and seeing are bigger than normal everyday life. Everything is big and loud and high and excessively low.

The music (of whatever type), the body heat, the breathing, the laughs, the groans, the crying into glasses of rum or bottles of beer, the slobbers dripping water from the mouth, at the women dancing or those playing 'hostess' or as well, from the peppery jerk pork (or chicken), the laughs, high and ribald, to prove (most of all to oneself) that a good time is being had.

And the soundless sounds. Which incorporates seeing and smelling and hearing and seeing and feeling. Like knowing that at this or that table, in this or that group, with this or that individual; in all this seeming frenetic activity silence reigned.

The dancing of the 'go-go' women. Icy never quite got up the courage to talk with any of the sisters but she always wished to know some of them. There were some who came out on that saucer of a stage, usually in the middle of drooling men and semi-embarrassed women sweethearts, with an apologetic, slightly embarrassed-imagined-'feminine' air. Icy always thought that those were the worst. She felt that they were neither good 'go-go' dancers nor (whatever they think) good material for wives, as far as most of the male patrons were concerned. Their hearts told them this, even as they hoped. So in their indecision and doubt, they would bring on to the little stage a backing-and-forthing. Never quite knowing whether to be 'go-go' dancers or wives in the making.

Not so with some of the other sisters. Some would come on to the stage like a bolt of lightning, some like the creeping rain. But they would be there to dance, and let no one doubt that. And they would choose with which man . . . or woman . . . or none . . . that they would rest after the stage.

Icy learned that some of the owners and regular clientele of the 'go-go' clubs deeply resented the trendy respectability of the Tit-for-Tat and Turntable. Many of these club owners looked down their noses at what they felt was the pretentious elitism of the other clubs' professional and office-worker clientele. The owners of the other clubs felt that the 'elite', Red Hills Road clubs must be making a lot of money, since they had so many big civil servants among their regular customers. But as a 'civil servant' herself, Icy well knew that the owners of the 'respectable' clubs probably had bills as long as all the arms of most of their customers. Bills stretching back to two or three months (at least) for each of these civil servant customers.

But, Icy always thought, if only the owners of both types of night-clubs could talk together! Because those of the so-called 'elite night-clubs' were also very suspicious of those of the 'go-go' night-clubs.

These thought that because these other night-clubs had one and only one commodity which they promoted – women – these clubs made more money than them and could laugh all the way to the bank. So they, both sets, continued in their confusion and unnecessary rivalry.

And the women bumped their backsides and wiggled the muscles of their vaginas under the quivering noses and drooling mouths of their inebriated customers.

ICY

S he would never know why it was called Red Hills Road. Especially since the hills which became visible only after passing the settled middle-class suburbs of Havendale and Meadowbrook were no longer red, if ever they had been. Some time during the development boom of the 1960s, any red earth which may have been on those hills was scraped away by the newly rich, some of whom were commuters to Miami on the five airline flights a day from Kingston. In many places on those hills, only the stark-white rock-face remained. Bare. Of red or any colour earth. Of trees. Of bushes.

Next had come the blasting dynamite. To make space on and within the rock for the towering concrete mansions. Home-and-Furnishing-magazine beautiful inside, some with more types of rooms than Europe ever thought of, even during the heights of empire and the vast profits from the slave trade. Outside, steep, bare drives to get to the houses. The only vegetation expensively and carefully nurtured rock gardens bereft of a nature-grown tree or untonsured bush.

No fallen mangoes or guavas on the ground for the maids and gardeners to gather for themselves, their families and friends.

Many of the maids had been brought as young girls from the country-parts and lived 'on premises' in less than splendid isolation in backrooms below ground level of the rock-face mansions. No visitors allowed – to them. Others travelled up the hill each morning from their modest residences down on Red Hills Road or as far away as Jones Town in downtown Kingston. These latter were not very many because employers of domestic labour only used downtown people as a very last resort. After all, they would agree among themselves at dinner parties, everyone knew that was where most of the thieves and burglars came from, you couldn't trust those people around your house, could you?

For their part, the maids and gardeners, once they were away from the mansions, would regale their families and friends with stories and anecdotes about the Red Hills mansioneers. They would shake their heads and say:

'What a funny world! We have to take bad things make laugh. How cum them people so edicated, how cum they 'ave so much money, how cum they in such high position, yet they don' know dat human being cyaan live pon rockstone? Lawd, them foolish, eh?'

Of course they would never say these things to the face of the mansioneers. Then it was all, 'yes Maam, yes, Sar, you right, Maam, quite right, Sar.'

Icy was house-hunting again. And she had set her heart on finding somewhere on Red Hills Road. She didn't want to live in one of the shacks on the side of the road. In any event, those were owner-occupied. Neither was she interested in renting one of those cold basement flats which were sometimes available on the hill, even if she could afford it. She had been looking towards that whole other community to the back of the road, in the interior on both sides, called Red Hills Gardens . Here were middle-class, cement-block and steel bungalows, set in wide gardens with trees and flowers.

For two months now, every Saturday afternoon and Sunday morning, she had been walking (whenever she couldn't get any of her friends who drove cars to take her) up and down the roads leading off Red Hills Road, knocking at every gate and asking: 'Do you know of any houses for rent in the area?'

It was always a 'no', if the residents deigned to answer. Now and again, she would come upon a house with no curtains in the window, a sure sign that it was unoccupied. Her heart would soar, only to be let down when, try as she might, she couldn't locate the owner of the particular cottage or house or flat.

And Dennis had given her an ultimatum.

DENNIS

As if you were stroking
a well-loved lover
your hands tenderly
caressing-out
the sounds

A comfortable intimacy
  between you
  and your drum.

Oh, the power and the glory of that first meeting and those early
days with Dennis! Well, it had not exactly been a 'first' meeting,
in the sense that she'd been seeing Dennis around on the music circuit
for a few months. You couldn't not notice him. He was such a fine-
boned, delicately sculptured little Black man. A very pretty Black man.

Too pretty, Icy thought.

It had even turned out that they had some mutual friends and acquaint-
ances. They knew very little about him, except that he was one hell-offa
musician; that he had taken himself off from the Jamaican scene to New
York and then to South America, to meet new people and learn new
rhythms. That he had gotten tired of these places too and had returned
to Jamaica, nobody knew for how long, this time.

A rolling stone, Icy thought. And took her mind off this pretty little
Black man.

But, apparently, they were destined to really meet. It was up in the
hills of Rockfort, off the main road to and from the Palisadoes airport.
He had gone to jam with Count Ossie and the Mystic Revelation of
Rastafari. Icy had gone with some friends to listen to the jazz session on
that Sunday afternoon.

At first, the Rastafarian musicians hadn't wanted to give him a look-
in. After all, he was a bald-head. And not only was he a bald-head, he
had tainted himself with foreign ways, living in all these foreign countries,
as he had.

It had been the Count himself, Dennis told her afterwards, who
insisted: 'Jah welcome all man with clean hands an' pure heart, let the
brethren play.'

And had he played!

98

She had written him this little poem as she listened and as he transported her spirit outside of the normally disused Water Commission social club nestled in a valley of those Rockfort hills. She had leaned against the wall at the back of the room but his eyes kept cutting a path through the jam-packed crowd, to her eyes.

She didn't like his eyes. They were too intense, too vulnerable. Such eyes belonged to men who needed not just lovers but, as well, mothers. Icy had no intention of being mother to anybody. She felt she needed a mother herself.

She didn't like musicians, except when they were playing music and she was listening to it. She didn't like them as people. And certainly not as her lover. She had a friend whose boyfriend was a musician. She was always bawling to Icy how badly he treated her. Hours upon hours of brooding, which he insisted was his way of composing his music. During this time, the friend must not only keep out of his way, she must melt herself into air, become dustless transparency but regain bodily form to prepare and serve him his organic food. She had to take on the role of unquestioning servant, psychoanalyst, psychotherapist, sister, aunt, secretary, maid, mother – and still find the energy to sparkle and to give him some good sex as well (when he had a mind for it, not necessarily when she wanted it).

No, Icy would often swear, she would never be a musician's woman.

The way women were always running after them! Much to their delight. Icy's friend was expected to understand this, even when the women began to invade the flat in which they lived. Her boyfriend needed his fans, did he not? And he had all sorts of theories, which wherever they started from, ended up that it was the woman who was wrong and backward, if she complained.

Icy had, so far, not come right out and told her friend that she was a fool but she swore that she would never put up with such a relationship. But here on this Sunday afternoon turning to dusk, in Rockfort, was this Dennis, a musician, heading for her at the back of the room after his set was finished.

She had fled outside before he reached her. She saw him coming down the steps to the outside of the building. There wasn't anyplace else for her to run. There was only precipice, then a steep rise on to the hills.

He had come beside her and said: 'Whenever you're ready, I am.'

Ah, so him bright! She had answered, 'Ready for what?'

'For whatever. Starting with leaving here.'

She had left with him. To her flat.

DENNIS

'Flat' was its name and flat was its nature. Icy had moved there two months before, after the new landlord at the other place defied the law, took the roof off the cottage and evicted her and all the other tenants in the cottages because he had wanted the place cleared to build townhouses which he could rent to foreigners for US dollars.

A colleague had told her that this flat was going to be vacant at the end of the month. The rental wås 150 Jamaican dollars a month, a little over half her salary, but she had had no choice but to take it.

It was one of twelve flats, converted from an old Great House, servants' quarters and stables, in Constant Spring, uptown Kingston. The Chinese landlord had bought up the property cheap, refurbished and rebuilt and now offered these flats to 'single professional' people.

The first time she saw it, she knew it wouldn't work, but she had to move. She had stepped from the concrete-covered yard on to the bed in the front room. Then crawled across the bed to get to the poky kitchen, then turned one foot around from the kitchen to get into the minuscule enclosure with the shower and toilet bowl.

This was where she lived and this was where she had taken Dennis. He had sat in the middle of the big bed and joked that he would have to do his exercises in the yard as he couldn't even stretch out his arms to exercise his Congo-drum fingers.

But it had all become all right that first night, once they locked the door, turned off the light and cuddled in the big bed. Once she had seen his hands on his drums, she had felt how they would be on her body. And while he had caressed her body, he had told her about himself. Things that the friends did not know and could never know. Like how he had felt stifled by the music scene in Jamaica; how much he loved reggae music but felt that reggae music was a world music that set the pace but also incorporated all the music of Black and Coloured peoples all over the world. How this was why he had followed the music to Africa and then to South America and how he had been happy in South America and had even found a woman he loved there. How he had returned to what he called his 'roots' in Jamaica only after someone stole his drums in South America.

He had looked at her out of his bony, sculptured, pretty face and said, 'Ice, I am a world person but I could never stay in a place where they would steal my drums. It better they steal my food. But not my drums. Ice, I been watching you ever since I come back to Jam-down. I love

100

you but same time, I love my drums. You think you can live with me and my drums?'

She had told him, 'Yes!' She had loved him, 'Yes'. And she had buried herself in his little body and most of all, in his smell, in that big bed which was the only real space in that little flat. Surpassing his prettiness, surpassing the excruciating ecstasy of the sounds which he brought out from the drum – was his smell.

As in the smell which rises from dusty earth when the rain thunders upon it. As in the clean, sweaty smell of sugar workers who bathe every day but also every day toil under a boiling sun. As of oranges put to roast on a slow fire and giving off a smoke of acrid lime. As of the cheesy, unwashed smell of neglected-behind-the-ears. As of musky oils from the glands of thick-haired armpits, inexplicably brown-haired crotch and standing love-ready penis.

As in the close, musky smells of dungeons where a minute of non-fear is snatched, made more precious, precious, because in the next minute the slavemaster will come and put to that moment an inevitable end. Put to an end the warmth and the joyous ecstasy.

Icy and Dennis laughed loud in this ecstasy. Not caring what the neighbours might think. Not caring what the landlord might think. Icy loved how Dennis laughed out, when he came to climax. She loved how he cuddled her and poured into her all his weaknesses when he let go his sperm.

She loved how he made a joke which only the two of them could understand, before he rolled off her and went to sleep.

DENNIS

She had been a musician's woman for nearly a year now. It had been sweet and bitter. It was so sweet when she sat or stood against the wall in a darkened night-club or at a dance hall and listened to him playing. Especially when that moment came that the rhythm of the drums took him over and he became an instrument for relaying its message. She would exult in her heart: 'He's mine! This supreme messenger of rhythm is mine! He will go home with Me, no matter how many of these screaming, rocking women want him to come home with Them.'

And after those times, when he played best, he really did need a mother. She had to make sure that there was some hot food ready when he came home in the early hours of the morning (because he couldn't eat heavy meals before a show but was ravenously hungry afterward). No matter how loud the applause at the show, she had to cradle him at home and tell him over and over how great he had been. It was not that she minded so much doing this (because most times, he had been great) but it slowly and then increasingly began to appear to her that the relationship was becoming one great adulation of Him, with very little or no consideration for Her needs.

Just about the point that this realisation was coming through to her, he had become more critical and demanding. He couldn't be depended on to help her get the food from the market and supermarket but he could be depended on to criticise the meal if it was not exactly to his liking.

He knew that she had been trying very hard to find a more suitable flat. He always had something else to do when she was walking around looking at possible places but his criticisms of the yard and the flat had become ever more consistent and strident:

'Battyman! Them is all Battyman,' he would rage in his descriptions of the male tenants of the other flats in the yard. Icy was becoming tired of these rages, especially since it was some of the same 'battymen' in the yard who helped her with all the million and one seemingly little daily chores (like replacing a blown fuse, fixing the refrig. when it went bonkers, and so on) which he was too busy being creative to do.

'Dennis, I don't care who they are sleeping with. Why should you? They are not sleeping with me. They know you are my man, they don't bring any argument to me. Why you worrying yourself so?' Icy would often say.

In his early days of coming to the flat, when he started his 'battymen' refrain and Icy responded thus, he would just grumble for a little while and then settle down quietly in her arms.

But lately he would charge that this or that one of her male neighbours had wiggled his bottom at him, had stuck out his tongue at him, had laughed at him, had embraced his male lover, deliberately to taunt him, while he was entering or leaving the flat.

In vain would Icy coax: 'Dennis, what are you getting so uptight about? Don't pay them any mind. Just go about your business and let them go about theirs.'

Those times had become very ugly times. Because he would turn his eyes on her, yet not quite looking into her eyes and say something like:

'Maybe why you and them get on so much is because them think you is sodomite too. Maybe them think all them woman who come here to you and who you always wrap-up with, is you lover. Maybe that's why them don't trouble you.'

At those times, Dennis would remain in a silent rage all night. His penis would refuse to stand, no matter how much loving care and massages it got. At those times, Icy felt that he was shaken to a foundation she never knew, and perhaps not even he knew that he possessed. She came to know that the best thing for her was to remain quiet and unobtrusive when he was like this.

She knew by now that the morning after those nights, he was not only insistent, he demanded, that she stop taking the Pill and have a baby for him.

On one of those nights, recently, he had said:

'This is it. Either you have my youth, or we have to break off this thing. If you say you love me, then you must want my youth. None of this sodomite business.'

Icy was of different minds when he said this. One side of her could not even contemplate losing him. But another side knew, for sure, that she didn't want to give in to what he was demanding.

When he gave this ultimatum, she was cuddled-up into him in the big bed. She could feel the fineness of him. She was inhaling-in his smells. She could feel his 'dick' in that so tender and sensitive part between and at the side of her leg. She didn't want to lose him.

But she certainly was not ready to have no baby for him. He had three children already with two different women. It's not that he was a bad father, but many times, with the up and down earnings of musicians, he could not provide the money that was needed to ensure that they were adequately supported. Icy had taken it on to herself (even if she was to provide it out of her own meagre Civil Service salary) to see to it that the mothers got some maintenance money every month. Most times, she had to put her foot down because Dennis was very bad at taking decisions, even the most routine and simplest ones, like budgeting a part of his earnings to mind his children (although he never lost any opportunity to boast about his two big sons and his beautiful daughter).

Of one thing Icy was sure. And it was that she didn't want to become his third baby-mother. Apart from anything else, would the fourth woman see to it that he minded her child? she wondered.

ICY

After the months of walking door to door, she had seen the advertisement in the 'Rentals, Duplexes, Flats' column of the Sunday newspaper. It said, 'two-bedroom cottage on own plot of land off Red Hills Road'. This was it! She determined that she was going to get it by the hook or the crook.

She had an advantage because she had a friend in the press room of the newspaper and he had given her the proofs of the advertisements on Saturday afternoon. She went to look at the road and the cottage.

You turned by one of those poky shops smelling of salted, dried fish, corned meat and kerosene oil, off Red Hills Road, on to this quiet road to the left. Five houses down was the sea-green two-bedroom cottage. It had a lovely little lawn in the front. To the side and behind, there were mango trees, one guava tree and an ackee tree. According to the address on the advertisement, the landlady lived in the bungalow in front.

But on that Saturday afternoon, she didn't try to speak to the landlady. She didn't want to take any chances. She just surveyed the area and the cottage. She had to have it. And this meant that she had to put a sneaky plan in place.

She was going to get her half-white American friend to have the interview with the landlady. She had met Marina during her evening classes at the University. Marina wanted to stay on in Jamaica after her student exchange programme was completed. Icy had told her that she would be willing to become her flat-mate. She had decided against telling Dennis about this. If only because she knew that Marina was one of those women he suspected to be her 'sodomite' friend.

Marina had grown up tough, in the ghettoes of Chicago. There was not sufficient 'milk in her coffee' to pass as white in Chicago. But in Jamaica, it was different.

In Jamaica she could easily pass for one of those Creole whites, descendants of the British plantation owners, who somewhere along the way from slavery and colonialism to Independence had gotten a little coffee in their milk bloodstream through cohabitation with one or other of the African slave women. To top it off, she was American. And an attractive and charming woman to boot.

Yes, Icy thought, if anyone could get that cottage, it would be Marina. For Marina had come to know middle-class Jamaica exceedingly well in the little over a year since she had come to the island. And she knew how to play them to get what she wanted. She afterward told Icy about her encounter with the landlady.

Marina had telephoned Mrs DaCosta late morning on the Sunday (after church), and had been invited to come around to discuss the matter of the cottage in the afternoon. Marina did not worry about the late appointment. Mrs DaCosta would not rent the cottage to any of those streams of prospective tenants who, no doubt, had been knocking on her gate from early morning, two months' advance rental money clasped in their sweaty anxious hands. If Icy had been granted that interview, she would have had to take out and iron her nicest dress, oil and plait her coarse black hair from the night before, make sure that her Afro was well groomed, borrow a pair of stockings from one of her few friends who still wore them in that hot weather and psych herself up to remember to speak only the 'Queen's English' – none of that bad Jamaican talk.

Marina bounced along to the interview in her faded jeans, T-shirt and sandals. Mrs DaCosta received her in a cool corner of the verandah. Settled her in the most comfortable chair and asked her what would she like to drink: tea? coffee? lemonade? fruit juice? A little wine, perhaps?

Marina declined them all and thus, from the beginning, established her superiority in the interview. Poor Mrs DaCosta had been so besotted with Marina's American accent and her endearing foreign gestures! Like frequently curling her lips, derisively sticking-up her nose, and splaying her fingers like she was holding an imaginary cup of tea on a New England patio. All this at appropriate junctures during Mrs DaCosta's complaining narrative about the amount of 'lower-class, ordinary Jamaicans' who had the nerve to come begging her to rent the cottage to them. Some of them even wanted to move there with children! She, of course, only wanted the most decent people to live there. And even if someone paid her three times the rental she was asking, she would not allow any of their natty-head children, dirtying the walls and trampling the roses in the garden.

Of course it was quite different with this nice American university student and her civil servant friend (whom she hadn't yet met but who, no doubt, was of the same type as the American lady, although she was Jamaican). And as to the two months' rental in advance, you know that was only to discourage certain types of people from applying. However, since from time to time she herself went up to New York, if the American lady and her friend were able to pay even a part of the month's rental in American dollars, this would be highly appreciated (you know how hard it is to get dollars nowadays, what with this crazy socialist government that some of them were foolish enough to put into power). The cottage was ready for moving into, she had gotten a woman to give it a thorough cleaning only just this week. If the lady and her friend didn't have their own domestic helper, she would be quite happy to recommend this woman – came from one of the shacks on Red Hills Road, you know, but a very clean woman and willing to work for only 20 Jamaican dollars a day. The gardener was something different. She wouldn't recommend him. He was too surly and wanted to demand all of 30 dollars a day. Marina swept her hands regally to the skies, 'ah, let's not discuss such a boring thing as money.' Mrs DaCosta was mortified. Of course they could move in and then sort out all these matters.

Marina, Dennis and Icy were on the big bed together in the flat of the Chinese man as Marina told her story. Dennis had not flickered an eyelid when he learned that Marina and Icy were going to share this new place. Perhaps because Marina was there and he was too intent on making a good impression on her.

But he didn't help them with the moving. He had a studio engagement and a very important show in the night. He stayed away for the whole of the first month after Icy moved into the sea-green cottage with Marina.

Icy missed him. But only in the late night after work and after she took a break from redecorating the cottage to reflect her personality and not Mrs DaCosta's. Here, an ink drawing of Ras Daniel Hartman. There, a painting of Kapo Reynolds, a poster of Nelson Mandela, a bust of Marcus Garvey and of course, the latest slogans of the Socialist Party.

Marina didn't care too much what Icy did or did not do with the cottage. Marina had a hot relationship going with Carl, and she slept in his flat most nights, only coming now and again to get more of her clothes from the cottage and to pick up any mail or messages.

Icy was very happy in the sea-green cottage. The happiest she had been in a long time.

Except for Mrs DaCosta.

Within the first two weeks of their moving in, Mrs DaCosta realised that she had made a dreadful mistake. The one she had thought was such a fine American lady probably came from Brooklyn or even Bedford Stuyvesant. She had been told that the 'bad-breed' Americans came from such parts. It could only be a bad-breed American that could take up with some natty-head Jamaican boy that was one step away from those Rastas. And as for the Jamaican civil servant friend! She was mixed up in them socialist politics and next thing she knew, the police would come knocking at her gate and asking about that woman. Or even worse, she would bring her socialist gunmen to intimidate her and take away her house and land. If she wasn't careful, very soon the socialists would take over the whole road and deprive decent people of all the property they had worked so hard to acquire. And, Lord, have mercy! Look how hard she had worked and look how long it had taken her to become chairlady of the Women's Auxiliary at church? Now all this was threatened.

Only last Sunday, after the morning service, Parson had told her to stay behind because he wanted to have a word with her. Parson had sat down and loosened his collar. Then Parson had said:

'Sister DaCosta, I know you to be a loyal servant of our great Lord, a perfectly Christian lady and a hardworking member of the Church. But some do not know you as I do, and they may misunderstand some of your actions. They may think that you have taken up with some of our errant sons, with whom our Lord is very displeased because they have gone astray from His Holy Word and have joined the worshippers of the Anti-Christ.'

Mrs DaCosta had begun to weep. She had to convince Parson that she was not one of those who had gone astray. Parson had repeated that he understood that but what was he to tell those others when they pointed to the fact that she had rented her cottage to communists? He, of course, could not tell her whom to take as tenants, especially since he knew that she depended on the rental money to supplement her meagre pension, her being a widow, and all. But it did not look good in the eyes of the Lord when she allowed such people to nest in her dwelling.

Mrs DaCosta couldn't evict them under the new Rent Laws the Socialist government had passed. They hadn't damaged the cottage. Far from it. They had brought in their own domestic helper, who, judging by how arrogantly she walked and the fact that she entered the cottage by the front door, was also a socialist. They had kept on that surly gardener, who now cut his eye at her whenever she dared to come outside her door while he was cutting the grass or pruning the trees. They paid their rent dead on time. They hardly ever talked loud in the cottage, much less to curse and fight. She had no intention of selling the cottage, which would have allowed the new owners to evict them under the law on the grounds that they needed it to live in. And she couldn't even raise the rent to a level which would drive them out when they were unable to afford it. Because, for that she would have to attend at the Rent Board and far from giving her permission to increase the rental, they might lower it below the amount she was now charging.

Mrs DaCosta went on a programme of daily fasting and nightly prayers to deliver her from these undesirable and ungodly tenants.

ICY

Ping-che-ting, ping-ping-screep!
Sound of knife and fork on plate.
Silence.
Broken only by the sound of knife and fork on plate.
And of chewing.
Silence.
Chomp. Chomp.
Silence.
'What's the matter, Dennis?'
Chomp. Chomp.
'What matter?'
Silence.
Ping-che-ting, ping-ping-screep.
'Why are you so quiet?'
Chomp. Chomp.
'The meat is too tough, Ice. I have to work hard to eat it. If I try to talk to you same time, I will eat my tongue with the meat.'

(He expects me to laugh at this. Perhaps I would have laughed before but not now.) There he sits in my sea-green cottage after staying away for nearly a month. There he sits around my little formica table, eating my brown-stewed beef and rice and peas, that I have taken my tired self to cook well enough in time that his stomach won't be too full by the time he has to go to work.

I sneaked out from work early. Hoping that we can have a real communion together. I thought I would feed him first. Then we would talk. I have been so wanting to tell him about the letter from my grand-aunt Jo in England. And to hear what he has to say.

In the beginning, we used to be able to tell each other all the things, little and big, which were worrying our minds. Especially after we had made love and were cuddling quietly.

This evening is starting wrong. Doesn't look like there is going to be much cuddling tonight. If I can't tell Dennis about the letter, whom can I tell?

Three times over this last week since he came back, I opened my mouth to tell him about it and all three times, I closed it back. For one reason or another, it was never the right time.

Perhaps I should just pull out the letter now, shove it under his nose and demand of him to read it! If I show him the letter, will he just read it, sniff, turn up his nose, remember an urgent appointment that he has or make a joke?

'Dennis, I'm sorry the meat is tough. I wanted to ready it in time so you could eat something long before going to work.'

Silence.

'Dennis . . . there is something I want to talk to you about . . . '

'It won't stay till tomorrow? I have to go see some Americans who want me to record some music for a film.'

In this moment, I hate him. I want to cuss and rage at him. It is times like these which make me know that our days together are numbered. Here am I facing the biggest crisis of my life. And he can't find the time to talk with me!? Americans and their precious film!

That's what I could never take with him. He never set his own priorities. If someone says, do this or do that, he would just go along.

I don't want to start an argument tonight. May as well bear my burden alone.

I clear the table. He is not going to talk tonight. I remove his plate with half of the food I put on it. I smash it against the sink. I really want to smash it on his pretty head and see the gravy nasty-up his handsome face so excited by the Americans and their film.

THE FOREIGNER-
JAMAICAN

It was the Sunday afternoon of the same week. She had the cottage totally to herself. She was thinking of the letter when she saw him from the verandah.

He was a tall, big, Black man. Nothing strange about that. There are many tall, big, Black men on Red Hills Road. But he had on a dark-blue suit and a light-blue shirt, with a necktie. He had on a felt hat. And he didn't walk like a Kingston-Jamaican. He didn't roll his hips and fling his feet, one before the other, caring not where each landed, as if all the road and the sidewalk belonged to him. He stepped as if each inch of the road contained a land-mine which he had to be careful to overstep.

Icy was sitting in the cane chair, with her feet propped up on the ledge which bordered the little garden. She could see his body and his movements, but she could not see his face.

She saw him peering at the number on each gate on the road. Now and again, he would peer into his hand as if he had a map there.

He came nearer. This tall Black man in his suit and tie. He was next door now. She could see him. The face was purple-black with granite-jutting forehead, under the grey felt hat. The jaws were strong and slightly less purple from a covering of dirty-looking, dark-brown hairs left over from shaving with a dull razor. She couldn't hear very well but whatever he told the neighbour caused her to point to the house next door. Her sea-green cottage.

He raised his head and looked across to the verandah of the cottage. She pretended not to see him. He began to walk towards her gate. Before their eyes would have the opportunity to meet, she went inside and locked the door.

THE FOREIGNER-
JAMAICAN

I t didn't make sense to try to fiddle the signing-in register on Monday
mornings. The Director would be sure to get into the Department
by a quarter to eight. He would open his office window very wide, on
the pretext that he was drinking in the fresh morning air but more because
he would be able to see anyone coming through the gate of the compound.
His 'good morning' would be loudest to those of his staff coming in after
8.30 a.m.

On this Monday morning, Icy was certainly going to be entering after
8.30. All of Sunday night, after seeing the tall Black man with the foreign
clothes looking for her, she had been unable to sleep. Her mind had
been like a tape-recorder perpetually on rewind. At about 6 o'clock, she
had fallen into a little doze. She jumped up at 8.00, glad that Dennis had
stayed at his flat. She poured one mug of water into the kettle and turned
up the gas burner high under it. She knew she had to hurry. But after
she had gobbled a cup of instant coffee.

She gave herself a 'dry rub', instead of showering, hauled on a skirt
and blouse and reached the bus stop on Red Hills Road by 8.25.

She had still been there at 9 o'clock. Two minibuses had passed her
there, on their way to downtown Kingston, the conductors hanging out
of the doors, people packed into the insides like sardines in a tin. The
drivers hadn't even bothered to stop.

She didn't reach the office until nearly 10 o'clock. As she entered the
gate to the compound, she could see the Director waving at her and
saying something which she could not hear. She couldn't be bothered
with him now. She would have to think up some story to give to him
later.

For there was the tall Black man, still in his suit and tie and his felt
hat, waiting for her just inside the office gates. Seeing him more closely
now, she was sure he was not a farm worker from America, he was from
England. His suit was very heavy and old-fashioned, the trousers bulky
and his tie a conservative dark blue, like his suit.

'Is you name Icy Barton?'

She was confused. He didn't talk like a foreigner.

'Not you is Icy Barton?' he repeated.

'Yes. And who are you?'

He just looked at her. She couldn't meet his eyes. She decided to get

112

very angry. Who was this damned country-bumpkin man in his England clothes? Why was he hounding her?

'Who are you? What do you want with me?' He just kept on looking at her.

'Look Sir, I am late for work. I don't have any time to waste. What can I do for you?'

'Do? Fah me?'

He raised up the felt hat from his forehead, took a big white handkerchief out of the right-hand pocket of the bulky trousers and wiped the before-midday tropical sweat from his forehead.

'You are wasting my time. Please tell me what is it you want with me.'

'You wase fi-mi time yestiday. Why you hide when you see me?'

She felt uncomfortable that he had asked her this question right-out. She didn't know what to answer. He had taken the initiative . . . and he followed it up:

'Why you don' write yu mother?'

Jesus Christ! The letter! But how did this man know about it?

'Yu mother worry bout you night and day cause she cyaan hear from yu.'

Mr Samuels, the office security guard, is her friend. He doesn't hear any loud talking between her and the strange man but he must have sensed her distress because he advances towards the gate scowling at the man. Icy is thinking that she cannot take a scene, this will attract too much attention. She goes towards Mr Samuels and says:

'It's all right, Sammy. He just brought a message for me. Everything all right.'

This emboldens the foreigner-Jamaican man even more. He holds on to her hand and says:

'Cum. Mek we go roun-a de restaurance roun de cawna whey we can talk bout everything.'

Icy pulls away her hand.

'I can't come. I'm late for work. The Director will fire me. Look, see him looking through the window there . . . '

The foreigner-Jamaican man gives her his deep look again. This time, it is an ultimately judgemental look, bordering on contempt . . . for her.

'Icy Barton, mek up yu mind.'

She goes again towards Mr Samuels.

'Sammy, if anybody asking for me, just tell them that I have a little family emergency that I have to deal with.'

They are seated in the restaurant. The man says he only wants tea. Icy doesn't want anything but she orders some orange juice.

'You know my mother?' she asks him.

'Yes. We use to work in de same ahaspital over there a-Inglan' togather. Nice lady. She even invite me to her birthday party an' A go to her house an' meet her husband.

'Even after she did lef' Dulwich, I use to see her at de Underground

113

station or sometime in Brixton market. She always dignify. Not like some of the other one-them.'

'So why you come looking for me? What's the message from her? How you get to know about the letter? How you find me?'

He laughed for the first time. He didn't laugh loud but his eyes danced loudly.

'How A fin' yu, is fi-mi secret. After a time, A didn't buck-up yu mother on the Underground or in the market. A ask roun di ahaspital an' somebody tell me dat she leave that work an' gone to another ahaspital. Den later on, A hear dat she down-a Birmingham. A have a cousin dat live pon Dudley Road a Birmingham. Me an' mi wife did go to spen' weekend with her. As God would will it, mi cousin live next door to Mistress Maysin cousin an' him wife, she is frien' to yu cousin Hengry wife. A see yu mother there. A tell her that A planning to go to Jamaica. When me an' mi wife leaving yu cousin Hengry house, she run outside an' call me one side from mi wife. She whisper to me that I mus fin' her daughter when A go to Jamaica. See if she arright. She always use to boast bout yu, from she was at Dulwich. Boas' bout her daughter who going to be university graduate. She give me a letter to give yu.'

He began to slurp his tea again. It is his second cup of tea. Icy is still sipping her first orange juice.

'How long ago was this?'

'Cyaan 'member. Maybe bout a year or more. Cause we didn' leave right away. A had was to sell the house dat we did buy in Tottenham an' mi wife neva did wan' fi leave Inglan'. Then we did book on the boat dat go to Spain an' all aroun' before it reach Jamaica. We buy a piece-a lan' in Wes'morelan' an' we bin building wi house likkle by likkle. A goin' back up-a Inglan nex' week an' A did want fi tell yu mother dat A fin' yu.'

'How did you find me?'

'Yu ask me dat arready an' A tell you is fi-mi secret. Yu de one dat sen' a black cake fah yu mother one Christmas, ain'-it?'

THE FOREIGNER-
JAMAICAN

I cy remembered the Christmas cake. It was the first cake she had ever baked. It was the second Christmas after her mother left for England. The first Christmas, she had only sent her a card, because she was grieving so much she did not have the energy to send her anything special.

From the August, she had asked the wife of the house where her mother had left her how to bake a Christmas cake. She had told her to get raisins and currants, lime peel, mixed fruit, flour, eggs, dark sugar, salt, baking powder, wine and white rum. She had shown her how to grind the fruits and put them to soak in bulk wine long before Christmas. She had started late and although she had given the fruits a month to soak, the cakes weren't ready until the beginning of December. She had put them in aluminium tins, waited for them to cool from the oven, then liberally doused them with bulk wine and white rum, so that they would be moist when they got to England.

Her mother had written in March to say that she had gotten them and how much she enjoyed them. That was a long time ago. She never sent anymore Christmas cake.

'How do you know about the Christmas cake?' she asked the man.

'Eh! Everybody know bout it. Lawd, yu mother neva stop talkin' bout it. She bring some slice to Dulwich Ahaspital for we when wi having wi tea. She even give piece to dat hoity-toity Nursing Sister.'

He stopped talking and looked at Icy. Raising his head from his tea:

'How come you neva send no more Christmas cake fah yu mother? How come you stop write her?'

The tears that she had been trying to restrain ever since this foreigner-Jamaican man began to speak about her mother now began to flow into her glass of orange juice. She raised the orange juice to her lips, hoping that it would block the tears. It was the tears which blocked the orange juice from passing down her throat.

'A neva know dat you could-a bake cake so good! Is the bes' Christmas cake A ever taste.'

'You just trying to make me feel good. It was the first cake I ever baked in my life. I can cook but I can't bake.'

The man looked at her, as he would at a lover:

'Though is one little slice A taste, A still tasting dat cake dat you bake fah yu mother. You mus' bake sum more an' invite me to eat a piece.'

Some people, especially if their skin is white, think that other people with black skins cannot blush. How ignorant, Icy thinks. For the word 'blushing' describes a rush of blood to the neck and face and this is possible in all human beings. No doubt, this happens with the 'lower' animals too. And, perhaps, even with plants, when sap rushes to a particular part of the stem and up into the leaves. Or even into the flowers and fruits themselves.

Icy's skin is normally like polished ebony. But when the tall Black man in the England clothes tells her how much he enjoyed the Christmas cake she had baked, there began an ebony rush of blood from all over her enclothed body, to show itself first in her cheeks, turning them darkest purple. And hot is her face, hotter than the Caribbean sun on its midday march.

'But why you don' write har?' The man is persistent.

'It's a long story. You wouldn't understand.'

She is now weeping openly.

'Cum, mi likkle one, don' cry. Howsomever it be wit you an' yu mother, write har. De two of you wi' work it out togather.'

He is digging deep into the pocket of the heavy trousers. He comes out with a crushed envelope.

'See de letter dat she give me to give yu. She say dat A musn' leave Jamaica till A get a answa from yu. A goin' back-a Wes'morelan' dis eveling an' A not coming back-a Kingston till nex' week when A go a Palisadoes airport fe go back-a Inglan'.'

Icy didn't want to open the letter. She was still thinking what to do about the other letter which had come in the post from her great-aunt, Miss Jo. She didn't want to open this other letter here in this restaurant, before this stranger, before the other strangers in the restaurant, before those of her office-mates who were now coming in for an early lunch.

'Opin it an' hear what yu mother 'ave fe say,' he commanded her.

She opened the crushed envelope. She had to stare hard to see what was on the one page inside the envelope, what with the dimness in the restaurant and her tears.

The one page said how much her mother was worrying about her. How she thought that something bad must have happened to her why she hadn't been able to get any answer to her letters. One paragraph of the one-page letter she found herself reading over and over.

'*Things are not so very good here. I would like to come home. I feel that if I don't come home soon, I will expire. I want to come home and live with you.*'

'Is my mother ill?' she asked the man. He was slurping his tea.

When he was good and ready, he answered:

'Well, she was walking an' talking when she give me de letta. She did look a little confuse an' worried but A would'n' say dat she sick, cause Inglan' is a confuse an' worried place.'

'What about Fitzie Mason, her husband? You saw him?'

116

'A ongly meet him one time. When she invite me to her birthday party. A don' know nothing bout him.'

He went back to his tea. His third. Icy felt that he must be a tea addict. She remained quiet. She didn't want anymore orange juice. Her co-workers coming in were looking at her strangely. No doubt, they were wondering what she was doing there with this man. She hoped they didn't notice that her black eyeliner was running down on her cheeks.

'What A mus' tell har when A go back-a Inglan'?'

'Tell her to come home. Tell her that I forget everything that happen in the past. Tell her that I miss her bad, bad. Tell her . . . that I love her.'

The foreigner-Jamaican man smiled and called to the waitress to bring the bill.

It was only when Icy was on the minibus going home after work that it came to her that she hadn't asked his name.

ICY

D ear Icy,
     Praise the Lord.

I hope when these few lines reaches your loving hands, they may find you in the best of health.

I don't know what is wrong with your mother. But the last time I went to Birmingham to see her, she would not let me into her room. Can you come and see what is wrong with her? Because I don't know what to do. I talked about it with Henry, but he don't know what to do either. We would be very happy if you could come and see to your mother. Let me know what you decide.

As always,
Your Aunt, Jo

This must be the hundredth time she was reading this letter, since it came by airmail post a little over a week ago. She felt that whatever it was that her mother was talking about in the letter which the foreigner-Jamaican man had brought must have gotten worse.

From she came home from work, she had been sitting in the drawing-room of the cottage, thinking about what exactly to do. Even after the evening sun had gone away and night had come down, she was still sitting there.

Many questions kept buzzing around in her mind, like the singing of mosquitoes which will not go away no matter how many of the mosquitoes themselves are caught, swatted or silenced.

Why should she feel any obligation to do anything about either of the letters? This woman had birthed her but did that mean that she owed her anything? What to do? Ignore the letters and go on with her life? What then? Suppose she died in England, wouldn't it be she who would have to see to her burial?

But suppose Aunt Jo was just being alarmist and she was perfectly all right? Then she wouldn't have to do anything, would she?

There began a knocking at the door.

'Miss Barton, Miss Barton!'

She decided not to answer. The last person she wanted to have to deal with now was Mrs DaCosta. Icy had not heard her coming up on to the verandah and to the front door of the cottage. No doubt, she had sneaked through the gate with no sound of its being opened (as she usually did), crept up on to the verandah, listened and peeped for a while, before knocking on the door.

When Mrs DaCosta sneaked into the yard during the day she would go round the side of the cottage and knock on the backdoor, after she had looked to see if there was any garbage mounded-up at the root of the mango tree, any water thrown from the kitchen to become stagnant and breed mosquitoes in the backyard, any dirt-encrusted back windows. Even if she hadn't seen any of these 'sins' she still had to knock on the backdoor, if only to point out to Icy or Marina (the few times that she could catch Marina there) that one little blade of grass that was not quite in place. Because even Icy was hardly there in the days, even on weekends, Mrs DaCosta had taken more to scheduling her visits in the late evening and early nights.

'Miss Barton, I know you in there. Why you don't turn on the light?'

Mrs DaCosta's 'knock-knocks' have now become 'boom-booms'. She clearly has no intention of going away. If Icy doesn't open the door, the neighbours will soon be turning on their yard-lights, opening their windows on to the road and the braver ones venturing out on to their verandahs to look where this noise is coming from.

Icy begins to weep with frustration and rage.

The Director had not bought her story about a sick aunt making her very late for work. He had seen her go off with the big, Black man. In his mind that could only mean one thing – a hot love affair. And perhaps he was thinking of all the times he had invited her to have dinner with him, in some discreet, quiet restaurant, of course. Or to have a drink together in the backroom of a downtown bar after work. He had even raised the stakes to a quiet weekend in one of those hotels in Flagler Street in Miami. Of course, when he upbraided her for being late, again, he didn't mention any of these invitations, which she had refused. He had been all for 'work ethic' in the Civil Service. He had said that, whatever members of staff chose to do and with whomever, outside of work-time, was not his concern. But, as liberal and kind a boss as he was, he could not have government employees under his supervision going off to consort with their visiting lovers during the work-day.

He had delivered an ultimatum to Icy: if she didn't pull her socks up, he would have to recommend her dismissal to the Civil Service Commission. And he reminded her that she couldn't expect the Civil Service Association to defend her. As she well knew, they were a responsible trade union and could not stick their necks out for those radicals among their members who by their own actions invited disciplinary measures against themselves.

Icy had just kept saying, 'yes sir, yes, sir,' as he spoke.

Then when she came home she had seen a note pinned to the pillow of her unmade bed. Dennis had come before, let himself in with his key and left her another ultimatum. The note told the same story as in the other flat, only this time it added how uncomfortable he felt 'sneakingin to visit and sleep with my own woman with your hypocrite landlady making-up her face and cutting her eyes at me'. If Icy valued their relationship, the note continued, she had to make a choice, it was either or either, etc. . .

Icy felt cornered, harassed, persecuted and hunted. She went to the door. And cracked it a little.

'Yes, what do you want, Mrs DaCosta?'

'Pardon me, Miss Barton, for disturbing you in the night . . . '

'Cut that shit and tell me why you are knocking on my door.'

'Miss Barton, you shouldn't use those words, they are of the Devil. I only come to disturb you because A get a letter today from me daughter in America an' she an' her family want to come home an' move into the cottage. So A was wondering if you and Miss Marina did find any place yet.'

Icy looks at this woman. Her skin is that indeterminate colour which comes from years of using bleaching cream. The strands of her hair are dead from decades of straightening; cold and hot. But she has mercilessly pulled the ever-lessening remaining strands to the back of her head and pinned them into a black cloth 'bun' to give the impression of a lot of hair.

Her body is the compact slim that she feels it is decent to be. She wears a girdle all the time.

Icy feels like cursing this woman as she has never cursed anyone before.

'What the raas-claat yu come to me door fah? Move offa me varandah right now before A have fe throw stale piss pon yu.'

Mrs DaCosta's eyes in that bleaching cream face become very dark and sad, as if they are weeping. She is so shocked that she moves back from the door to sit on the ledge of the little verandah. She is speechless.

Icy wants to close the door and just leave her there. Then she hesitates.

'Mrs DaCosta, come inside.'

Mrs DaCosta is still sitting on the ledge.

'Come, let me help you.'

Icy stretches forward her hands and one of them grasps one of Mrs DaCosta's hands. 'Come inside. I won't use any more badwords.'

MRS DACOSTA

She is still hesitating.

'Mrs DaCosta, come inside before people start to look what happening on the verandah.'

This apparently has decided her. Icy seats her on the couch.

'Let me boil a little mint tea for you.'

She opens her mouth, perhaps to decline the offer. But Icy is already in the little kitchen off the back of the drawing/dining-room.

In another few minutes when Icy puts the ceramic mug steaming fragrant mint tea into her hands, she manages a slightly weak:

'Thank you, Miss Barton.'

'If it's too sweet for you, I can throw it out and mix another one quick-time. The mint tree just outside the door.'

'A know, Miss Barton, is I who plant it there.'

She doesn't respond as to whether the tea is too sweet or not. But she is sipping it.

'Is you who plant most of the trees in here, Mrs DaCosta?'

'Yes. When me and me husband come on this road, only two more houses was on it: Mrs Banton who live down near the end and Mr Armstrong and him family, right beside you there. Mi husband was a builder and him did know how to take opportunity when them present themself. So him manage to get them two piece a land on the road, opposite to one another. Him did build our house but him die before he could start on this one. Is mi daughter and her husband who help me to put up the cottage after mi husband die.

'The boy him gone all part of the world. The last time me hear from him, him was somewhere down the Middle East. I don't even know if him dead or alive now.

'Is mainly Macca tree was here when we start to build. The little old man who you see over there in the garden, sometime – is mainly him who help me plant up the yard . . . '

Her voice trails off and she assumes a shame-faced look, as if she feels she has said too much.

'Mrs DaCosta, I want to apologise for the way I spoke to you tonight. Please forgive me. It's just that I am under so much pressure, I just can't take another one.'

'Miss Barton, A don' want you to feel that I am against you and Miss Marina. My daughter older than oonu and I don't want nobody to disrespect me.'

121

'A sorry for how A talk to you, Mrs DaCosta. A truly sorry. But don't we take good care of the place? How we discommode you, Mrs DaCosta?'

She is quiet. So silent, Icy is forced to speak again. And to put the question 'on the table' or, more accurately, on the rug which takes up the centre-space in the front room and stops just a little short of the feet of the couch on which Mrs DaCosta sits.

'Is our politics you don't like?'

Mrs DaCosta gives out one loud sigh and puts down the mug on the side table.

Icy takes up the mug. 'You want some more?'

Mrs DaCosta shakes her head.

'Politics, Miss Barton? Politics is not for poor people like me. Politics is for rich people and university graduates.'

Icy laughs.

'You laughing at me, Miss Barton? What A say sound foolish to you?'

'No, Mrs DaCosta, is not that it sound foolish. A laugh because that's what people always say when them want hide what them really stand for. But them have them politics too, just like everybody else.'

'Miss Barton, me don't mix up mi-self into politics. Me just go to mi Church.'

'But don't Parson political? Don't him tell you that the socialist-them is bad people? What part of the Bible tell him that?'

'Miss Barton, I never come over here to argue politics with you. I just come to tell you that mi daughter and her family coming to Jamaica and A want the cottage for them.'

'How long them coming for, Mrs DaCosta?'

'That's not your business, Miss Barton. All you want to know is that A have to have the cottage for them.'

'But nothing couldn't work so, Mrs DaCosta? What about our rights? What about me and Marina rights?'

'I have a right to get mi cottage when A want it back. And A want it back for mi daughter.'

Icy gets up to make herself some mint tea. Again Mrs DaCosta declines any more. But she hasn't gotten up to leave.

'Mrs DaCosta, A think that A understand about you daughter and so – after all, is she and her husband who help build the cottage.

'But A don't think you looking on my side as well. Look, look! I just get a letter from England. I don't even know what happening to my own mother!'

She shoves Aunt Jo's letter at her. Mrs DaCosta doesn't decline to read it. Although having to screw-up her eyes.

When she is finished, she folds the letter up neatly and hands it back to Icy.

She pulls up her knees so that she is sitting straight up in the couch, with her back leaning slightly forward. She clasps her hands on her lap and begins rubbing the palms together.

'Miss Barton, A never know you mother was in England?'

'We not too in touch, Mrs DaCosta. A lot of water went under the bridge.'

'But Miss Barton, yu mother is yu mother, whatever water gone under the bridge. So what yu going to do?'

'That's what A was thinking bout when you knock. That's why A was so vex with you.'

'A didn't know about yu mother, at all, Miss Barton. Then you no going have to go over England to see how she doing?'

It is more a statement than a question.

Icy is hesitating.

'You don't have the money to pay yu fare, Miss Barton?'

'A don't really. But is not so much that because friends in mi Party will help me, lend me the money or so. Is only that A don't even know if A know her anymore. A don't know what A going to find. A don't know what A going into. A don't know anything.'

'Miss Barton, you don't go to church. Or you would know that the good Lord will reveal all in His own good time. Just trust in Him.'

'That is all well and good, Mrs DaCosta. But is I who have to go face it. And now you tell me A going have to start look place again to move?'

'Well, now is April. A don't think mi daughter and her family coming till August. You could go look for yu mother, spend a month or so to straighten things out, and then come back and look for a place. You don't have to face that, till when you come to it.'

Icy feels as if a net curtain has been lifted off her face. Everything is so much clearer now. She begins to chant:

'It doesn't matter
that the Dawta doesn't
know
the Madda

It doesn't matter
Dat de dawta tinks de
Madda sell her out

She mus' go to Inglan'
An' to Inglan'
she is bound to go

She must go
to Inglan'
An to Inglan'
She mus' go
or die.

She is boun'
to go

123

to Inglan'
or she will not ever
find her pas'
she is bound to go
to Inglan'
to convince herself
she is a human being.'

Icy is dancing all around the room, stopping at the dining table now and again to drum out the rhythm to her chant.

Mrs DaCosta smiles, gets up off the couch.

'Don't bother to stop yu singing, Miss Barton. It remin' me of a old church song. The Lord knows best, just follow His will. If you need the money for the fare, jus' let me know tomorrow morning before you go to work an' I will get it from the Credit Union. Don't bother to come to the door, I will let myself out. Just remember to lock up good before you go to bed.'

ICY

She doesn't have much memory of the airplane flight. She must have slept through most of it. The immigration officer at Heathrow seems satisfied with her explanation that she has come to visit relatives. He reads the letter her Director has given her confirming that she is expected back at work on such and such a date. He stamps her passport and waves her through.

Her memory of Heathrow is of cold, white light. When she comes out of Customs, at first, she does not recognise Aunt Jo and Cousin Henry. The big fat Black woman and the little shrivelled-up Black man look vaguely familiar. But she doesn't think it's them until Henry exclaims, in an unmistakably Jamaican voice,

'Is she, man. Is little Icy. But what a way she grow big! If it wasn't the long neck an' the big bright eye-them that she have from she little, I could-a never tell that is she.'

All this is quite embarrassing because he is talking very loud. But she sees that nobody is paying them any mind.

Aunt Jo tells her that she lives in a place called Finsbury Park. She seems very proud of it. Cousin Henry has come up from Birmingham to come to the airport to meet her. He has to go back before-day-morning.

The house looks like a doll's house from outside. It's very cold inside. They call that time of year 'Spring'. She calls it damned cold. Aunt Jo insists that she should not leave for Birmingham until after Sunday dinner. She complies and is glad. Some of her friends and the people from her church come around at dinner time. The house becomes warmer.

Icy travels to Birmingham alone. There are some journeys which can only be undertaken alone.

She is standing before the house. This is a bare street. But there are big and small buildings on it. Is house-paint short in this country? she wonders. Or do house-paints here only come in browns, greys and colour-less?

It is a big building. Three storeys with an attic. A big building on a wide, grey street. It appears to her like one of those phantom buildings with which horror movies abound.

She puts down her load – suitcase and two bags with all sorts of provisions she feels her mother has not eaten in a long time.

She raises her hand and squeezes the bell.

PART FOUR

MRS MASON

Alone in the world, with only God to call on . . . Is this the time that the Eckna is going to catch the oilskin tablecloth afire? Perhaps I should look to see if the oilskin is burning. I wish they would turn off that music. If I look if the Eckna catch the oilskin, I will have to leave it . . . her . . . on the landing. Shut the door. The voice in bodily form say she is my daughter. Maybe it . . . she . . . is a little mad?

('Maybe you the one who mad, Val, kyaak, kyaaa, kyaak, ieeee, ieeee.')

It's the man-Voice, mocking me.

Why the other voice coming now, at this same time? I don't want to have the two of them here at the same time.

('I always here, Val. You will never escape me. You run from London to Birmingham to get away from me. I won't let you get 'way . . . you know A love . . . love . . . love you . . . ')

It must be that voice that send her. To get me to come back to him. To keep on the confusion in my life.

'Young lady, I have no daughter. Just leave me alone. Let me have some peace in my life.'

She is still making like she want to hug me up. But she looks like she stunned. Like somebody creep up behind her and give her a big blow in the head. A blow that don't fall her but scatter her brains like. She just looking on me . . . into me.

She don't know what to say. She taking down her hands. She turn to brace her back against the railing. She gripping the railing with her two hands. She now not facing me in front. Her side is to me but her black eyes still boring into me. Her face screwing up. She don't know what to say.

'You look like you are not a bad person, somebody must put you up to this. Somebody must send you to torment me. Who send you here, young lady? Who it is that tell you to come here?'

Oh, Lord, she starting to cry again. Is not a good sign when spirit cry. She must be a spirit or she couldn't live in my head. What a botheration. Why she don't just vanish and leave me in peace? What a worries on me here now? She . . . it . . . now weeping. Who it is that send her here? I prefer when she did stay in my head and did not take bodily form. I could never stand that type of weeping that she going on with now. It may make me soon start to weep too. Perhaps this is the only form they could send that would have any effect on me. I should go back into the

room and bring out my Bible. Read some Psalms, make the sign of the
cross and spit behind me (I can't spit into the room?) . . . and after that,
she . . . it, bound to go away.

('Kyaak, kyaaak, kyaak, kya, kya, kaaay, ieeeee, ieeee. You think is
the Devil that send her? Is God that send her. God know A love you,
you is me wife . . . that A married . . . but you run away and leave
me. Whey you ever hear any good woman run away and leave them
husband . . . is God that punishing you . . . ieeee, ieeeeee, kyaaa,
kyaaa, kyaaaaka . . . ')

I sink to my knees . . . right in the door frame. The Voice seem to be
lost in her own world. I start to mumble the Lord's Prayer. I stop looking
at her. I pluck myself away from her black eyes. I have to concentrate
on my God . . . if I am to come out of this one. I make the sign of the
cross . . . on my knees. I repeat my protection again: 'dead before me,
rotten before me . . . '

MRS MASON

Thank you Jesus! My prayers taking effect. The Voice-spirit sort of swaying before my eyes.

She crumpling-up on the chaka-chaka carpet! It must be God that strike her down. God know that I bear enough in my life. God know that I go through enough in this country. Too much evil all around. Too much covetous people.

The other Voice quiet now. It not laughing and taunting me anymore. Perhaps it's gone. Unless it hiding in the room, waiting to see if I will crumple up too.

The burn-smell so high, high. It could be that the Voices come now to burn down the room . . . put a finish to everything. Finish-off every one of them. Starting with them lower-class ones downstairs. How anybody can reach anywhere if you always surrounded by them? They going to make mi head burst with the music. They turn it up even louder now. Just to torment me. Boom, Boom, Boom, beating inside my head.

It's them . . . and the Voices which bring me to this. My husband Fitzie was a nice man before him come to England and mix-up with them. Take for instance how he behave at the first birthday party I have after I come to England, he would have never behave like that in Jamaica.

I never keep any birthday party the first year I come to England – I couldn't invite any decent people into the little room him did rent on Acre Lane in Brixton from the Indian man? With the hallway always dirty, no matter how I try to clean it up and the toilet outside. In Jamaica, I would hold the party in the yard, but no yard wasn't here?

I never did get over the shock when Fitzie come for me at the airport and take me to the little room. Him was embarrass too. Him always did get vexed when him embarrass. Him shout at me and ask me, what me did think? If me did think that me was coming to mansion in England? Him ask me if me never know that the white people don't rent good place to Black people in England. Him say that we was lucky to get such a 'nice room'.

Him say that is only the Nigerian-them and sometimes the Indians, who would rent their place to Black people. According to him, the Irish-them would rent to Black if they did have any place to rent but plenty of them was in the same position as Black people. Him start to stammer as him was telling me all this. Him say that we very lucky that the Indian man and him wife did rent us the room because them was very particular

131

people. Me had was to keep my mouth shut because only God Himself know what Fitzie would do if him get too shame and embarrassed.

But I wasn't satisfied. Because I never come to England to kotch on anybody eyetop, whether they be white, African, Indian, Irish or mi own people. Luckily I did get the little job at Dulwich Hospital and I did try to get on well with the white topanaris. I was always willing to take over them duties when they wanted to drink tea or chat with the doctors. They thought that I was a 'good girl, Val-e-rie' (that's what them did call me, you know, eh, eh). The Nursing Sister and some of the other nurses show me how to get around the Social Security, what to tell them. And that is how we got that nice flat in Clapham.

Fitzie was so ungrateful! Maybe him was just jealous because is me did get the flat and look how long him was here before him send for me? He was always complaining that plenty Black people don't live on that road. But that's why I did like it. I don't want to live round too much of them.

I invited all of my neighbours to my birthday party. I make sure and tell the Nursing Sister and some of my other workmates, in good time (white people don't just get up and jump go anywhere, them plan everything from long before, even to go to party). I warn Fitzie to make sure that none of his lower-class, rowdy friends come – they were not invited.

They would want to be knocking dominoes down on my nice new table. I would have to find white rum and red rum to give them and then make-up whole heap of rum punch. They would want the drinks flowing so that they could drink till they drunk. They would want curry goat and rice, just like if they were in Jamaica. They would be talking and laughing loud! Not caring at all that the neighbours not used to this sort of thing and they might call the police. These type of people wouldn't be satisfied with just sitting around and having low civilised conversation. They would want their loud music. They would want to jig-up themselves (say they dancing) on my nice new carpet.

I wasn't having none of that. I make sure that I tell Fitzie from I planning the party. We would be having just a little red and white wine. Maybe a little lager as well. But certainly no rum. Fitzie puff up his face and got very vex when I told him. He said that he wouldn't come to the party if his friends couldn't come. But I wasn't keeping out all of his friends, only the ones that would embarrass me or get me into trouble with the white people.

He thought that I was going to change my mind. But on the day of the party, he saw that I was serious when I put my best tablecloth on the table and laid out the table with little sandwiches and nuts, some cold sliced meat, green vegetables, bread and cheese.

He asked me if I had bought goat meat in the market. I told him, a strong 'No'.

'You couldn't get no goat meat, Val?'

'I never ask for it, Fitzie.'

'You buy the sheep mutton? Is not the same but A suppose it can do if you have some good Indian curry and pepper to season it with.'

'Fitzie, don't bother me. I don't buy no mutton, at all. We not eating any mutton. You not in Jamaica now, you in England and you have to eat what the English people-them eat.'

He stood there, looking as if his brain scatter. As if he was in another world. As if he couldn't believe what he was hearing. Before he could find his tongue, I told him that there wouldn't be any 'dance music', because it was not a 'dance', it was a party. There would be only a little low, soft classical music.

That's when he slammed the door and went out to that ungodly pub in Brixton that keep open illegal, even when the law say that they should close. I never feel bad. Let him go to join his rowdy friends. None of them could bring their mouth to me. It was My Birthday Party. It wasn't Fitzie birthday. If I couldn't have my own birthday party how I wanted it to be, then what is the use of working so hard and taking all the cold weather in England?

Canute did come to the birthday party. I did invite him. Fitzie never feel good that I did invite him.

When Fitzie did come back from that pub and see Canute in the house, him did start to stammer. But he wasn't rude to Canute. He controlled himself. Anyway, it was me he was vexed with.

You did try to make me feel guilty, Canute. I don't forgive you for that. You did ask me where Miss Jo was and where Henry was. And you did ask me where was all the other Black people that I meet in England. You did ask me if I didn't have any Black friends.

It wasn't my fault. I did invite all of them, except the rowdy ones. I did glad that it was only the one West Indian porter at the hospital who come. He knows how to behave himself. You always did blame me Canute, that the only Black people at the party was Mr Wright, the porter, and you and Fitzie. But it wasn't my fault?

Whatever you want to say now, I still say that we had a nice, quiet party. You going to ask me what about the part when one of them said that too much immigrants coming into the country and them was going to be taking away jobs from white people?

But remember, them was quick to tell we that is not us them talking about but some of the others? Cho, you and Fitzie was too touches! You always waiting for the people-them to say the wrong thing and always vex when them talk what is really in them mind. Then you are the same ones who turn around and say, 'you never know what white people really thinking.'

If you and Fitzie did keep oonu mouth shut, then the party would end up successful. Or maybe it was my fault. But them was mi friends and neighbours. If I couldn't tell them what was in mi mind, then who I was going to tell?

Is the Nursing Sister who start it. Is she who did ask me if I did like living in England. And before I could answer her, she answer her own question herself.

'Val-e-rie, you are getting on all right, aren't you? You couldn't get this job back there in the West Indies. Our Val-e-rie is very happy here. Val-e-rie, tell us how you have a party in a mudhut back there.'

You, Canute. And you, Fitzie, can blame me for this part. I lose mi head. I shouldn't did tell them what was really in mi mind.

'Ann, I didn't live in a mudhut. We don't live in mudhut in Jamaica. We is just the same like you. Some of you live in big house and some of you live in little house. Just the same like we. Some of you rich and some of you poor. Just the same like we.'

The male nurse, Robert, say,

'Oh, really.' And push up his eyebrows. This did get me real vex. Maybe this is why I didn't pay you and Fitzie and the West Indian porter any mind, when you start to signal me through yu eyes to keep quiet. So I go on talking-out what was in mi mind.

'I didn't come to England to live-off-a England. I didn't come here to clean hospital floors and to wash you old people shit. I come to England to take-up back my studies and to become an SRN, just like you, Ann.'

Ann did choke on the piece of ham that she was eating. Robert did give-out a laugh that never even move his face or his eyes. Some of the others did remember that they train going to be leaving soon.

But you did behave bad too, Canute. You didn't have to slap Ann in the back so hard? You could have massaged her back gently to clear her throat. You handled her so roughly, she got all red in the face. I bet she was vexed with you? That was why she called me, 'Missis May-son' – normally she calls me 'Val-e-rie'.

I didn't blame her when she said,

'Well, Missis May-son, it might not be so easy for you to become an SRN. You have a good position now, better be satisfied with that.'

Fitzie did behave even worse than you, Canute. I was so shame! He give out a big loud laugh and he start to curse so much Jamaican badwords that I did want the floor to open up and take me in. Only Mr Wright could understand him, apart from you and me. But the white ones-them certainly never think that he was telling them how nice they were. Although they couldn't understand the language, they are not fools? They could understand full well that he was cursing them.

But still, it never had a man that I love like I did love Fitzie. Other men did love me. You, Canute, did love me.

Canute in America. That's where him went after him came to England and I wouldn't leave Fitzie to go back to him. Because in spite of all that was happening, it never had a man that I did love like I did love Fitzie.

Still and all, I can't forget you, Canute. Even now that you come in the form of a Voice, I can still remember the first time that I met you.

She hadn't known that a flower grew atop the sugar-cane. Even when, as a child, she had known the sweetness of the sugar-cane.

With the sugar-cane came many other memories. On a day after the June rains before her baby was a year old, Henry had come to visit her on his little donkey. Grannie Lou and herself had been able to make up the fire though it had been hard to light because the sticks were still damp. Henry had brought flour and rice, salted mackerel, corned fish and even a little piece of fresh mutton.

Grannie Lou had been happy. She said that all this food would last the three of them for a long while, especially since Icy was still taking her mother's breast milk.

She hadn't been able to tell Grannie Lou before, that she was going. She was afraid to hurt the old woman's feelings. But Grannie Lou could not expect her to live on this hill all her life. Grannie Lou should understand that she had to get back into the world. Whatever that world had to offer to her and her child.

Henry's donkey had been tethered, fed and watered. They were having a feast outside under the hairy mango tree. From where they were, they could see all the way down into Ducksies. Where their vision blurred, they knew was the Caribbean Sea where it washed Old Harbour Bay.

Grannie Lou was content. Grannie Lou's legs were crossed at the ankles of her rainy-season boots. She had taken off her tie-head after the meal and was allowing the cool night breeze to caress her coarse black plaits. She hadn't eaten any of the mutton. She had boiled-down some of the salted mackerel in the milk of the dry coconuts that the storm had blown off the trees. She had made flour dumplings, so tight they could break the teeth out. But the toothless Grannie Lou had had no problem with using these hard flour dumplings to wipe and scoop up the coconut custard and mackerel rundown from the Dutch iron pot, to direct the dumpling with the rundown on top into her mouth and to chew it with the greatest satisfaction. Henry and Putus had curried the mutton and boiled white rice to go with it. All of them had drunk the Seville orange lemonade that Grannie Lou had made. The woodfire which cooked the meal was now just lazily burning embers. Grannie Lou took out of her bosom her piece of tobacco hemp. She took one of the seemingly dying firesticks and lit her hemp. Drawing-in deeply. When she was sure that it was lit by a smouldering fire never to be put out, she turned the lighted part of her tobacco hemp cigar inside her mouth, clamped tightly between her black lips.

It had been a magic night up there on Grannie Lou's hill. The dying woodfire light and the moonlight fought with each other to light up her cured-black, ebony face. Her whole body was relaxed and quiet.

Henry was at peace. He had the young Icy in his arms and kept rocking her and talking to her in a sort of half-chanting, half-speaking voice about things that the baby could not have understood. But the baby kept gurgling and laughing. On other nights, the baby would have been in bed

135

long ago. Nestled by her breasts in the cot Grannie Lou had made up in the hut for the baby and mother. On this night, the baby would not go to sleep. Henry had taken her in his arms around the fireside.

Putus was not at peace. She was happy that Grannie Lou and Henry were happy. But she had kept seeing the place beyond their blurred vision from that hill. Where the Caribbean Sea came to Old Harbour Bay. The vision and the joining of this sea with her land were clouded in mists and fogs. But she wanted to be down there. From this hill. To where the Caribbean Sea joined her land. But to go from there, to the other lands which the Caribbean Sea washed. And more so, to go where it joined with other seas and oceans. She could not be at peace until she followed her sea into where it joined with all the other seas. She was bound for the mansions of the world.

'Grannie Lou, I going. I taking Icy with me.'

Henry stopped rocking the baby. There was silence for a while. She had wondered if she should explain further. If she should tell them how she really felt in her heart. Would they understand? Or would they think she was just ungrateful?

Henry was still silent. The baby was still. Like a little lump of rock in Henry's arms. Grannie Lou leaned forward. Stoked up the dying fire. Leaned back. Recrossed her ankles. Took the tobacco hemp from her mouth:

'God go wit yu, Miss Val. Walk good. Be careful of the bitterness in the worl'. Always remember dat the same ting dat sweet one time, can be bitter a nex' time. The same ting dat sweet one place can be bitter in annoder place. Walk good, but neva figet yu fambily. Is ongly dem yu got. So neva figet yu fambily.'

Putus had taken the baby and left with Henry the next morning. To Old Harbour. She had declined Henry's offer to stay in Ducksies until she knew what she was going to do. She had declined Henry's offer to take her and the baby to Mama Belle. She would go on, she had insisted, bypassing Brown's Hall and going straight down to Old Harbour.

She was later to know the bitterness of the sugar-cane which grew on the estates down from Grannie Lou's hill.

These grew in miles of fields, bigger than Brown's Hall, bigger than Grannie Lou's hill. Estates that would swallow up Grannie Lou's hill. Would swallow up Grannie Lou herself and not have to pass her out as waste matter. Would swallow up Henry and the knock-kneed donkey on which he had first carried her, pregnant, to lodge with Grannie Lou. Could swallow her up too. And, if that happened, would swallow up her little Icy as well.

She hadn't gone to the sugar estates right away. When she had come down to Old Harbour, she had been hoping that she could get a job as a messenger-girl and helping out with the filing when she wasn't running errands, in the doctor surgery, the courthouse, the agricultural Co-op

Bank or the hardware store. Failing that, she would even be willing to sell tickets on race day at the Little Ascot horse-racing track.

None of them wanted anybody to work, no matter how willing. They needed people to pick fruit at the Bodles citrus farm. But only for two months at the height of the harvest season. And then, only a few days' work could be gotten. When that job was finished, somebody had said that they needed women to work on the sugar estates at Bernard Lodge and Caymanas in the Spanish Town area. The estate owners could sell more sugar to England and they were anxious to bring more fields into planting. She hadn't gone right away.

She had tried her hand at whatever she could find after leaving Bodles. A domestic day-work here and there, while a cousin kept Icy. Selling pieces of ready-made children's clothes in the Old Harbour market on Saturdays, with Icy ma-ma-ing away beside her on the market stall or nodding away on the ground in a hamper-basket.

She had not been able to earn enough to rent a room for Icy and herself. And by this time, the cousin had started to show her bad face. Having a vexed-up face when she had to stay in the yard. She had to pretend that everything was all right. Although when she spoke to the cousin, she pretended that she didn't hear her. The cousin made all sorts of complaints about the bad behaviour of poor little Icy. Moaning down into her belly when Putus could only give her a few copper and silver coins instead of paper pound notes. Putus had known in her heart that it would be just a matter of a very short time before the cousin asked her to leave (if she was in a particularly good mood) or threw Icy's and her things out into the street, if she remained in the mood she had been in for some time.

But sugar estate work? Is this what she had come to? How far she had fallen! They needed women to cook. And they needed women to plant cane-tops, her friend had told her.

She had turned up at 6 o'clock one morning to sign on to join the other women planting cane-tops at Caymanas Estate. She had by then tried to overcome her shame by reasoning with herself that no honest labour could make her a low woman. That she could only become a fallen woman if she tried to live from the sale of her body or turned into a thief.

They had taken her on at the Caymanas Estate. But when the foreman, a little, short, fat Black man was counting off the women and separating them off into groups to begin the planting, came to Valerie, he said that she might be more suitable for the staff quarters. They needed two cooks there and a domestic servant.

She only got the job because the chief cook, whom everyone (even the big boss) called 'Aunt Ina', spoke up for her. They wanted Valerie to 'live-in', just like all the other domestic staff. Some who, like Aunt Ina, were born on the estate. Valerie said that she couldn't live-in because she had a young child and she had to go home every evening to take care of her. The big boss hadn't liked this at all. And neither did the Mistress. But Aunt Ina had assured the big boss and the Mistress that she thought Valerie would work out very well as her assistant. And since she (Aunt Ina) never went anywhere in the nights (as they well knew), she didn't need Valerie in the nights.

In these two years, she came to know the bitterness of the sugar-cane. As a house servant, she was 'privileged'. She didn't, like the women dropping the cane-tops, have to be bending, bending, forever bending, her back in the broiling sun, big basket, heavy with the cane-tops, weighing down one arm, the other arm feeding sugar-cane tops to the moist, dark earth.

She mainly worked in the house. It reminded her of the time when she was at Aunt Sisi's in Old Harbour. She mainly worked in the kitchen of the big house with Aunt Ina, preparing two meals for the day (Aunt Ina prepared their breakfast). Sometimes the boss or the Mistress would send her on errands or the Mistress might want her specially to iron a dress for her.

Still, she was very dissatisfied. The women in the fields looked down their noses at her whenever they saw her. And somehow she felt shamed (for no reason at all) whenever she came into contact with them. Valerie thought that they probably thought that she was a concubine to the big boss or one of the foremen.

The men were rude and feisty, she thought. From the big boss right down to those in the fields. They had taken to calling her 'office-hands'. She hadn't cared. She had tried not to pay them any mind.

With the money she earned, she could now rent half of a little room with another woman in Spanish Town. It was very convenient. She or Icy didn't have to come into much contact with the woman, who worked as a barmaid at night and mostly slept in the days. She was at work on the estate in the days and Icy was staying with an elderly woman on the next street, who was satisfied to take good care of her for only three shillings a week.

Before she was on the estate for a month, most of the men, from the big boss down, began telling their one another, 'don't joke with this one, is pure vinegar that!' But now and again one of the braver ones would make as if to touch her. Then she would straighten-up her back, plant her strong legs into the earth, or the floor (depending on where she was), scowl at the particular one so much that, after a while, none dared to touch her.

So when one day, this one driving an old Ford pick-up drew up beside her at the gates of the estate and asked her if she wanted a drive anywhere she had clasped her hands behind her back, knitted-up her brow, pointed-out her mouth and growled,

'I don't want any drive from any of you, leave me alone and go on your ways.'

He hadn't left her alone. Even if she didn't see him one week, he would turn up the other, always asking her, did she want a drive to Spanish Town? When she said no, he would drive off.

One day she had said yes, she did want a drive. Maybe because the next day was a holiday and Miss Ina had told her that although the Master and Mistress were having guests, it wasn't necessary for her to come. Maybe because she was extra tired and couldn't bear the thought of the long walk to Spanish Town. Maybe because she was beginning to respect him since he didn't press his case and took no for an answer. Maybe whatever.

She had climbed into the front of the little pick-up. He hadn't said a word to her all the way to Spanish Town hospital. She hadn't said a word to him either. When he had turned up into the Port Henderson Road, just after they passed the hospital, she had wondered what he was up to. One side of her said, 'scream out and let him stop'. Another side of her said,

'He don't look like the type that would rape a woman. Plus, if him try anything, I can always bawl out or lick him down. Is broad daylight.' She had eventually said to him:

'That's not the way I living.'

He had said:

'A know. A know the yard that you live into. I have a cousin who used to live there but she move. The landlord too thief and miserable.'

They had driven on a bit more on the Port Henderson Road, passing on one side of the road, only bush interrupted by a house here and there and on the other, sugar-cane fields.

She had spoken again:

'A have to go home now because I am picking up mi little girl from the lady who keep her for me.'

'A know. A will get you there in full time.'

She thought that he knew a lot.

Then he had looked at her as the van ricketed its way over the pot-holed dirt road and said:

'Don' worry yu-self. A just want to show yu something.'

She had relaxed after that. As much as she could anyway. What with the constant rattling and bumping of the old pick-up. What with her fear. She hadn't been able to help remembering that the last time that she was this close to a man, it ended up with her being thrown out of her family's house. Ended up with her suffering shame and starvation. Ended up with her fall to the bottom of this pit she was now in. Ended up with Icy. She wouldn't give up Icy for nothing.

He had driven into the Bernard Lodge estates. But he hadn't stopped at the staff houses. He had passed the barracks and gone right on to the further fields. He had turned a corner. And all of a sudden, they were in front of a sugar-cane field but a different type of sugar-cane field. Here the cane plants were like a whole troupe of hundreds of green-costumed ballet dancers, swaying gracefully in the breeze. And on some of their

139

heads, an elongated, white-silver jewelled crown had sprouted, a crown as if made of and hung with little pearl and diamond drops.

'What they plant here?' she had asked him. 'What kind of plants are these?'

He had turned off the engine of the pick-up and brought his body round to face hers in the cramped seat of the pick-up.

'Is the same sugar-cane. The same one-them like the one-them that they plant at Caymanas. Is just that this one is another breed. This is the one that grow flowers at the top at certain time of year.'

She had had to catch-up her bottom lip. It had been hanging open in surprise. She honestly never knew that a flower grew atop the sugar-cane.

He had held out his hand as if to shake her own.

'Canute Davis, at your service, Maam. Not you name Valerie Barton? A check out yu name with mi friend in the pay office. Well, Miss Barton, A hope that we will be no more strangers.'

MRS MASON

And we did become no more strangers. All the time I was with Canute he was like a true father to Icy and more than a father and a brother to me.

Canute was as good to me as he could possibly be. He wasn't a rich man. He didn't have no big education. And he wasn't extra handsome and goodlooking. But he had ambition and he wasn't fraid of work. He try his very best to make me and Icy comfortable. Canute did love me.

Must be that's why all these years he never leave me alone. When he not there in physical self, he come as a Voice.

You never did forgive me for leaving you, eh, Canute? You never did understand. You did think and you still think that it was because they come and take you to jail that morning leaving me and Icy alone. You think that it was because I didn't have you to provide for we anymore. You don't remember that I was still working at the textile factory after I leave Caymanas. I could manage to support me and Icy, especially when I get overtime work.

Is not that I didn't want no jailbird for a husband, why I went and take up with Fitzie. You wrong, wrong, wrong. As I always did tell you when we buck-up in England. I did tell you that is just love, I did love Fitzie. I did tell you that it wasn't that you didn't treat me and Icy good. It wasn't that I didn't know that you have ambition. I did know that you plan to work on the sugar estate till you get a truck to join with the pick-up. Then you would leave them and start you own haulage business.

But you did make them catch you, Canute. I couldn't lie in the bed with you again after what them do to you that morning, when they come for you and say that you was taking out the estate rum and selling it on the side. You was all brave when them was knocking loud, loud, on the door. You was the one who did say to me, 'Let them in, it don't make no sense to pretend that we not here.'

But when they come in and gunbutt you in yu stomach. When I see you fall to yu knees, I had was to hide Icy face in mi nightie. She did want to run to hug you up. I didn't want them to gunbutt her too. And I didn't want her to hear all the nasty things-them that they were shouting at you, spitting at you. I didn't want Icy to hear them calling you a thief and a criminal. That's why I take her out of the room and leave you in there alone with them.

That's why I only come to look for you one time at Richmond Prison. It was so far away anyway, it would take me the whole day to go and come back. Still, I could have come more than one time. The truth is that I couldn't bear to see you like bruk-foot bird in a cage. The whole time Icy kept asking for you. I told her that you gone to stay with your mother in Portland for a little while and that you soon come back.

She was satisfied with that story till Fitzie start to visit. All I tell her what a nice man Fitzie was. All I tell her how much land him family own in Clarendon. All I tell her that Fitzie was the one who could take me into the mansions of the world. She just never like Fitzie. She just never trust Fitzie.

MRS MASON

'Never mind that now. Dat is ole time story. Pick her up an' take her inside the room.'

But Canute this is not the Icy that you did know. If anybody should know the real Icy, ain't you? Fitzie was her stepfather for most of the time she growing up but you did know her more than him. Remember how you used to just know when she not feeling well, even if you were at work. You forget that she would quicker tell you if something on her mind than tell me? So how come you don't know that this one is a spirit that them send in her form to confuse-up mi head? Cho, man, use yu head.

If I just leave her there, she will melt away. Then I'll be free . . . free. Nobody ever want me to be free. Nobody ever help me to be free . . .

'Woman, stop the nonsense chatting an' pick her up.'

That's you. That's Fitzie. That's Boysie. That's Mama Belle. That's Henry. That's Miss Jo. That's the one who call herself 'Mistress Dixon', from downstairs. That's the feisty, eggs-up boy, Rasta. That's the staff nurse. That's the Nursing Sister. Even the poor mirasmi-looking white man at the greengrocery down the corner, feel that he can come give me orders. Do this. Do that. Don't do this. Don't do that.

So who I be? Me not somebody too? What about me? I not somebody too?

Well, all of you better listen, if any of you are interested to know, I am my own big woman. I make up my own mind. My mind tell me to leave this young lady there. Yes right there, on your chaka-chaka carpet. I would never have picked such a carpet for myself, if you did not bring me down to this level. Yes, I will leave her there. So do your next best, Mr Voice.

(Kyaaa . . . kya, kya, kya, kya, kyaaaaaaa . . . !)

Fitzie come back. That's him laughing at me. Canute gone. But I didn't tell him to go. Is that why Fitzie come back? I know the two of them could never stand to be in the same place together.

It cold, eh? Jesus, A trembling all over. Cold bumps all over mi body. I never notice that it was so cold, before. Is like a grave open. A don't hear any sound from downstairs. Them turn off the loud music. The little bulb on the landing turn on. Usually it don't give any light when it turn on. But it bright, bright now. It don't even seem that is it the light coming from because it's only 25 watt for the whole landing. A ball of light shining from somewhere. The music stop but another music coming from somewhere. No, it's not really music. It's like a whole heap of birds twittering and chirping and some singing. It have another sound too, like tree leaves rustling-up themselves. But no trees not near here? Much less birds.

Before, the cold was like a still wind but all of a sudden, it feel like it getting warmer. I wonder if they turn on the heat? It almost warm like Jamaica now.

(Cum, mi likkle mudder. Tek her up. Tek her up before she dead in front yu door.)

Lord Jesus, is who say that? Sound like Grannie Lou. But Grannie Lou dead. 'Dead before me, rotten before me', if that is not Grannie Lou voice. But how could that be? Grannie Lou dead. I get the message in Kingston the day before I board the plane at Palisadoes airport to come to England. I couldn't go to her funeral. What them did expect? I couldn't just cancel the ticket to go to Grannie Lou funeral. I was booked to come to England already. All the years I in England, I never even dream Grannie Lou. She never come to me before in a Voice.

Is her Voice though, that just speak to me. I can't see her, the light very bright in mi eyes. Some of the birds now start to whistle a tune. Sound like one of them song they sing in the clap-hand church.

(We one-big-appy-fambiliee, so A cum fah to carry yu 'ome.)

Home, Grannie Lou? Home? But A don' have no home?

(Putus, is a long, long time, yu no 'ave no nice time. So A cum fah to carry yu 'ome.)

Grannie Lou, A know that yu vex because I didn't come to yu funeral. Yu think that I put England before yu. I couldn't help it. Mi ticket was booked already. They would charge me a whole heap of money if I did cancel it, and I wouldn't have the money to pay. I never forget yu Grannie Lou. But I can't come with yu now. Don't bother to call me. Sorry, but I not going. I know enough to know that yu dead. If yu going to carry me home, then I have to dead too. Bad as everything be, I not ready to die yet. So go away. I still love yu. But go away and leave me alone.

All the birds stop their music. The trees quiet-quiet. Only the Voice remains. It's humming the clap-hand church song. Then it gets deeper and more serious. And impatient.

(Cum, cum. Putus, whey yu sense gone? Yu lose all-a-it since yu cum a-dis-ya place? Use yu head, girl. If A did wan' yu fe dead, A wouldn' tell yu to tek up yu dawta afore she dead. I cyaan lif' her up an' tek care of her. Is ongly yu can do dat.)

But I don' even know if is mi little Icy there before me. Grannie Lou, they send them in all sorts of shape and forms to confuse me. How I know is Icy?

(When yu feel her in yu han'-them, yu wi' know her. Don' worry bout dat. Just pick her up, quick, quick!)

It's beginning to get cold again. I must pick her up and go back inside the room before the warm wind forsakes me. And before the birds and the trees go away.

144

MRS MASON

I try to pick her up. It's either that she is extra heavy or I am extra weak. Every time I try to lift her, I threaten to fall down on my knees. If I stoop to lift her, I am not sure I could stand up again with her in my arms.

I pull her inside the room. I kotch her up in the armchair. I take a pillow off the bed and I put it behind her back. Her long neck seems very weak. It cannot hold up her head. Her head keeps falling down on her chest.

The burn-smell is even higher now. I must attend to the Eckna before the room burn down. The little kettle is black-red. All the water burn out. The edge of the oilskin tablecloth already start to curl up.

I am so tired. Just pulling her from the landing inside the room did make me very tired. I don't think Grannie Lou would mind if I just leave her in the armchair and go to my bed. I want to sleep. I must get my rest.

('Turn off the Eckna. Cool it down. Turn off the Eckna. Cool it down. Cum, turn off the Eckna. Cool it down. Cum cum, cum.')

Lawd! Mek me sleep. I tired so till.

('Get up! Turn off that Eckna an' cool it down.')

Must sleep-walk, I sleep-walking. I turn off the Eckna. The paraffin oil must be near finish now, anyway.

I hear a little sound from behind me. I turn around. It's her. She is sitting-up straight in the armchair. But she still looks weak and sick. She is holding-up her stomach. Her eyes are trying to tell me something. She is opening her mouth.

Lord, have mercy! All over the front of her clothes. Splash on to the armchair. Good thing I did turn around. Because it flash as far as the hot Eckna and sizzling on it. None don't catch the bed though, so far. Good thing.

I must get out the basin quick, quick. Before she spurt-out her stomach again!

I take out the basin from under the washstand. Throw a little water from the goblet in it and then put the basin on her lap. I put one hand behind her back to make sure she keep her mouth over the basin.

Don't make no sense to take-off her dress yet. Because she still retching. With all that come out already, you wouldn't think that anything could possibly leave in her stomach.

Big chunks of heavy food. Little balls of chewed-up food, which she

145

never digested. She bring them up and they sticking-up on her dress, on the arms of the armchair, on her stockings and shoes. She splash them all over the floor in front of her. But still she retching. After all the heavy food come out, yellow bile pouring from her stomach. Through her lips, over the bridges of her lips and on to her dress.

I want to clean her up. I still don't know if I want her to stay in this room with me but I can't have her so dirty in my chair. I don't want her to die here. I don't have any telephone to call the doctor. I don't know if the doctor would come anyway.

I going to have to take care of her myself. I will wait until she stop retching. Then everything she have in her stomach will come out.

She stop retching. She lean back in the armchair weak-weak. Nothing, not even anymore yellow bile could leave in her stomach. Her stomach is still as she lean back. Cold sweat washing her. Her skin is grey.

I can take off her clothes now. Clean her up a bit. Put her into the bed. I don't have any hot water. I can't light the Eckna again to warm-up water. Maybe the cold water will help revive her. Make her feel better.

I lift her out of the armchair. She is lighter than when I tried to lift her from the chaka-chaka carpet to bring her inside the room. Or I am stronger. I lift her up in my arms. I don't want her clothes to put vomit on my clothes. I don't care. I lift her up.

She is a woman.

But she is like a baby in my arms. She is so little, and meagre and delicate under her clothes. Maybe she doesn't feed her body well. I should put her in an old nightie after I clean her up. Just in case she start to vomit again.

Why am I putting her in a new nightie? All the time that she was vomiting, her eyes were wide open. Looking, looking. I clean her off. Put her in a new nightie. Lay her down in the bed. Cover her up good-good. I pull the eiderdown right up to her neck. All this time, her black eyes keep looking at me. Looking into me. With an icy stare.

I give her a piece of ginger to chew to settle her stomach. She take it meekly into her mouth. She not saying a word.

I clean off the armchair. I pull it up to the front of the bed. I will watch her sleeping.

MRS MASON

I t's Icy. Is mi little Icy. Come to me here in England. Them send her
in a different form than the one I did know before. But is Icy.
Grannie Lou was right.

I start to know that it was she from I take her up in my arms. But I
still wasn't sure. Cause is such a long time since I take her in my arms.
I get a little more sure when she did start to vomit. She always used to
vomit whenever she very upset about anything or whenever I discipline
her hard.

But still I wasn't fully sure. Until I was sponging her down and A see
it. I saw the special mark. She has a mark right beside her navel. I gave
her that mark when she was in my womb. One day when I was up at
Grannie Lou pregnant with her, I did want to eat some steamed doctor
fish so bad, that I keep scratching by my navel. Grannie Lou had chuckled
and said, 'yu still hungry fi tings yu cyaan have, eh? Mind yu mark yu
pickney.' So say, so done.

When she born, a little mark come out at her navel. It was the shape
of a little doctor fish. It's still there. After all these years. Those who
don't know about it might not see it. You can hardly see it now because
her skin get blacker than when she was little.

How come she get so black? She was so clear-skinned and brown when
she was little. She did almost take after the Portuguese people in my side
of the family and the English people in her father's side of the family.

Up to the time I leave her to come to England, she was brown. Now
she turn up here black as midnight. Maybe that's the new form them
send her in. But the birthmark is still there. And her icy stare is still
there.

I know is Icy. But I can't take her in this black form. I have to get rid
of her quick, quick. It's for her own good too. If she stay here, she going
to become even blacker. Them won't know that she have white blood in
her and they will treat her just like how they treat all the rest of the
black-black ones. Just like how them treat me.

Is Icy. Is my little Icy. So help mi God, A don' want them to treat her
like they treat me. That's why I have to send her back out into the night
now that she stop vomiting. One of the other Voices will take her in and
put her back on the airplane tomorrow. After all, ain' them who send
her here? They should take care of her. They can't depend on me to do
their job for them?

As God is my witness, I never did want to leave her. But what could

I do? I couldn't be a good mother to her unless I finish my own education. I had to come to England to finish my own education. The only way I could help her was to leave her. Then I would come back with full education and we would be happy together.

All the same, if I didn't leave her, they wouldn't have the chance to take her over and make her into a spirit that they now send to bring me down to the last bottom of the bottomless pit. They manage to get me into the last room. But I am not going to fall on the floor. I am going to stand up in this room. They heard me saying that. They heard me praying night upon night, for God to protect me, to keep mine enemies from dragging me to the floor of the last room. That's why they send Icy. To help finish me off. They could only send somebody that I love so much. To help them carry out their plans against me.

I must send her out, quick, quick. They tried everything over these eighteen years. They changed Fitzie and used him against me. Because they know that I love him. They bring Canute to England to haunt me. They send the Voices. Everywhere I go, everything I try, they always send someone to try to pull me down. They send them in all different guises. To try to conquer me. Sometime they send some of their own people, white topanaris people who look through you like you wasn't there, like you was just air. Sometime they send half-white people, they call them 'half-caste', those ones that are neither fish nor fowl. Sometime some of them who they send were Indian or half-Indian.

Sometime they send some of my own people, Black like me. Some of them Jamaicans like me. When they send those ones, I had was to use my head good-good, so I could recognise them. It wasn't all that hard, cause by this time I know they always send someone to try to pull me down as soon as I start to rise up. So whoever come, whatever the colour of they skin, I could always know when they come to pull me down. I reject all those ones, even if I did know them from long time and they look just like me. I reject them. All of them fail, whatever colour and form they come in. They could only pull me down part of the way, not all of the way. That's why I retreat-back to this room and don't let none of them into it. That Mistress Dixon downstairs and the boy Rasta who always playing the loud ungodly music try many times to come in but I keep them out, eh, eh! They think I am a fool.

I not surprised that they now send Icy. For she to succeed where all others fail. It's only Icy they could get into this room. And that's why I know it's Icy.

ICY

Her bed feels good. At least in this little god-forsaken room, she still has a good bed. The nightie is of cotton. It feels like a house over me. A house that won't be washed away by any storms or hurricanes. It smells good, too. It smells of newness and camphor-balls.

She sponged me down with a little rough wash-rag, soap and a basin of icy cold water. It's like when she used to put water in the zinc washpan to warm in the sun at the back of the yard in Jamaica and then say, 'come, let me bathe yu skin.' This water was not sun-warm. It was snow-cold. And it was only a small basinful. But it has bathed my skin.

I can't remember when I have felt this way. So empty. So clean. Almost virginal (whatever that means, eh, eh). I am so tired. But I can't sleep. I want her to think that I am sleeping. But I can't sleep. This is too much for me. I never expected anything like this. Nobody in Jamaica would believe me if I ever told them that anybody in England lived like this. Jesus Christ, what am I going to do? I wasn't prepared for this. I have seen wattle-and-daub huts in the countryside of Jamaica. I have seen corrugated-zinc and cardboard shacks in Trench Town and other parts of Kingston, but I have never seen a building like this. Much less a room like this. How could anyone live like this? At least in the one-room shacks in Jamaica, you can see and feel the sun. It is warm and you can be in the yard or go out into the streets, whether it's night or day, only coming back into the shack to sleep. She has to shit and wash and cook and live, in this room. Because, knowing her, she wouldn't use the one bathroom and toilet for all the people in this big building. Jesus Christ!

There is nobody in Jamaica who would believe me if I described this room to them. Everybody that I know believes that everyone in England or America lives in a mansion. No wonder she told the policemen to tell me that she was quite all right, when I phoned from Jamaica before coming. No wonder she couldn't write to tell me about this room.

This room is like a coffin. Only a little bigger. It is totally enclosed and of itself. The wallpaper is browny-grey. It can barely hold the bed, a wooden wash-stand with goblet and basin, a small table with a paraffin lamp, the armchair and a bigger table with the Eckna. It has one window which is covered over with a thick curtain. There is a little carpet on the floor. There is a bulb enclosed in a moth-eaten lampshade in its ceiling. She hasn't turned it on. She has lit the paraffin lamp. The room reminds me of that horrible flat that I moved from to go to the sea-green cottage, only it's smaller.

The room is clean. No bad smells. No dust. No dirt. Smell of Dettol. It's clear that she has scrubbed it down.

I have to admit, to my eternal shame, that I would have thought her a liar, if she had written to tell me about this room. I would have thought that she just didn't want to have me with her in her nice, new life. I think I am beginning to understand why her letters were so . . . alien. What a fool I must have seemed, when I wrote to her asking her to do this and that for me. Wanting to join her when she became a qualified State Registered Nurse in England!

No nurse lives like this in Jamaica! Thank God, she didn't bring me here. How could I ever survive in a room like this?

I have vomited out that tasteless, soggy airplane food. I have even vomited out the tasteful rice and peas and chicken which I ate at Aunt Jo's. I have vomited out my shock.

I am pretending to be asleep. She is sitting by the side of the bed. I cannot see, as I could before, her wasted breasts. I cannot see that her clothes have gotten too big for her present body. I cannot see her eyes. The paraffin lamplight is like a reticent half-moon light which shadows threaten to overcome. But in which a silhouette forms the only substance. Like a shadow sculpted into the armchair.

She sits there for a while, watching me. Then she gets up and goes to the trunk at the foot of the bed. She is searching in the trunk. Tumbling out sheets, bedspreads, blankets, pillowcases on to the floor. Whatever she is looking for is in the bottom of the trunk. She finds whatever it is. She returns to the armchair with some sheets of paper in her hands.

MRS MASON

Fitzie and Canute think that I am a fool. They never think that I was a fool in Jamaica? Is only when they come to England that they start to tell me I am a fool.

They used to tell me that I love the white people-them too much. They used to say that you can't trust them. And that I believe in them too much.

All the man-them were complaining about the Teddy boys. But how they did expect me to understand, I never meet any Teddy boys yet? I don't walk street at night. I never walk street at night in Jamaica and I don't walk street at night in England. I did see Mrs Haughton son with his ribs break-up and his face so black and blue, it did look like bad-baked potato pudding. The mother did tell me that is Teddy boys beat him up. But I didn't believe it. England is a law-abiding place. They wouldn't allow that to happen and they don't arrest somebody. Unless Mrs Haughton son was wrong in the first place and he don't want to tell his parents.

I never believe that no Teddy boys would ever do that to Fitzie. He has his nasty ways sometimes but he is a decent man with his good job as mechanic with British Rail. He not one of those who always stretching out their hands to the white people begging something.

I always did feel that so long as him keep himself quiet, him would get along and reach very far. He wasn't like me, who did want to carry on with studies, he had his profession already. But him always getting in trouble with the people in their own country. Sometime with the boss, sometime with the trade union. Him say that some of the topanaris in the trade union behave same way like the guvnor. I couldn't stand his constant complaining against the people-them.

I remember the time that he never come home for two whole days. I was worried out of mi head. When him turn up, him was so bruised-up and dirty, I couldn't think where he did go. He wouldn't tell me anything and I think that he must have been under some bridge with some dirty woman. When he go with his women and they don't please him or when he want to bring in any one of them and I always suspect something, he try to take it out on me. When they do him anything bad at work, it's me he come home and quarrel with.

I should-a did keep my mouth shut when he turn up after the two days. For when I start to curse him and his dirty women, he give me one dirty look, as if he scorned me. Then he spit right on the floor and said he

151

don't know how he could-a did married such a foolish woman. I did feel to leave him right then and there but the flat in Clapham was in my name and I wasn't going to leave him in it and go sleep on the street. I decide I going to hold on till I could get a better job and save-up to buy a house. Then I could send for Icy. And we could live together.

I nearly changed mi mind. Because after he stay quiet for over a week, he come and put his head down in mi lap and tell me that the police did lock him up and keep him in Stoke Newington jail. He was crying but he bury his face in my lap so that I couldn't see that he was crying. Still, I feel it in the way his body was so soft and broken-up. I did start to cry too.

Him tell me that the Teddy boys back him up as he come out of the tube station in the night. He said that he swore on his mother's grave that it was either them or him. He said that it was about six of them. They knock him to the ground. They were going to kill him. He said that he pulled out his knife while he was on the ground and stabbed the one that was leaning over into his face (I never did know that Fitzie carry knife). He said that this did get them vexed. One of them lift a piece of iron bar to smash his head in. But all of a sudden, a car headlight light-up the place. It was police. The Teddy boys ran, holding-up the one who Fitzie stabbed.

He said that the police threw him into the back of the car and took him to Stoke Newington police station. He tell me that they were worse than the Teddy boys.

I didn't believe him. I didn't believe all of them others too. Some of them was telling me that them keep down their children in the school. I think is their fault. Nobody never tell them to bring all they pickney here. I leave my own back there. Cause she was getting a good education already and I didn't see no reason to move her. Lawd, too much pressure! Too much pressure in this country! I wanted to go home. But I couldn't go home the same way I did come?

MRS MASON

After the birthday party, they told me that they didn't need me anymore at Dulwich Hospital. They said that I hadn't been working well (they didn't tell me that before?).

My friend the Nursing Sister said that I would do better at Tootin' Bec because there were many of 'your people' working there. I did ask her if they would transfer my application to go to evening classes to further my studies.

She looked at the beds, she looked into the roof, she looked out the window which was locked because it was winter but she didn't look into my eyes. She said,

'Missis May-son, you will be much happier there.'

They put me on the senile dementia ward. All dead people. That was when I really start to get confused. They didn't give me the time-off for my evening classes. Lawd! They tried to mix me up with the dead people. As if I was dead too.

You had to do everything for them. It's not that I did mind that so much. Because I am a healer. Some of the dead people would come alive as soon as I stretched out my hand to them and say, 'rise'. Some of them who were cursing me before and calling me 'black bastard' wouldn't make the other nurses touch them.

The other nurses were jealous of me because the old patients loved me. But some of them was too satisfied to be dead. And I couldn't stand that. It made me feel as if I was dead too.

I used to come home and tell Fitzie how much the patients loved me. He would look at me and say,

'Val, yu don' understan'. A wonder if yu will ever understan'.'

Maybe Fitzie was right. I couldn't understand how I couldn't laugh and have fun anymore. Then the Voices started to come. I didn't listen to them at first. I was holding on.

I was on the night shift. Then Icy send this letter to me. I wrote back to her while I was on the night shift. Icy is all I have.

I did want her to be all right. I didn't want to tell her that I was not all right. I had was to read her letter two times before deciding my mind what to answer her.

Dear Mama Putus,
   I hope when these few lines reach your loving hands, they may find you in the best of health and good spirit.

153

I received your last letter and was very happy to get it. Thank you very much for the 10 pounds. I used it to buy a pair of school shoes. I know you always used to tell me that cheap things are not good and that it is better to buy one good thing than many cheap things. But Nathan's had a sale downtown (you remember Nathan's store?) and they were selling out all sorts of things. Even shoes from 19/11 to two pounds, nineteen and eleven. So I bought a nice pair of brown, laced-up shoes (it even has pointed toes). I put the rest of the money in my saving-pan. Maybe I will spend some of it when Christmas comes. I will try to send a bottle of sorrel for your Christmas but I have to find out if anyone knows anybody who is coming over there and they can take it to you for me.

You did not tell me in your letter how your nursing course was going. I hope well. I hope that you and Fitzie are getting on and that he is managing all right.

Every time that you write to me, you ask me if everything is all right with me. I don't know if you notice that I never answer your question straight. If you read between the lines, you could understand what I am saying although I don't say it out straight.

Sometimes I think that you can't understand me anymore since you went to England. The more you are away, I am having it harder to picture you and to talk to you. Things have gotten to a bad stage so I decided to tell you straight out what is happening, for you to understand what I am really going through since you left to go to England.

I am not happy at all. I miss you very, very, much. Don't worry yourself because I am not sick and I am not starving, also the teachers say that I am doing well at school. I will take my Senior Cambridge examination next year. I am not good at Maths and I think I will drop it and take up Bible Knowledge to make up my subjects for the examination. My headmaster says that there may be a problem with that because they don't do Bible Knowledge, Health Science, Home Economics or Woodwork, in the A and B stream, only in the C and D stream. As you know, I am in the A stream. I get all As in the subjects such as English Literature, English Language, History and General Knowledge. I have problems with Latin and French but I think that I will pass them in the examination.

Last week, a man came to our school who said that he was living in Cuba for thirty years and he has family there. It was in our General Knowledge class. He talked some Spanish to us. Mama Putus, it is a nice language. I think that I would like to learn it but they don't teach it in our school. Somebody told me that they are going to introduce it in the D stream but I don't think that they will bring it into the B or the A stream before my examination. I told them from the beginning that I could not do Physics and they didn't bother to let me take it.

I know how much you worry because you want me to do very good at school. I am trying my best. You told me that you were pleased with my Reports. So don't worry about that.

However, I am very unhappy at home. If I tell you that the people I am living with beat me, physically, I would be telling you a lie and I don't want to tell a lie. I must say to you that they beat me psychologically. They treat me as an outsider and I am very lonely. All I can do is read books to keep me company. Sometimes they say bad things about you and I cannot stand it. They even make me feel that I am committing a crime when I read, saying that all I live in is books.

The other day, the wife came to me when I was washing my school uniform. She told me to wash the husband's and the son's clothes because the maid didn't come for the week. I refused. I was not going to wash all those iron-khaki pants for the husband. The son has a lot of nastiness in his underpants and I could not put my hand on that. After I refuse, none of them did not speak to me for days. They told me that I think that I am better than anybody else and that it is you I get that feeling from.

They take it out on me because in spite of the money you are sending, they refused to give me any to buy a new dress to wear at my friend's wedding. I had to wear an old dress, one of those that you left me with. When I told the husband that I didn't have anything suitable to wear to the wedding, he told me that I will end up looking men on the street, if I only keep my mind on pretty things. He said I should concentrate on my lessons so that I could turn out to be somebody. I didn't answer him but it was in my heart to tell him that I am already somebody because I am flesh and blood. He knows that I am doing well at my school work because he takes my school report to curse his own children with, telling them look how I am doing and they cannot even pass their term exam. It was in my heart to ask him what they do with all the money you send every month, why I can't get a new dress or new dressing shoes and have to wear the old ones which have a hole in the bottom to church or wear my school shoes. But I kept my lips sealed because I did not want him to say that I was rude to him and for him and his wife and his children to treat me bad.

I cried the whole night, because I feel like a motherless child. I cried even more the next night when I saw that he had bought new dresses for his daughters, new suits for his sons and new shoes for all his children to wear to the same wedding. But I didn't say anything because I had enough to cope with when his children curse me many times and call me orphan.

155

On top of everything, they don't allow me to go anywhere but school and church. I know you told them not to allow me to run about, but I don't want to run about. I don't think it is running about to want to go to my school fair, or for my school friends to come and look for me at the house or to go to a matinée show with my friends. The only person they will allow me to go out with, besides them, is Mr Seymour (you don't know him). They say he is an old friend of their family. They allow me to go out with him some Friday nights. He tells them that he is carrying me to visit his sick wife who likes me to read to her. He lives with his wife and her younger sister and they also have a man boarder in the house. It is a nice, big house in upper St Andrew. You should see how the husband grins up his face when Mr Seymour comes to collect me on Friday evenings. Maybe the husband thinks that Mr Seymour is taking me straight to the house and we will all have tea or soft drinks with his wife. But many times, Mr Seymour don't go straight to his house, he stops at a place that sell patties and ice-cream. I like the patties and they have about 10 different flavours of ice-cream.

Last week Friday, he stopped at another place. It didn't have any patties. It didn't have any food at all. It only had rooms. Mr Seymour told me that you couldn't get patties or ice-cream in the front but you could get anything you wanted if you took a room. He told me to wait in his car outside and he would call me when he got a room.

When he called me and took me into the room, I saw that there wasn't any patties there. There wasn't anything in the room but a small bed, a little washstand with a basin and goblet, a towel and a bar of soap. I sat on the bed and Mr Seymour sat on it too. He tried to touch me in the chief one of those places where you told me never to let any boy or man touch me. I began to cry and make a big noise. Mr Seymour put his hand over my mouth. I was so upset I began to vomit on his hand and on to the old sheet on the little bed. He forgot to order the patties and said we should leave right away.

Mama Putus, please, please, I beg you, take me away from this place. At least put me at another place until you pass your Nurse examination and can come back to take me. I am so unhappy I am going to die if I stay with these people. Mama, please take me away to be with you in the place that you are (although I don't think I will like it). Please come back and let us be together again.

Anticipating a very quick reply from you;

I remain . . .

Your little Icy

P.S. Sorry for the bad handwriting. Say hello to everyone with you. Hoping to hear from you Soon. Take good care of yourself.

Your loving daughter

Icy (Icylane)

MRS MASON

The letter come from Icy in Jamaica when I was just getting confused. Every day, they was just on mi back. Every minute I had was to prove that I was a human being.

After a while, I did know that they treat me better if they think I am a fool. So I pretend to be a fool. I pretend that I don't understand when they talk to me.

After the birthday party, I start to understand more what Fitzie and Canute usually say to me. But I couldn't tell Icy that? How I was going to tell Icy that England wasn't the mansion of the world? I had was to tell her to be satisfied with what she have.

I wrote a letter to her. Her answer make me even more confused. In fact, I nearly died when I got her answer. Many times, even after I leave London and leave Fitzie, I read her letter.

> Dear Mother,
>
> I hope that you are well.
>
> I know that you must be wondering why I have not answered your last letter. I want to tell you that it took me such a long time to reply to your letter because I was sick about your letter, in reply to my letter.
>
> At first, when I got your letter, I said, never would I reply to it. I felt in my heart, that maybe since you had become a different person from the one I know, that it must be that new person talking. I took out your photograph that you sent me from England. I did not tell you before but I didn't know the person in the photograph, so I said to myself that it must be the person in the photograph who wrote that letter to me. I decided that I would not answer the letter because that person would not understand what I was talking about anyway.
>
> It was Miss Mighty who told me that it was just you and that you were only fatter and have the weave-on hair on your head. She said that I shouldn't pay any notice to the clothes, that was how people there had to dress because it was so cold there. Every day over these months, she was asking me if I answer your letter yet. In the end, I decided to reply to your letter and tell you what is in my heart.
>
> After I tell you everything what is really in my heart, maybe you

will never write to me again or talk to me again but since I am writing you, I have to tell you.

First, what I want to tell you, is that I was right to kill you in my heart from the day you went on the plane at Palisadoes airport. I knew in my heart that you were telling me a lie when you said that we would still be together and that as soon as you finished your nursing studies, you would come back.

When I got your reply to my letter, I killed you totally in my heart. I know that you, or the person in the photograph, may cry and ask me why. So I decided to write and tell you why.

You told me in your letter that you were very proud of me. I am glad for that. You didn't have to tell me that the main thing that I must have on my mind is passing my Senior Cambridge so that I can go to University. I promised you that and I am doing my best to keep that promise.

I don't know what you mean when you say that I should behave myself and obey this family where you put me. I want to ask you one question which is this: how can I just obey them when I am so unhappy and they don't care about me?

You are sending money every month for them to keep me and I just ask you to put me somewhere else and send the money to that family. You didn't say anything about that in your letter. How could you agree that they shouldn't buy me a new dress for the wedding from the money that you are sending them?

How can you want to see your daughter looking less than the others, because, you say, I should not have my mind on temporal things? How can you agree with them that they should only let me go to school and church?

You said in your letter that I must be careful that friends don't lead me astray. You asked me what am I doing with a friend who is going to be a married woman and who have so many children. You said that Miss Mighty was too old and too experienced to be my friend.

I want to tell you the truth, because maybe you have forgotten since you are in this strange place. Miss Mighty has the shop near to the home where you left me. I would have died if she did not befriend me. Since you have been away, it is only this woman who I can talk to. She helps me in every way.

Mas Tom who she has five children with, is like a father to me and Miss Mighty is like a mother to me.

When I told Mas Tom what had happened with Mr Seymour on the Friday night that I told you about, he told me that I was not to leave the house with Mr Seymour on Friday nights when he came to collect me. He said that I was not to pay any mind to the husband or the wife when they are pressing me to go with Mr Seymour. Mas Tom told me that I was to pretend to be sick and go in my bed.

Miss Mighty was so vexed that she started to curse and say that she was going to talk to the husband but Mas Tom told her not to do that but just to counsel me on the way I should act to protect myself.

I wrote to you before about Miss Mighty but maybe you forgot. Remember that I told you that she was the one who explained to me everything about my monthly periods (you just gave me the small clothes but you didn't tell me what it was all about). She told me that I did not have to put up with that terrible smell or that rancid water to dip my hand in, to soak and wash and bleach the cloth napkins every month. She showed me some napkins in a plastic bag and taught me how to put them on (they don't need any safety pins. They have something like a sticking-plaster that stick on to your panties and they even come with a belt that you can knot the ends of the napkins on to.) You don't have to wash them, you just tear them up and flush them down the toilet or burn them after you use them.

I cannot understand how you could not understand that I would want to dress my best and look my best for Mas Tom and Miss Mighty's wedding.

You say I must behave myself. But you don't tell me how I am misbehaving myself. I want to be a good girl. I think I am a good-behaving girl. It is only you and the people you put me to live with, that think that I am a bad-behaving girl.

I feel very bad because you did not curse Mr Seymour. When you were here, nobody would not try to do anything like he did with me. You would have put him in his place. It was you who told me that no boy or man should touch me in the place that he tried to touch me, but you did not say anything against him when I told you in my letter that he tried to touch me in that place. You said that he was a good family friend of the people you had left me with and that they are upstanding people in the society, so that maybe I misunderstand Mr Seymour.

Well if you want to think so, that is up to you. I know what I know. All you had to say was that I should behave myself, obey the people you had left me with and respect Mr Seymour. Respect Mr Seymour! Whether you want to know it or not, he is not worthy of respect.

If you want to write back, you can do so but from now on, I count myself as a motherless child. As well as being a fatherless child.

Yours sincerely

Icylane Barton

ICY

The shadows in the room have become like a sea. Only it's not the Caribbean Sea. I know because the Caribbean Sea is forever lit, either by sunlight or moonlight. The Caribbean Sea is forever warm, whether by night or day.

This room is cold. I am so cold even though I am tucked-into the covers of her warm bed.

This sea must be the Arctic Sea. I have never seen an Arctic Sea but I had to read a lot about such seas in school and university. And they told me that such seas are forever cold. Perhaps this is the Dead Sea or a dead sea.

She is an iceberg in this sea. An immutable rock-iceberg. Then she changes. And she is like a piece of eternal driftwood, grey-black, battered by the waves but not yet cast adrift in the Arctic Sea. Then she is transferred to the Dead Sea as a piece of black coral but she is one of the few living things in that dead sea.

Then she is like a boat, navigating the Dead Sea. She begins to rock and moan. I am trying to understand what she is moaning. It is not easy. I have the feeling that her moans are older than Brown's Hall. Older than Jamaica. Older than England.

Older than the Arctic Sea. Older than the Dead Sea. Older than even the Sahara before the time that it became a desert.

She is rocking back and forth, like a canoe. I still cannot see her eyes. But I can now see her mouth. Perhaps my eyes have gotten used to the paraffin shadows. Her fleshy, full top lip forms an awning. Her bottom lip has come up to nestle under that awning. Together they form a fleshy, black-purple mountainous giant pout. A giant pout of her mouth protruding from the plane of her face.

'Woooy, woooooy, woooy. Woh, woooooh, wooooy, woh! Woooy, woh, wooooy, woooooy, yoh!'

This is intense and high-pitched. Then she rocks back. And she looks at me as if she knows that I am only pretending to be asleep. I now see her eyes. They are looking into me under the covers. She opens the sheets of paper she has taken from the trunk. She screws up her eyes in the shadows of the room. I know she is beginning to read those sheets of paper she has taken from the trunk. I pretend to be asleep.

I think I know what those sheets of paper are. Of all the letters that I sent her before, of the few I sent her after, those two letters have been like a bone in my craw. How many times has she read them over these years? I wonder.

I remember those letters very well. Sometimes, over the years, I have been glad that I wrote them to her, sometimes I have been sorry. Right now, I am of two minds about them. When I see her rocking and moaning while she is reading them, I feel like a worm. She is so clearly hurt by them. I didn't mean to hurt her so much.

Then again, what about me? What about my big pain and heartburn? I had to tell her the truth. She should know the truth. Should I suffer because she doesn't want to face the truth?

I hope that she doesn't try to talk to me about the letters. I want to talk to her. I want her to talk to me. But I don't want to talk about those letters. That is water under the bridge. My life has moved on since then and what is gone is gone and cannot come back.

She seems to have finished reading the letters. They were the longest letters I ever wrote to her. She is now just staring into the little space of this shadowed room. Her rocking has changed rhythm. Before, the rhythm was erratic, like that of a canoe cast adrift in turbulent waves. Now the canoe is still adrift but the seas are calmer. It is rocking gently to the drum rhythm of the heartbeart.

She starts to croon a song. Is it to me or to herself? I cannot be sure. It is a song I have never heard before. But it is of a rhythm that is familiar, though I know I have never heard it before in my own life. Maybe it seems familiar because it is pulsing to the same time as the blood circulating from my heart all round my body. She starts the song low down in her belly. Then it eventually comes through her pouted mouth. And all the time she is rocking to the command of an eternal heartbeat.

It is a heartbeat which eventually comes out in words, or rather parts of words:

Dey, de-de-de-de
Dey, de-de-de-de
Dey, de-de-de de-dey
  For Your Face
(for your face)
Is like the Seville orange
for your face
Is like the Seville orange.
    That orange
S . . . E . . . V . . I . . . LL . . . Eeee
Springing from the belly
  (springing from the belly)
Of European Kings and Rulers
       O'er us.

Your face is like a Seville
orange . . .

On and on and on . . .

ICY

Still crooning her Seville orange song, she gets up and puts the back of her hand on the Eckna. It seems to have cooled down because she doesn't quickly pull her hand back.

She tries to light it again. It seems to have run out of paraffin. She looks towards the bed and says,

'A nice cup of tea would be good.'

I am still not sure if she is talking to me or to herself. Even if I were sleeping before, she must know I could not be sleeping after her singing. But tea is the last thing on my mind. I am still chewing the piece of ginger she put in my mouth. It has settled my stomach.

I want to talk but I don't know where to begin. I wish she would stop singing this mournful song. I don't want her to begin rocking again when she returns to the armchair. She will return into herself completely.

'I wonder what time it is?'

She is standing at the table, looking down on the Eckna, when I say this. She turns around very slowly as if she has to make sure where the voice is coming from. She does not answer for about a minute. I am fearing that she is not going to answer.

Then I see she is going towards the head of the bed. There is a little side-table there. I had not noticed it before. She takes something from the table and holds it up to the one valiant ray of light coming from the struggling paraffin lamp.

'I buy this clock out of the first money I earn in England.'

When she says this, she is holding something up in her hands. If she says it is a clock, I suppose it must be. But it just looks like a blob of darker shadow. She shakes it.

'It stop working. I wonder when it stop working? Must be when I move from London to Birmingham. Or must be when I went out to the store the other day that they break into the room and mash it up. Just to give me a hard time.'

I don't want her to begin to talk like that again. I want her to speak to me, with me. When she tidied me up she left my own watch on. I can't see its face clearly.

'It doesn't matter. I don't really need to know the time. I don't have any appointment with anybody. It's you I came to look for.'

I have the feeling that she is just at the point of being transported out of this room altogether, although her solid body would remain here. She seems to pull herself back. She goes to sit again in the armchair in front of the bed. She begins again her rocking motion.

'Mama Putus. Mama Putus.'

She stops rocking and looks at me.

'Mama Putus, what happened to you here? Why you never send and tell me the truth? All the time that you write back home, you said that everything was arright with you. It's only in the letter that your work friend brought and the letter from Aunt Jo that anybody would know that something was wrong . . . '

She only looks at me. She looks at me for a long time. Even in the dim lamplight, I can see the whites of her eyes. They are making me very uncomfortable. Perhaps she still doesn't know who I am.

'Mama Putus, you don't recognise me? Is me Icy. Is just that you don't see me for eighteen years. Is just that I grow much bigger than the last photograph you have of me. That was a teenager picture, I am a big woman now. But is me Icy, same one.'

She is perfectly still now. I am wishing now that she had continued her rocking and chanting. The stillness in the room is oppressive.

I can't bear it. What kind of night is this which has no sounds? All nights have sounds. I don't expect the chirping of crickets or the mournful howl of pattoo. This is not Jamaica where numberless mongrel dogs would be trying to outbark each other as soon as darkness falls. But surely there must be some living thing outside this room on this night? I don't expect sound systems disturbing the rest of early sleepers. But does no one snore? These old buildings must creak, mustn't they?

Are there no people whom sleep has deserted and who must have their most alive and active times while others slumber? If there are, don't they make any sound? Does no one walk or drive the streets on this night? Doesn't anyone cry out in the heat of love or hate? Isn't anyone being born? Isn't anyone shrieking in the agony of dying?

Perhaps this night does not exist outside this room. I will never know. Or perhaps I will come to know. I would very much love to know.

If I should speak again, I know my voice would sound so loud in this soundless night that it makes me afraid to speak. It makes me afraid to be. I fear that this fear is making me mad.

I feel like getting up off the bed and turning the table over. Then afterwards I would throw the Eckna with all my might at the covered window. I want to hear glass breaking and smashing. I want to hear loud talking, shouts, howls, moans, groans and hysterical uncontrolled laughter. I want to hear sounds, even if they be the sounds of anger, hate and death. I am being killed by silence. I cannot stand this silence.

I want to hear her sing again. I get up from off the bed and grip her arms.

She turns her eyes fully on to me. The look she gives me flings me to the floor between the armchair and the bed. She did not struggle when I gripped her arms. She has not pushed me away from her. But somehow,

165

I have landed plop on my bottom on the floor and I have hit my back against the bed. My head is dizzy.

All I can see is that look. It is not a look of hate but it contains so much raw hate it's like a blast from a welding torch. Yet it also contains love. Like a helpless love. One which oughtn't to be but cannot help being. But most of all, it is a look of absolute frustration, sorrow and surrender. Surrender of what, I don't know.

And yet, it is a look which seems to say, 'if you could only know, then you could live.'

I've had enough. I am weak. She can do with me whatever she pleases. I don't care if I survive this night.

At last, she speaks. And it is terrible to hear.

'You didn't hear I tell you not to come here, Icy? Why you didn't listen to me? I tell them to tell you not to come here. The police didn't give you the messsage? Why you come here? You think I have whole heap of money to give you? You come to live off of me? I tell you not to come. Why you didn't listen, Icy?

ICY

Eighteen years! Eighteen years she has been away. From she left Palisadoes airport in Kingston, she never put her foot back home. And she has the nerve to ask me why I have come here?

It's like she has forgotten everything and everybody back home. She never even came home when Mama Belle died. She sent 50 pounds in postal orders to help with the funeral expenses. It arrived after the funeral. She sent a cablegram claiming that she couldn't get the leave from her job to come because she had just come back from her holiday.

Ah! who would believe that? Tell that to the birds. Everybody knows that any employer, no matter how hard-hearted, would give a person leave to go to their mother or father's funeral. Even that dreadful Director at my office, he became so helpful and humane when he heard that my mother was sick in England. All I had to do was cry two tears (which wasn't pretending), and he immediately arrange it for me to get part of the leave with pay and part without pay. And he wrote such a nice letter that I didn't have any trouble going through Immigration. So what she talking about? It couldn't be that different in England?

Her excuse about not getting the leave was bad enough. But worse still was what she said in her letter which came with the postal orders, about, 'since Miss Belle is dead already, it didn't make sense to lose my job just to come to the funeral'. I could have killed her when Boysie's son Mannie read out her letter at the 'Nine-night' and I saw Boysie smirking. Nobody said anything. Everybody was too embarrassed. Everybody was too sorry for Mama Belle whose eldest daughter did not think her funeral important enough to come to. I knew that they were thinking that it was better that she hadn't sent any money if she was going to be putting the money in place of her own coming to pay the due respect to her dead mother.

I have to wonder: 'Is what this woman really a-defend?'

It seems to me that just like the time when I wrote that letter to her, now I have to tell her what is really on my mind.

I get up and stand before her so that she can't have any doubt that it is she that I am talking to and not to myself.

'Imagine, you take a holiday. You pay money to travel on ship to the Caribbean and you don't come to Jamaica. You go to Trinidad. How come you go to Trinidad? We have anybody there? You have any family there? You one child was there? Trinidad better than Jamaica?'

She doesn't answer me. She is looking at me in a waiting way . . . I suppose waiting for an answer to her question as to why had I come here. I am getting really vexed with this woman. I am thinking of all those times when I needed her and she wasn't there. I am thinking that if it was some other daughter or son, they wouldn't even turn the black of their eyes when Aunt Jo wrote about her. They certainly wouldn't scrape up all their little savings and borrow money to make up and come and look for her. What an ungrateful woman!

My knees have become very weak. I sit on the bed.

'If yu going to sit on the bed, don't sit on the edge. Sit at the foot or it will sag the mattress.'

Jesus Christ! That she should be thinking of her precious mattress at a time like this.

'I don't care one backside about your mattress. Answer me! How come you never came home?'

She gets up out of the armchair. She comes to stand before me. Before I can quite figure out what she is going to do, she lifts up her hand and smashes me one blow to the side of my face. It spins me around and drops me laying down into the bed.

She lifts up her hand again. Lawd God, she is going to kill me!

She is not meagre and wasted anymore. She is big and tall and strong. If she chooses, she can smash me to pieces. Her hand is like a sword. If it descends, it will surely chop my head off. She holds it up there, for a long time, level with her head and over my head. The whites of her eyes are turned up in that hate–love look again. She eventually lowers her hand. But she is still standing.

In a deadly calm and chilling voice which echoes around the little room, she says:

'Not you. Never you. Never use those words to me again. Others may forget. Others may not know who I am. Others may insult me and take step with me. But never you. I will not tolerate it. I am still your mother, however brought low. You are still my daughter, however big and high you have become. I forgive you for your letter. But don't do it again. Never speak to me like that again or I will smash your teeth down your bad-manners throat and you can swallow them.'

And then she slowly sits down in the armchair again.

I C Y

This is a different woman. This is not the mad, confused woman I met since I climbed those stairs.

This woman is Mama Putus Barton. Daughter of Miss Belle Thomas from the line of Kayam and Grannie Lou. Daughter of Mas D Barton, from the line of Ma Tata, Da Da Barton and Great-Grandfather Barton.

For the first time since I came to this building, to this god-forsaken room, I know this woman. I have no doubt now, it is the same woman.

The side of my face is hurting but there is a bigger hurt. I want to know about those missing years. I want to know about everything that happened since she left me crying at Palisadoes airport. I want to know who is the babbling, disturbed woman I met earlier. I want to know where did Mama Putus Barton go. And how and why she has come back. Most of all, I want Mama Putus to stay.

The Mama Putus before she came to England only ever hit me twice and never like this. Oh, that Mama Putus would threaten every day to beat me because almost every day I was a rebellious child. But she only ever hit me twice. And it was more 'spanking' than 'beating'. As far as I can remember. Once was when I was about nine years old and I went off for the whole day to jump with the Junkonoo Bands at Christmas-time, while she was at work at the textile factory. I had really meant to come home long before she came off her two-to-six shift. But the Junkonoo Bands with their fife and drum music was so sweet, I hadn't come back home till nearly 9 o'clock. She had taken a strap, told me to hold out my hand and brought down the strap two times on each hand. She had ended up crying more than me.

The other time was after I got the Island Scholarship to High School and she got to find out (I still don't know how) that I was telling my school friends that I lived in the Taylors' big house which was two houses down the road from the one we really lived in. Lord, I had never seen her so vexed! This time, she hadn't told me to hold out my hand. She had, with a mighty force, laid the strap over my shoulders and on to my back. But only one time, saying, 'If I don't mind sharp, I will kill you an' I don' want to do that. Promise me, promise me that you won't tell them kind of lie again.' Of course, I had promised, if only not to see and feel the strap descend again.

She had never hit me after that time, not physically anyway, up to when she had left to join Fitzie in England.

169

Still, the blow she has just given me reminds me of that second time. Only that this time, she is even more vexed.

She is quiet, sitting in that armchair. Her face is like the crags of rock-mountains which I have only ever seen in geography books. She has shut me out.

I want to reach her. If I don't reach her, I will expire. Now that I have seen her, I have to face-up to the knowledge that I won't be able to live with her rejection. I won't have her rejecting me again. I don't want to leave her now. I love this woman.

I go on my knees in the middle of the bed (I hope it won't sag the mattress). I have forgotten how to pray. I gave up praying long ago. First, when it couldn't bring Mama Putus back to be with me. Later, when I saw how some people who went to church and prayed all the time turned out to be just a set of hypocrites. Still later, when I couldn't bring myself to pray to a god who looked so different from me, in fact looked so much like the people who colonised my country and were even then taking our bauxite and sugar for little or nothing.

I knew that I couldn't pray to their god whose picture is in all our churches. But now, I feel a great need to pray.

I kneel in the middle of the bed, concentrate my thoughts. What comes out of my mouth surprises me as much as it would surprise all the people I know and who know me . . . or think they know me:

Jah! Rastafari!
Jah . . . Rastafari.
How excellent is thy name

Jah!
Rastafari!
Jah Rastafari
How excellent
Is Thy Name
In
All
Of
Earth
I have spoken your name
without realisation
in the congregation
Don't leave me now
Nor forsake me
Jah guide.
Jah, help me
Teach me
Teach me
How to fight for her.

170

ICY

From somewhere a clock is chiming. I wonder where it could be and how come I didn't hear it before. The sound is like that of a small or faraway cathedral bell. But much mellower. I am trying to remember if I saw any churches with bells on my way to this room.

I cannot recall. But everyone I have met since I have come here tells me that the people do not like noise of any sort. Perhaps this includes church bells.

Is there a 'Big Ben' in Birmingham?

The clock is still chiming. I haven't been counting the 'boings' from the beginning. I probably didn't even hear the first 'boings', because I suddenly became aware of the chimes after my loud prayer and while I was quietly meditating on how to get through to Mama Putus.

'God be praised. It start to work again!'

Mama Putus jumps up from the armchair and goes to the little bedside table. She is looking down at the clock, the one she said she had bought with her first wages in England. The one she had shaken in frustration to try to get it to work. The one she said stopped working when she moved from London to Birmingham. The one she said somebody must have smashed.

'It working! Icy, it working. I did miss it so. It don't work for such a long time but it working now.'

She begins to move her foot in time with the chimes. Even in the shadows of the room, I can see that she is laughing. A soundless laugh but a real laugh. The laugh I remember so much. Like happened when I passed the Island Scholarship to High School and Mama Putus showed me the letter from the Ministry of Education. Like happened when Fitzie's letter came telling her to join him in England. She forgot about her two, too-big buck teeth in the front of her mouth, pulled back her black lips, making purple plums of her cheeks and just grinned.

Before, she would have let a high sound come unhindered out of her belly, now only the grin remained. But Mama Putus's grin nonetheless.

'Twelve times it sound. But A don't think is 12 o'clock. It not telling the right time. Don't matter that. It chiming again.'

When she says this, she turns around to face me full. I sit up in the middle of the bed.

'So how come the clock just start working?'

'Maybe because you pray for it. I glad to see that you remember to pray. I did hear that you reject God. No matter how high and mighty

171

you be, you can't reject God. That was the time I really worry bout you, cause if you reject God, God will reject you and that's the last of you when you make God reject you.'

She pauses here. She is not grinning anymore. Her face has become like the heavy rainclouds over the St Catherine hills. At the same time, she has a perplexed look on her face. Not the vexed and hostile look of earlier but a look which is disapproving but begging to understand the seemingly impossible to understand.

'But you turn Rasta? Is Rasta you were praying to. How come you turn Rasta?'

I have to think this one out. I don't think that I turn Rasta. But she right, I was praying to Rasta.

'Mama Putus, I am a socialist. I am not a Rasta.'

'But is Rasta you pray to. Everyone pray to their true God. Is Haile Selassie you praying to? That's where you reach? Lord have mercy! But don't you know that Haile Selassie just a man? You don't know that Rasta only smoke ganja and play drums? Police have to beat them up and kill them all the time. Is that you want for yourself? Is that you go to High School and University for? To get degree in Rasta? Jesus, have mercy!'

'Mama Putus, I don't know how to explain it.'

'What you mean, Icy? How you can believe in something that you can't explain? No nonsense that?'

'I trying to work it out for meself and I can only take the little-little pieces of how I think and put them together and see what comes out.'

She is quiet and waiting.

'You know that I grow up in the Church. But after you leave to go to England, I couldn't pray anymore. Then after I join the Socialist Party and they said that no God never made the world and that everything came about by science and the action of man, I felt such a great freedom. I didn't have to have nightmares anymore about burning in hellfire. I didn't have to be afraid of ghosts anymore. I only had to fear the burglar and the gunman who was a person like me.

'Mama Putus, you can't imagine how good it is not to have any fear of the supernatural. It was like I was released from bonds of iron and could run free and barefoot even 'mongst the prickles.'

'But nobody can live without God? You couldn't come and see me here alive, whatever you want to think bout how I live, if I did live without God, I would dead long time. None of we is only flesh. We is both flesh and spirit. And God is a spirit, so everyone should worship Him in spirit and in truth.'

She said this with a finality that brooked no debate.

'I lived without your God until now, Mama Putus. Not only that, I had to live without father for most of my life and without mother for a big part of my life. Yet, don't you see me here alive? Before I pray to your blond-hair, blue-eye, weaky-weaky-looking man-god, I prefer not to pray at all.'

'So you prefer to pray to Haile Selassie? But Haile Selassie not man? Like Fitzie, like Canute, like Robert, the male nurse. Just like all the other man-them who sit down on woman and blight our prospect. Is because him Black, why you pray to him?'

'Mamaa, I don't understand it good yet but I don't think that I did pray to Haile Selassie, the Man. I think that I did pray to the Idea of a God who look like me, who sympathise with me, who fighting the same battles like I fighting . . . and who want to win out like I want to win out. Maybe it don't make much sense but that is how I think about it.'

'Well, all A can say is that it better you pray to Haile Selassie than don't pray at all. And since He make mi clock start working again (eh, eh), Him probably in touch with the true God.

'It late. A don't know what time it be but bedtime gone long time. You should get yu sleep. Come, let me cover you up again.'

MRS MASON

I put her under the eiderdown again. I pull it up to her ears and to the back of her head. Only the front of her face is out.

She not sleeping but I pretend that I think she sleeping. I go back to the armchair. Lord, what all these things she telling me? Poor little soul. She don't understand. She always was good on her mouth though. Even before she could talk properly, she could-a use-up words that not even big people did know. I glad to see that she still good with her mouth.

'Mama Putus, you not cold? Why don't you come into the bed?'

'I used to the cold. You not used to it, so better you stay in the bed. Go and sleep. I will catch my little sleep right here in the chair. Don't worry bout me.'

She don't look satisfied.

'Mama Putus, something been worrying my mind.

'I fraid that you might get vex again if I say. But I have to say it.'

Is what this girl bothering me for, eh? I still don't make up my mind what I going to do with her. I can't put her out, it too late. I don't know what will happen to her out there and I don't want to have it on mi conscience. Better she just keep quiet and sleep.

'Mama Putus, you not as confused as you pretend to be? How come one time you seem like a mad woman who don't know anything and then another time, you remember everything and you know everything that you should know?'

Kyaaaa-kyaa-kyaa-kyaa-kya-kia. Kyaaa-kyaaaa-kyaa-kya-ka! The girl was always a smart girl, you know? She is mi daughter, in truth.

ICY

I don't know if the joke is on me but it is so good to hear and see her laugh like that again. We had shared so many such laughs, she and I.

I remember after Canute was taken to what I now know but didn't then, was prison and before she met Fitzie Mason, life was very hard. But she always kept me in school. And she always kept me in Sunday School. I had one pair of shoes, a black, laced-up bootie, and it had been falling to pieces on my feet.

After she had scraped-up the money to try to buy me another pair of shoes, it only came to the amount that could buy me a pair of crepe-soled canvas shoes. I remember her taking me into the Bata shoe store in Spanish Town. The store had been busy so she had to wait. She waited. Calm, dignified, tall, patient.

So much so, that it was the Jamaica-white Store Manager himself who came up to her and said, 'Can I help you, Madam?'

Looking down on him (although he was taller) as if he were her servant, she had answered:

'Yes, you can. I want to buy my daughter a pair of tennis shoes.' I was wondering what is this 'tennis shoes' and where Mama Putus had seen it before. I had thought that we were buying a pair of 'crepe'. It was even more of a wonder to me when I saw this white Jamaican 'Madam-ing' her up and taking a chair out of his own private office for her to sit on while he looked for these 'tennis shoes'. The white Jamaican Store Manager even pinched me on my cheeks, said what a pretty, well-behaved little girl she had . . . 'Mrs . . . Mrs . . . ?'

Without a blink, Mama Putus answered, 'Barton, Mistress Barton'. The Manager gave me a Paradise Plum sweetie to suck while he looked for the best crepe-soled 'tennis shoes' for the daughter of 'Mrs Barton'. He even gave her a discount on it.

One week later, 'Mrs Barton' was back in the store, asking calmly but firmly to see the Manager. She was holding me by her side, dressed-up in my one nice lacy dan-dan dress but with my feet bare. She had the 'tennis shoes' in the other hand. She had come to tell the Manager that the lace of the 'tennis shoes' had broken the first time that I put them on. That she was sure that the Manager hadn't known that these shoes had not been properly made. That she had brought her daughter, barefoot, to emphasise the way she would have to appear on her gym lessons if she was to depend on this rotten shoes.

By the time we left the Bata shoe store, I had a lovely pair of 'church shoes' on my feet and Mama Putus had brand-new, expensive 'tennis shoes' clutched under the arm which wasn't holding me.

When we got home, she had laughed like she is laughing now. But it still wasn't like how she laughed after the 1955 National Election Campaign.

It was in the days before the big political violence. It was also in the days before the big drugs violence. A few burglar bars were beginning to appear on a few of the larger Chinese wholesale grocery shops in the downtown Kingston area but most of the houses still had plain glass windows or board windows.

It was also still the time when supporters of the People's Party could feel free to go and heckle and have a laugh at the meetings of the Union Party, and vice versa. Supporters of the winning party in general elections or local government elections would express their joy at being on the winning side and their contempt for the losing candidate by marching to his (it was usually a he) house with hastily made brooms and branches of trees to 'sweep him out'. Now and again, in the height of an election campaign, when tempers got high on all sides, stones would be thrown into an opponent's political meeting. On rare occasions, someone might be stabbed with one of those wickedly sharpened pointed knives or chopped with a glistening machete.

But in those days, political meetings were in general great fun. Especially the speeches of the different leaders and election candidates. And the way the crowd would sing! They just transferred the choruses and Sankey hymns from the Church, inserted the name or names of their favourite political leaders and sometimes, loudly, as in a raucous shout, sometimes crooningly, as in a love moan, declared their undying allegiance to the leader and to the Party.

It didn't matter that by election day they might have changed their minds and voted for the other party and leader. In that moment, drunk on the smell and heat of the sweat of each other, the prickly chill of the night air, the rantings of impossible promises, the belly-cracking jokes of the speakers, they would gladly promise to follow leader x or y, 'until we dead'.

'Mama, is that one you going to vote for? eh, eh?' I had asked excitedly, as I jumped up and down to the singing.

'Hush yu mouth and keep still, girl. You should never tell anybody who you going to vote for. That is nobody business but you and yu God.' All the different canvassers had come to our house. Mama Putus had listened to all of them and made the right sounds without telling any of them who she was going to vote for.

Then she had heard that the Union Party was giving away a whole ten pounds to each person who committed themselves to voting for them. When the canvasser of the Union Party knocked at our gate, she brought her in to have some Seville orange lemonade. She chatted up the woman ever so nicely. Though, if she had thought carefully, it would have been clear to her that at no time had Mama Putus told her that she was going to vote for the Union Party. The woman gave her the tcn pounds. And even promised her a big job and a house, if the Union Party won.

More fool her. As it turned out, Mama Putus was supporting the Party that was bringing in scholarships to High School for the children of the slaves, as she put it.

The elections took place. I don't think she even told her husband Fitzie whom she had voted for. But on the night after the count was taken, she marched with the victorious crowd to the house of the losing candidate of the Union Party. She did not take any part in the 'sweeping', but no one could by then have had any doubt that she more supported what the People's Party stood for.

Mama Putus was in a good mood at home after she came back from celebrating the victory of the People's Party. She didn't nag me to 'go to yu bed' or 'don't drink too much of that cream soda, it will give you gas in yu stomach.'

She just kept laughing. Fitzie thought that she was drunk. But I knew that Mama Putus had only been drinking water and lemonade.

Fitzie was holding court on the little verandah, a glass of estate rum and coconut water in his hands:

'Yes man, things going to better now. People power time now. Marcus Garvey word must come to pass now.'

Mr Stanley, from the room round the back, was quiet. The other two big women there were quiet. Fitzie hadn't liked this.

'What happen, oonu vex because oonu old-clothes government lose!? Kyaah, kyaah, kah. Cho-man dash way that de Party now. Is bout time you join the Party whey can help we fe turn doctor an' nurse an' big profession people, eh?'

Mama had laughed even louder.

'You really believe that, Fitzie? Then you fooler than the woman who give me the money to vote for her Party. If anybody tell we that them can make all a we turn big professional people, is a lie them telling. God make the high and the low in the beginning. And so shall it be to the end. Is only one thing I asking of this new government. Help me to get a steady job so that A can feed meself and support mi pickney. Fe able to hold up mi head with dignity. That's all I ask.'

Then she had started to laugh again. And when she could catch her breath, she had said,

'You have to know how to fool them. I fool the Union Party people-them but is not because I think that the People's Party-them care bout me anymore. Them looking-out for themself too and them pickney too. But at least them willing to give fi-mi pickney something too. And that is why I fool the Union Party woman. Kyaaaa, kya, kya, kya, ka.'

That had ended the party. Everyone got up and began to drift to their rooms even before she said, 'Come to yu bed, Icy.'

MRS MASON

London Bridge is falling down
    Falling down
    Falling down
    Falling down!

London . . .
Bridge . . .
Is falling down
On my fair lady.

Eh, eh! Kya, kya, kya, kya. A not a fair lady. But it fall down on me too. Kya! kya. I don't want it to fall down on Icy, though. Tomorrow morning, DV, I going to send her back home. I never work so hard and bear so much and travel so far, for she to have to bear the weight of London Bridge, just like me.

I want to make sure she understand. If is one thing that she have to understand, is that she must go back home. Tomorrow morning. No later than that.

'Icy, it hard for you to understand. That is why I never did want you to come here. After I really learn about this place, I swear on my Bible that I wouldn't let you come through this same Icy-Lane that I was going through.

'I never plan that for you. Da Da never plan that for you, although he could never know what it was like here, cause he never live here.

'Since you say you want to know the truth, since you insisting on knowing the truth, I going to tell it to you.'

A say that A going to tell it to her but I don't know if A want to tell her all of it. They say in they courthouse about, 'the truth, the whole truth and nothing but the truth'. But the whole truth is a hard thing to swallow. Most times, it better you keep back some of the truth and don't give out the whole of it.

A have no choice. The only way A going to get her to board the plane and go home tomorrow morning, is if A tell her the whole truth. Maybe that's all A can do for her, at this stage.

'Icy, all the time I was in Jamaica, Lawd, I did love England! When A just come here, A go and stand outside Buckinham Palace when A have the time, to see the changing of the guards. I did love how the

178

English people-them talk. So refined! So civilised! Not like how we chew-up our words or bawl them out at the top of wi voice.

'In all of the hospitals, they always have pictures of the Royal Family, even in Tooting Bec. In the beginning, I love them so much! Mi heart would beat strong, strong, whenever I see the Queen, the Duke, they children and all they family.

'You remember, Icy? You remember how I used to love them?'

ICY

I must have fallen asleep. It is one of those times that I am not sure whether I am sleeping or awake. So I don't know if what I am seeing and feeling and going through is reality or dreaming.

I am a schoolgirl in Spanish Town, Jamaica. I am in the First Form in High School. Royalty is coming from England. It has been practice every day for the last week, at the Anglican Cathedral and in the Square with its Rodney statue. I am in the Girl Guides. We don't have to march as smartly or as much as the Cadets or even the Boy Scouts. But our dark-blue uniforms have to be crisp, not even one little crease allowed anywhere. Every button and badge must out-glisten even the sun. The brown shoes must be like a mirror. Better to get a new pair of dark-blue regulation socks since the old one is sagging slightly, Mama Putus says.

She carries out her own inspection of everything I will be wearing to meet Royalty in the Square. She meticulously checks from underwear up. She vetoes the panties (they are not new enough).

'Suppose you take sick and have to go to hospital?'

She insists that I wear brassières, which I haven't quite gotten used to yet and which I do not particularly like anyway.

'Can't have you little breasts jumping up an' down,' Mama Putus says.

The sun is not yet up but I am almost ready. Everyone has been told to be in front of the Cathedral, latest 7 o'clock in the morning. Even if anyone had dared to ask the Headmaster, the Form Teacher or the Guides Mistress when exactly Royalty would come to the Square, they wouldn't get an answer. If only because maybe no one knew, certainly no one at the school. They could only warn that 'anyone coming after 7 o'clock will not be admitted into the line-up.'

I reach the Cathedral before 7 o'clock. Many reach after seven but before the half past. By 8 o'clock, all the uniformed groups are in their places, stiff as ramrod. Schoolchildren in their ordinary, everyday school uniforms are being packed in by hurrying teachers behind a rope barrier on the side of the Square further down and opposite to the Cathedral.

The Military Band strikes up the folk song made popular and 'respectable' by Louise Bennett, 'Dis Long Time Gal, Me Never See You, Come Mek Me Shake You Hand'. The schoolchildren begin to sway, in place. The uniformed groups dare not. Even eyebrows must be steady.

Nine o'clock and the sun is growing hot. I begin to bless Mama Putus for the big breakfast she insisted that I eat before leaving home. The Police Band takes up from the Military Band, then the Alpha Boys

School Band. Crowds of big people are gathering. Red-seam police of the Jamaica Constabulary Force and blue-seam special constables of the Island Special Constabulary Force herd the crowds behind another rope barrier further down from where the schoolchildren are.

'I wonder who that platform over there so for?' I whisper to my schoolfriend and fellow Guider, Velma. By now it is possible to get away with whispering. More and more of the children are fidgeting, despite the disapproving scowls and constant commands of masters and mistresses to 'keep still' and 'keep quiet'.

Velma assumes her superior intelligent look:

'You don't know that is for the Custos and the Mayor and the MHRs and all the other special people? They are the ones who Royalty will meet.'

I am wondering what Velma means, if I and the other people in the Square will not meet Royalty too? But the Guides Mistress is again inspecting her ranks for the hundredth time. So I have to become ramrod again.

Eleven o'clock and I don't know the exact numbers of children who have fainted but now, more often than before, the St John's Ambulance Brigade nurses can be seen hurrying somewhere with their stretchers.

The special platform is full. I wonder how the Mayor must be feeling in his robes and the others in their dark suits and top hats, since I am so hot and uncomfortable in my thin Guides uniform. I curse Mama Putus for insisting that I wear the brassière. It is too tight across my back and it is squeezing and itching me in the heat. Royalty is going to be meeting one sweaty bunch of people by the time She gets here, I am thinking.

Something is happening. Everyone still standing on their feet in front of the Cathedral and at the Square, must stiffen-up again. Absolutely no talking. Absolutely no moving.

'Ahtenshun!'

'God . . . !
Save . . . !
Our Gracious Queen!
Long Live Our Noble Queen
God Save Our Queen.'

Outriders in their red, white and blue dress uniforms. A line of cars. Excitement in the Square. I am trying to keep ranks at the same time that I crane my neck forward to see what is happening.

There is cheering. I am waiting, for I don't know what.

It is nearly an hour later when we are told to disperse. Royalty has come and gone.

'You did see her? You did see her?', several of my schoolmates ask. Before I can decide what to answer, they say,

'You never see her waving an' smiling at we?'

I hadn't, in fact. But since everybody else had, I had to add my little bit to the descriptions of the Royal wave and the Royal smile as we walked home.

181

ICY

'Lawd, Mama, you should-a see the Queen!'

'What she look like, Icy? Then you see her near-near? What she have on? How she comb her hair? She keep it long or she cut it an' wear it short? Then the Duke was with her? She say anything to oonu?'

'Mama how you asking me so much question, one time? By the time A to answer one, A won't remember the other one.'

Mama Putus is sitting on the back steps facing the kitchen in the tenement yard where we lived with Fitzie. Evening dusk is coming on. Fitzie is on the night shift at work. We have just eaten our dinner together, alone. I am leaning my head on Mama Putus's shoulder. Her shoulder is cushioned with fat but not lumpy. I can more smell than feel the heat rising from out of her bosom into my nostrils. It is the smell of baby powder, caked-up with the sweat under her fat breasts.

Mama Putus sprinkles baby powder between and under her breasts each night after she has bathed herself in the big wooden tub in one section of the shed in the backyard. That's also where I have my bath each morning. She has long forbidden me to use the common shower in the little zinc enclosure to the side of the house.

'Well now, Mama, let me see what A can remember bout the Queen visit.'

'Remember, girl? But how you could forget so quick? No just this morning you meet Missis Queen? But see here, what a way you boasty? Anyhow, A can understan', because when I was your age, me never even know anything bout Royalty much less to actually meet one. The nearest me ever come was to see them on lantern slide and that was when me was big, big.'

'So how she did look when you see her on lantern slide, Mama?'

'From what A can remember, she did so refine, it make you feel big an' fat an' Black an' ugly. But then, she did smile so nice an' she always give this little wave. You could see the blue blood in her right away. A did see the Duke too. Him tall an' handsome.'

'But me never see no blue blood, Mama.'

'Girl, don' be a idiot. What you going to High School for? Them not teaching you anything there? Blue blood is Royalty. Them say that all of them Royalty have blue blood. That mean them born special. Them born to be rulers. Them born to rule over we.'

'Then Mama, is only Royalty one have blue blood? Or is all white people have blue blood?'

'Lawd, you ask too much question. Go brush yu teeth and do yu homework. Is soon bedtime.'

I nuzzle my face into her neck and keep quiet. Mama Putus hugs me around the shoulders. I know that I can stay there for a while longer, so long as I don't ask anymore questions which Mama Putus doesn't know the answer to. In any event, after standing in the square for so much of the day, I am now tired of Royalty, blue blood or no blue blood.

I am quite satisfied with the scent coming from Mama Putus's breasts. I prefer it to a million blue blood. I burrow my nose betwixt those breasts. Mama Putus doesn't seem to mind. I fall asleep.

MRS MASON

'Icy! Icy! Wake up! Wake up!' She fall asleep on me. Just as I make-up my mind to tell her the whole thing.

'Icy, you groaning too much in you sleep. Wake up! Wake up and shake-up youself. A want to talk to you.'

She jump up. Her jaw wet. I don't know if it's from mouth-water or if she was crying in her sleep.

'Lord, Mama Putus, I never even realise when I fall asleep. I glad that you wake me though.'

'You were having a bad dream, ain'-it?'

'Not really. You remember the time when I was in High School and I did go on parade for the Queen? I was dreaming bout it. Only that . . . '

'Me used to dream bout the Queen too. Only that after A come here and really get to know what going on, A couldn't understand how she allow some of her subjects to get all them bad treatment.'

'But Mama Putus, the Queen don't have to personally know what going on? She just a symbol up there. For we to worship. Well since I never did worship no one . . . '

'You think you know everything, eh? You was always like that. If you believe anything, you just stick to it, no matter what anybody say.'

'Lawd, A don't have nothing gainst you Queen? But how you can expect me to worship her when is she and her family and friend-them all through the ages, that take away our land and wealth? And them kill so much a-wi on top of it? Who them don't kill, they try to turn into them slave.'

'No bother come to me with you socialist politics. If you keep quiet and listen, I goin' tell you bout some real reality. Even some of yu big-time politician-them who say they want to help us, don't know them realities. Or maybe if them know it, them decide that them better just ignore it and look out for themself.'

She clamp her mouth shut and she just looking on me. Maybe she can cut off her words-them and just listen to what A have to say now.

'Icy, promise me something. I will tell you the whole truth but you have to promise me that after A talk to you, you going to take the plane and go back to Jamaica tomorrow morning. Cause A don't want you here.'

'But Mama, you was the one who write and tell me what a nice place this was. How much opportunity you did have here to further your studies. How you could always get work here and earn money. It was all a lie? How come you live like this?'

A shame so till! That's why I did try mi best not to make her come here and see me. That's why I was hoping that when she hear back from the police, she would decide her mind not to come.

'Icy, I never live like how you come to find me, all the time that I was here. At first, it did start out bad. The room that Fitzie bring me into in Brixton, I never live in a room like that all mi life. Not even when I did rent the half-room with Zelfa in Spanish Town.

'Since I did even start Commercial School and could do little typing before I leave Jamaica, I did think that it wouldn't be too much problem to get a job as a clerk in a country like this. Especially since is them same one set the exam-them that we have to do back in Jamaica. I did think that I would get a little light job, go to College in the evenings and before long, I would get a Certificate. Mi first surprise was where Fitzie did live. Mi second surprise was when I go out looking job. It did look like the only job that them had to give we was cleaning job. At first, A say that A would take it. Because, as you know, A did do some domestic work in Jamaica, from time to time, when things get hard. But that was not my ambition.

'The first cleaning job I take here, I never take anymore after that. Early, early, long before-day-morning, when it dark and cold, you have to reach there. And Lawd Jesus! The sort of things you have to clean-up! And the way when the Boss come round him look on you!

'And at the end of the week, what I get in my hand as pay, couldn't even pay the rent for the little room on Acre Lane. The next week, I decide that I wasn't going back.

'The next week, when Fitzie never see me hustling out before-day-morning, he ask me what happen. I tell him that I leave the job. He say that A can't expect everything as I would like it and that I just have to take what I can get. I tell him that I don't mind that, as he know from Jamaica. I tell him that anybody can do any kind of job to get by, cause nobody need to be shame of honest work – so long as the people who you working with respect you. I tell him that them never respect me. I ask him how the little "monkey-money" that them giving me after all that work, could help we.

'Him just turn him back on me in the bed and stay quiet. I remember it when afterward all him could do is eat-off mi ears with him complaining against them.

'But, Icy, it did take only few months after I come here to know how to deal with them. Fitzie always fighting them. I decide that I was going to be like them. Play their game.

'Fitzie was surprised when I got the job as Auxiliary Nurse at Dulwich Hospital. He said that it was just another "cleaning job" in another form. But I never paid him any mind. Cause he was the same one who make-up his face on me because I wasn't working and bringing-in any money.

'I didn't bother to tell him how I got the job. By this time, I learn enough here, to know that the best way to get that job, was to pretend to be an idiot. Pretend to worship white people, starting from whoever interview you. I had been making the mistake before of telling them that I was a graduate of First and Second Jamaica Local Examinations in Jamaica, set by Cambridge University in England. I did make the mistake to tell them that I could type and do "Business English" (they don't like that at all!).

'I never make that mistake when I went for the job at Dulwich Hospital. I made sure that I was clean. But not too well-dressed. I kept my head down all the time the cold-eyed Hospital Administrator was asking me all sorts of questions – most of which was not his business, anyway.

'I grinned my teeth: they like when you grin your teeth. When you keep your face serious, they cannot trust you. They think that you must be thinking and planning something against them. I gave them a bad-luck story (they like bad-luck stories) about how, if I didn't get this job, my family would starve and we would be living on the streets. The Hospital Administrator thought that he had something over me, which he could use against me whenever he felt like it. I got the job at Dulwich Hospital. And Fitzie was happier. Except when it came to the time of the birthday party.

'After the birthday party, everything changed in my life, though A didn't realise it full, at the time.'

MRS MASON

'Icy, you listening to me? Or you sleeping?'

'A listening good, Mama.'

'A sorry that A can't even make you a cup of tea, but is so it go. That's life.'

'A don't want no tea. A don't want anything. Just go on.'

'After the birthday party, the first thing that happen was that they fire me from Dulwich Hospital. Then after couple months, A get a letter from the Social Security that say that I was to be "rehoused". They said that they wanted the flat for a family and since I never have any children and was employed, they had was to bring in a "family". They offer me a little room in Battersea. But Fitzie say that he was not going to go there, so we rent a room again in Brixton.

'It was about this time that Fitzie start to take-up with the white-women-them. It have plenty of them who will work and give they money to a Black man. And the Black man-them turn idiot when them along with them.

'I did want us to save whatever little money we working and buy a house. So that we wouldn't have to go beg anybody to find a place to live. But all Fitzie could think bout was driving around with the white women in the car that we did put together and buy. I couldn't talk to him. I couldn't make him see reason. He start to behave so bad that I had was to pretend that I was on my own and I decide to make it by myself.

'I never make anybody at work know what was happening. I just go to work and I work same way as usual. I try to still keep my goal in sight. I was just stopping here, before I go on to better things.'

'Then Mama Putus, you never have no friend here that could help you? You never have anybody that you could even exchange thoughts with? How come you were so alone?'

'Icy, you don't know how things stay here. Most of the time I was working so hard, I didn't have much time to keep friends. Just work, work, work all the time. Then again some of you own people here just looking out for themself and trying to bring you down.'

'But all of them couldn't stay like that, Mama? It no must have some good ones? How come you never meet them?'

'I try to keep myself to myself. That was the best way. I never go to pub and I never go to them club and them dance, so plenty of them never like me.'

'Then what about those in you church? Them don't go to pub and dance either? You never have no friend in you church? You never have no special friend at work?'

'Them in the church! Is them is a set a hypocrite! I would-a never tell any of them mi private business, make them take it turn pulpit talk. After a while I did stop going to the church, especially after what did happen at work . . . But leave that alone . . . '

'Mama Putus, what did happen at work?'

'Hear me, Icy, A say leave that alone. You can go back go sleep now, morning soon light.'

'Mama Putus, is work it did happen? The thing that bring the big disgrace?'

MRS MASON

'How you could know bout it, Icy? You meet Him in England since you come here? Him did come to Jamaica for holiday? Is there you meet Him?'

'Who, Mama Putus? Who you talking about?'

Maybe I shouldn't did tell her all those things that I tell her. I should-a follow my mind like when she just come and I never trust her.

'Icy, tell me the truth, is Him who send you here to find me? Tell me the truth. I want to know if you ever meet that dirty bruk-kitchen wretch! If you and Him is together, I will kill you right here in this room and I wouldn't care if they put me in prison or in the madhouse and throw away the key, cause I wouldn't have anything else to live for.'

'Mama Putus! Mama Putus! Calm down. Is the God's truth I tell you. I don't know who you talking about.'

'Then how you know about the disgrace? You just say it to me. Don't you use the word disgrace?'

'Yes, I did use that word Mama but it was because of something I did see in my dream. I never tell you about everything that I did see in the dream. In case you think that I keeping back anything from you, I will tell you now. After I was seeing again in my mind that time in Jamaica when the Queen did visit, it seem that I did fall into a deeper sleep. I did see you naked in this big room. Everybody know that when you dream bout nakedness it mean disgrace. That is why I was crying in my sleep. That is why I ask you about the disgrace. Believe me Mama.'

Maybe she telling the truth. Because is only Him and Me know bout it. I would-a never tell Miss Jo or Henry. They would bawl and create a whole heap of excitement!

Him did go on leave from the next day. And when Him come back, Him was walking bandy-leg. Him tell them that Him had a bad riding accident. Him never tell them what did really happen. I don't even think Him did tell his priest. And I certainly never tell anybody. Fitzie don't know bout it. Fitzie couldn't understand when I run away from him and come to Birmingham. Him think it was because we was always quarrelling since him treat me so bad. Him think it was because I was more ambitious than him. Him did think that it was because I did find a rich man in Birmingham who could bring me into the mansions of the world.

I couldn't tell any of my own people-them. Parson and the church-people would want me to go to the police. I couldn't do that. It would bring more disgrace.

189

I couldn't tell Canute, even though I usually tell him every little thing that's worrying mi mind, even things that I never talk about with Fitzie. Canute did gone to America by that time, anyway. If I did write and tell him, he would want to take the next plane from America to come and beat Him up. He would want to stir-up one stink and all complain to the government and that would just bring more shame on me. And it wouldn't even did help to put anything right. They would just put Canute in prison here. Like they put him in prison in Jamaica. This time, they would throw away the key. They would put me in the madhouse and throw away the key.

No. I couldn't tell Canute.

I couldn't write home and tell anybody. They wouldn't understand. They would wonder if it's not me who did bring it on myself.

I didn't have anywhere to turn for help. So I just look after myself, bear my burden and keep it between myself and my God.

But I couldn't sleep with Fitzie anymore. Him had other women with me. Him even slap me couple times – a thing he never did do in Jamaica. But that's not why I leave him finally. I leave him because I did feel too dirty, no matter how many times a day I wash and bathe, I did feel dirty after what Him did do to me. I couldn't even go back to my church. I did feel they would find out just by looking at me.

It was one of the times when Fitzie and me did get back together after I did leave him and him come begging me to come back, saying that him was going to behave himself now. But after it happen, I told Fitzie that I would sleep on the couch. Many nights he would come to me wanting love. Begging me to come into the bed. I couldn't go into our bed. I didn't have any love to give anymore.

MRS MASON

'That white-man tore me up, Icy. With all that was happening, is Him that bring me down to this level. I didn't want to tell you about it. But maybe you should know about it, so that you can be warned.

'Because I would never did think that somebody like Him could do something like that. Is Him that did interview me when I did go for the job and every time that He buck me up after that at the hospital, He used to give me this sweet smile and ask me how I getting on, as if Him did really care.

'He wasn't supposed to be there in the hospital at that time of night. A staff nurse was on duty and I was only supposed to be there to help her. The staff nurse only came when the shift just start. Then she disappear.

'They did call me "Auxiliary Nurse" but the only thing I never do was give injections. So I was used to the nurses coming at the beginning and giving the injections and then going off. To have tea, to chat with the doctor or whatever they wanted to do. I was used to running the ward by myself at night. That's just how it goes, whatever you hear they say.

'The geriatric ward was usually like a graveyard. Only that sometime the patients cry and scream so much, you would think that you was in Hell with all them old people who during all they life never did make their peace with their God before dying. The patients were not yet dead but they were travelling through the valley of the shadow of death. Their screams were awful.

'I didn't expect to see Him on the ward. He hardly ever come to the ward, even in the days. He was one of the big topanaris in the office and usually if He wanted to talk to any of the staff, He would send for them to come to his office.

'When He appear-up on the ward that night, I was very surprised. I wanted to ask Him what He was doing there but that was not in my place. That would be insubordination, as they call it. I was just glad that I was doing my duty when He came. It would have been a hell-of-a-trouble for me, if I had been catching a little rest with a cup of tea.

'Still, I was hoping that He did come to see if the staff nurse who was supposed to be on night duty was there. I would never report them, anyway it's me who would get the wrong if I report them. But I was thinking that if the guvnor Himself could see that the staff wasn't doing their work then maybe He would discipline them and change things around there. I would be glad because they would have to stop putting

191

all their work on me. Some of the patients were so bad-minded and ungrateful! Always cursing me and calling me "black monkey", that sometimes I said to myself that it served them right, the way some of the staff nurses treated them. But I am a healer, so I didn't pay any mind to what they were saying. I wanted them to get better treatment, no matter how they treated me.

'So when I saw the guvnor come on the ward, I feel that if He saw how the situation really was, He would change things and the poor patients would be glad because they would get better care.

'I made sure that I was doing everything that they tell me to do. By the rules. It's all well and good if the staff nurses or the Nursing Sister complain about me but this is the Man that could dismiss me from the job right away. I couldn't afford to lose this job? I did hang on at this hospital, even when I felt that I was going to get mad with the pressure. I felt that if I stuck it out, sooner or later they would support me to register in the nursing course. I knew I would pass it good if they give me the chance. After that, it would only be a matter of time before I could send for you, Icy.

'When I saw Him come on the ward, I even felt that I could ask Him personally about helping me to get on the nursing course.

'He went into the dayroom. It had pictures of the Queen, the Duke and the other ones of the Royal family. We use all these pictures to try to get the old people to remember their life. The therapist say that since all of them love the Royal family, the best way to get them out of the confusion in their minds was to remind them of the Royal family.

'He called me into the dayroom. He started to ask me how the patients were doing. Then, all of a sudden, He grabbed me. I didn't know what to do with myself . . . or with Him. He wrestled me down on the floor.

'He began to blow hard and gasp out that he loved me. I hated Him now.

'He hooked his fingers into my panty and tore it off my body. He pushed his fist up into me and opened his fingers inside me. He clawed-out my insides with his fingernails. I couldn't stand the pain.

'But is the pain that get me really mad! I decide that I wasn't going to bawl-out and give Him that satisfaction. I just lay there on the floor of the dayroom, looking up at Him, scorning him.

'His little teelis was jumping up and down, trying to stand up, while he was ramming his fist into me. He began to puff and blow even harder, saying, "Give it to me, Black bitch! Give it to me!"

'A don't know where A find the strength from, with all that pain and bleeding, Icy. But A find it. Them days, A used to keep mi fingernails long, and A sink one of mi hand into the root of the little teelis!

'He jump-off of me. And He start to bawl-out and scream louder than the old women who couldn't sleep.

'But I will never, never, forget his eyes, Icy. If He could-a kill me right there and get away with it, Him would do it. Jesus Christ, Icy, when his eyes turned full on me, mi blood run cold! Them was like blue-glass. Them was like a mountain make-up of pure blue-glass. And no matter how deep you look, or how wide you look, is only more and more blue-glass you can see! Endless, endless blue-glass.

'I never before in my life see eyes that have so much hate in them. Jesus Christ! Those eyes did blast some hate at me! It was me under Him, with all mi pain and mi bleeding but the way He look at me, you would think that is me was making Him bleed.

'I couldn't understand why He hated me so. He must did hate me even before I did sink my fingernails into his crotch. Or He wouldn't did come to rape me. I never did Him anything all the time I was at the hospital? If anything, I did like Him and bow-down to his name. I never cursed his mother? I don't even know his family, much less to have done them any harm? He doesn't know me? None of mi family know Him, so they couldn't have done Him any wrong. So how come He did hate me so? I couldn't understand, Icy. That, more than anything else, get me confused.

'I did ask Him what was the reason why He hate me so? I did tell Him that Him was behaving like a piece of machine that somebody make only to destroy others. He is still wriggling-up himself in pain on the dayroom floor. And giving me his hate-full look. But as I am walking out back into the ward, He turned those dead eyes on me again. He tell me,

' "You Black bitch, I am going to get you. You tell anyone about this and I will tell them that you are mad. I will have you as a patient here, if it's the last thing I do."

'I look on the picture of the Queen with the Queen Mother and the Duke on the wall. And I know that they can't help me against this Man.

'I left Him on the floor and I went to wash the blood off of my feet.'

ICY

Lord Jesus Christ! Lord Jesus Christ! I could never did even imagine anything like this! Happening to Mama Putus? Not to some leggo-woman who tease man? To Mama Putus?

No wonder she turn so confuse. No wonder she tell me in her letter that she going 'expire'. If I did only know! Then I wouldn't be so vex with her. I would come up here long time and find a way to deal with that Man who violate her so.

I don't know what to do. I want to hug her up. But I crying too much. I fraid that she going to push me away and become Mrs Mason again.

'Mama Putus, Mama Putus, tell me where I can find that bitch! Tomorrow morning, as daylight, I going to London to find Him. I going to the hospital. If He not there, I will find somebody who can tell me where He is. I going to find Him . . . '

'Icy, that pass and gone. Is only because you ask me why I tell you about that. Especially since you did say that you dream bout the disgrace.'

'I promise you, Mama Putus, I am going to find Him. I don't know mi way round this country but I will go look for Henry and Miss Jo. They will help me find Him. Mama, you can't make Him get away with what Him do to you?'

It's she who come to hug me up. I bury my face in her breasts. My tears are running down between them.

'Icy, Icy! mi little Icy, don't cry. Don't sorry for you Mama. I know that you saying what you saying because you well vexed. But you going to get yuself into trouble if you go and look for that Man. I glad that with everything that happen, you still love me enough to want to do something to that bruk-kitchen who damage me . . . '

The whole of me choke-up. I don't want her to think that I am going to do anything foolish but she must understand that I just can't go to sleep, go back to Jamaica tomorrow and forget about everything that she tell me.

'Don't worry, Mama Putus, I won't attack Him in his office. If I go to his office, it's just to look upon Him. Perhaps I will go and pretend that I looking a job at the hospital, just to look into his stinking face. To identify Him . . .

'After I identify Him, then I will point Him out to some friends of friends that I have up here, so that they can know the wretch. Once they know him, then they will take care of the rest. And nothing will save his rotten soul!'

MRS MASON

She crying so bad, I fraid that she going to cry herself to death. Like that Irish woman. I bear it. I get depressed. I come down in the world. But I never cry miself to death? That is just what Him would-a did like.

I have to talk to Icy serious, serious. So that she can understand herself good. I don't want her to get herself mixed-up with Him, for no reason whatsoever.

Knowing her, even if I cry to her, even if I bawl at her, even if I box her again and tell her not to go to London to seek revenge on this Man, she going to do it. So I better tell her the rest of the story and see how she will react.

'Icy? Icy? Stop you crying and listen to me.'

'Mama Putus, I don't want to hear, if what you going to tell me is to leave that Man be. I want to see Him dead, dead with his tongue long out. Dead in the worst way!'

'And what good that would do, Icy? They would just lock you up. And then what would happen to you? I don't even worry about myself any more. But what would become of you? Them would get you too. Him, Himself might survive and sign paper for them to put you in the mad-house.'

'A don't care! A don't care!'

'But I care. And that is why I want you to keep quiet and listen to me. Because the story don't end there. I want to tell you the rest of the story.'

MRS MASON

She listening. It's not no lie I going to tell her. Is what happen in truth.

'Icy, after Him do me that in the hospital that night, I had was to come to work the next night. I was still in pain but I couldn't afford to lose the job. I was so fraid the next night! I was on mi "Ps and Qs", in case Him come and order me off the job. But Him never come. Is afterward that I find out that Him did go on leave from the morning after the dreadful night.

'I stay on at that hospital for a while. But even with everything, it wasn't the same as before. Every time one of them come near to me – whatever they come for – mi whole body tense-up. It was just like I was in the dayroom again. Mi hand would start to shake and I would drop anything that I was holding in my hand. I know that they would soon have to fire me again.

'But I didn't wait for them to dismiss me from this job too. Specially since I didn't know when He would come back from his leave.

'I leave and go to Birmingham. I don't see Him since I run to Birmingham but I know that I damage Him, for life.

'Since I in Birmingham, I hear about Him. I buck-up on an orderly who was at the hospital when I was there. I ask him if all the staff that was there when I was there, was still there. He tell me that some gone and new people come. I ask about Him, in a sort of round-about-way and by-the-way style.

'You know what the orderly tell me, Icy? He tell me that the Man is still there. But only because He is a permanent civil servant and they can't just fire Him so. Him is no use to them.

'The orderly tell me that the Man not his usual self. He tell me that the Man turn a drunkard. Everybody laughing at the Man behind his back, and some before his face. The Black staff in the hospital saying mongst themself, that He must do one-a we something bad and we obeah Him.

''Cause He just walking and talking to Himself and sometime his spittle running out of his mouth and down on his shirt-front. From what the orderly say, Him is a sorry sight. Him mash-up. Just like how Him try to mash me up.

'And Him still walking bandy-leg. The white staff say that it look like the riding accident damage Him permanently. In both body and mind, eh! eh!'

'Kyaaaa-kyaaa-kya-kya-kya! Kyaaa-kyaa-kyaa-kya-kya!'

196

MRS MASON

She laughing now! Thank God. Eh-eh-eh-eh, wuy!

'Icy, A glad that you see the funny side of it. It don't make no sense to go to London to kill that Man. It have plenty like Him here and you would have to be killing and killing and killing. You don't want to spend the whole of yu life killing and killing and killing? Better you work yu brains pon them.

'Hear me. Go home tomorrow and forget about the whole thing.'

She laughing and crying same time. But she say to me,

'Mama Putus, I not going to Jamaica tomorrow. When I go back to Jamaica, is the two of us going to go.'

'Lord Jesus! You still want to go to London and kill that Man?'

'Nah! Him bearing his own tribulation already and it worse than death.'

She bright no hell!

'So what you going to do tomorrow, Icy?'

'I going to stay here, in this room. We going to talk some more, so that we can know exactly what to do. Where to move from here. Everything not clear in mi mind yet, Mama Putus. But what I know is that we going to gather all them people who is friend and family to you but who you never pay any mind. We going to gather all of them. Aunt Jo, Henry, the "foreigner-Jamaican" who bring yu letter to me, Canute from America, the West Indian woman who let me in the door to come and see you, the Africans-them who you call "uncivilised" and all the others who care bout you. We going to invite them to come to a party in this room.'

The girl must be mad! The things that A tell her must be make her get off of her head!

'Party? Here so? With all them lower-class people? In this terrible little room? Over my dead body!'

She turn on her icy stare. I remember it. I know that it don't make no sense for me to argue with her. In any event, she going have to be the One.

The One that going to have to take up what me couldn't carry. I have to use Mama Belle favourite words:

'Nothing more to be said.'

So all A can say is:

'Arright, Icy.'

GLOSSARY OF
JAMAICAN
TERMS

ATOMAN: An ottoman.

BALD-HEAD: Usually referring to persons, especially Black men, who cut their hair instead of wearing Dreadlocks. Used in a negative context, it refers to the oppressors of African people and/or Black people who support the ways and culture of the oppressors, the cutting of the hair being seen as one outward sign of this 'treachery'.

Used in a positive context, it can refer to a Black person who is not a Dreadlock, or even to a white person whose heart and actions are supportive of justice for African peoples and other oppressed peoples.

BAMMIE: Cassava cake bequeathed to the Africans who were transported by force to the American continent, by the Arawak Indians; most times eaten with fried fish in Jamaica.

BATTYMAN: Homosexual.

BRUK-KITCHEN: Scoundrel; untrustworthy individual (as one who would break into a family's kitchen and steal their food, leaving them to starve).

BRUK-NECK FOWL: Fluttering about blindly, as when the neck of a chicken is broken but its body is not yet dead.

BUCK-UP: Meet

CALLALOO: The most popularly eaten green-leafed vegetable of the spinach family. Also refers to a thick, one-pot, very nutritious green vegetable soup in the Eastern Caribbean.

CHAKA-CHAKA: Overused and worn; unsightly.

COMBOLOS: Friends; of the same social class and behaviour.

COMBRUCKTION: Crisis; tremendous happenings.

COONU-MOONU: Fool; person who allows herself/himself to be made a fool of. Not possessing any sense or powers of reasoning and making up one's own mind.

CROCUS BAG: Particular type of burlap bag.

CROWBAIT: Individual who behaves in the lowest and most treacherous way to others; idea being that such a person is bait for the scavenger bird, the John Crow.

CUSTOS: Appointed official who is the representative of the colonial Governor in each parish of the island.

DEAD HOUSE: Morgue. Depending on the context, can

198

also refer to the house in which a member of the family has recently died whose yard and house became a centre of gatherings of other family, friends and well-wishers.

DID TONGUE AND TEETH MEET?: Were there any conflicts and quarrels? There are two main ideas here. The first is that two people who have to exist together in a close space are likely to have conflicts as a matter of course. The second is that if teeth do not exercise due restraint or if tongue provokes teeth unduly and brings on a confrontation, then this must assume proportions of bloodshed, given the separate natures of tongue and teeth.

DREADLOCKS: Allowing the hair to grow and form naturally into permanent braids. Among Africans in the diaspora it is associated with the Rastafarian religion/movement, which is based on the objective of the redemption of African peoples. Also used to describe a person with Dreadlocks.

DRINK MAD-PUSS MILK: To have temporarily lost one's senses/mind.

DUPPY: Ghost.

ECKNA: Small, one-burner kerosene oil stove.

EGGS-UP: Ingratiating; to ingratiate oneself.

FEISTINESS: Rudeness.

FLOUR BAG CALICO: Originally the bag in which wheat flour was packaged. After being soaked, washed and bleached, the calico cloth was used to make garments, bedsheets, pillowcases and tablecloths. Those which used to be worn by the prisoners were not properly bleached and sometimes still bore the markings of the flour bag.

GRUDGEFUL: Covetous; hostile towards the real or imagined successes of others.

HAWTY: Well, hearty.

INJUN-KALE: Green leafy vegetable of the spinach family – named after the indigenous peoples of the American continent.

JACKFRUIT: A large, usually elongated fruit with a thick, green bumpy skin and sweet, hard yellow pulps inside. The seed inside the pulp can also be eaten when roasted.

JUNKONOO BANDS: West African masquerade played out by costumed groups at major festivals. Taken and adapted to 'New World' conditions by the forced transportees, this became a main Christmas-time attraction, especially for children.

KOTCH: To be somewhere for a very short time; 'not kotch on' – not to be dependent on.

LANTERN SLIDE: Silent movie.

LEGGO–: Loose, idle, lacking in personal discipline, purposeless.

LEGGO-BEAST: A superlative state of the above.

LICKY-LICKY: Opportunistic, greedy.

MHR: Member of the (colonial) House of Representatives.

MIRASMI-LOOKING: Physically weak, ill; ineffectual-looking.

NINE-NIGHT: The wake which takes place after the burial. This signifies the family and friends saying their goodbyes to the bereaved ones and returning to their own homes to get on with their lives.

OBEAH: Describing a group of African religions, spiritual customs and practices originally brought by West African transportees to the Americas and the Caribbean. The slavemasters and colonialists had a policy of brutally suppressing the practice of these religions, including incorrectly grouping all of them under the term 'necromancy' and making this a criminal offence. The word 'obeah' can be used as a noun or a verb.

OIL NUT: Castor oil nut.

OONU: You, your.

PATTIES: Jamaican meat-loaf; can also be vegetarian.

PATTOO: Owl.

PEENY-WALLIE: Glow-worm; dragonfly.

PICKNEY: Child or children, depending on the context.

PUSS EYES: Eyes which give the impression that the person is sly and cunning.

RED-NIGGER: Usually refers to a person of mixed Black and White race. Owing to the patterns of racial hierarchy established by the white colonialists, such persons are thought to be most assimilated into the oppressive structures and colonial culture. The term is therefore usually used in a negative context especially to describe those who behave like the white oppressor.

RUNDOWN: Jamaican dish made with coconut milk, salted and pickled mackerel or other fish; usually eaten with boiled green bananas.

SET-UP: The wake which takes place closest to the night after the actual death of the person.

SLIMBER: Slim, flexible.

SWIPS: Go quickly without any delay. The act of moving so quickly that motion is seen only as a blur.

TAKING STEP: Insulting; treating one less than one's worth.

TAN-TUDDY: Be calm. Don't do anything rash.

TOPANARIS: Upper-class; the big boss. One who is high or thinks him/herself superior to all others.

TOUCHES: Overly sensitive; quick to take offence.

WAITER: Tray.

WASH-BELLY: The youngest and last of a woman's children.

WRENKIN': Rude; impudent.